FOREWORD & TRIGGER WARNINGS

DEAR READER,

Welcome to the mayhem of the Disciples MC and the Five Points' Mob world colliding. It's been a BLAST and here's hoping you fall hard for Cindy and Cade!

As always with Serena's Irish characters, here's your pronunciation guide. :P

Pronunciation Guide:

Neev — NEE-av/ Neev

Róisín — ROH-sheen

Catriona — cah-tree-nah

Trigger Warnings:

Substance abuse/overdose with medical intervention/scenes of violence/domestic violence/child abuse.

With that being said, bring on the mayhem!

Love

Cassandra & Serena

xo

PLAYLIST

If you'd like to hear a curated soundtrack, with songs that are featured in the book, as well as songs that inspired it, then here's the link:

https://open.spotify.com/playlist/0ve8F7b0Nd4VH4zortJE6a?si=
5e538cfa3ef04787&pt=70b2a681274d467b552ec29e2a1ff578

PROLOGUE
CADE

CINDY DAVIS IS hell on my dick.

Not that she knows it.

When she serves me coffee with a disinterested glance and inadvertently flashes me a set of tits that I'd be A-OK suffocating in…

When she leans up on her tiptoe to grab extra sugars from a shelf in the diner where she works and her skirt pulls taut to reveal an ass that's begging to be spanked…

When she dips down to retrieve a spoon that's fallen on the floor and looks over to laugh at something one of her co-workers says, I know one thing and one thing alone:

She's running from her father, my job is to drag her back to New York, and somewhere in the middle, I have to fuck her.

I just have to.

As a career criminal, I know it'd be a crime *not* to dick her down and make her see heaven, hell, and everything in between.

I watch as she wanders past a booth where the brothers from the Disciples' MC sit, a longing expression overtaking her features when she peers at one fucker—Ryder.

My hands ball into fists as she flirts with him.

Or tries to.

I don't think she even knows she's doing it, and he looks awkward as hell with the attention because, from weeks of stalking Cindy, I know he's very much taken.

The funny thing about this world is that when you watch from afar, you literally *see* ticking time bombs before the explosion.

Cindy is that.

She's hot and spoiled and used to getting what she wants.

Therein lies the problem.

Ryder *doesn't* want her.

"Hey," I call out, raising a hand to gain her attention.

She shoots a bored look at me, literally giggles at whatever shit Ryder says as if he's the funniest comedian in the world before turning her attention my way.

"How can I help you?" she inquires, resting her hand on her hip.

That sass—it can't just be me who wants to tap that.

What the fuck is wrong with these Disciples asswipes?

Deciding that their loss is my gain, I smile at her, packing on the charm. The one-hundred-megawatt Frasier charm that has gotten my brothers and me into trouble since we were ten.

She blinks.

Her breath stutters.

Her lips part.

I've got her.

Then Ryder chuckles at whatever bullshit his buddy is spouting and her focus fades.

She jerks as if she's been shocked and this time, she swallows back tears of longing.

I know what it's like to want something you can't have.

I've been staking this place for three weeks now and *she* is officially that.

Maybe the stakes are different for me. I get the feeling this is a long-ass crush she's fighting, but that's the joy of being Irish—I kissed the Blarney Stone when I was born and Cindy Davis is about to be bombarded with Irish charm.

Sure, she might get my ass killed, but some women are worth burning for, and Cindy Davis is exactly that.

So I'll make my retreat, stalk her pretty ass until I know every single one of her secrets, and when she's ripe for the plucking, that's when I'll make my move.

This filthy little Disciple has no idea what she just unleashed upon herself, and I can't goddamn wait to watch the orgasm hit her pretty eyes when she realizes that Irish checks American every.

Fucking.

Time.

1

CINDY
LOS ANGELES – CALIFORNIA

"CINDY?"

A light tap on the bathroom stall has my eyes darting to the door.

I take a deep sigh and slowly exhale.

"Coming."

"Honey, I don't want to be an ass, but we're slammed. Hurry up." Joy, my fellow waitress and good friend, taps once more on the door then leaves with a muttered, "Christ."

"Okay, pull your shit together," I whisper, unlocking the door so I can head over to wash my hands.

With a groan, I take in my reflection in the large mirror.

You ever have one of those days where you just shouldn't get out of bed? Where it'd be better to crawl back under the sheets and hope tomorrow sucks less than today?

That's my day.

One little thing after another led to me hiding in the bathroom because I. Hate. People.

"God."

It's a declaration, a prayer, and a curse.

I turn off the water and spin on my heel to grab a paper towel. Irritatingly enough, I even tried to fix myself up today. I straightened my hair then added beach waves and everything. What a waste of time.

Maybe I'm just hormonal? Because yesterday I was fine. I even went to a meeting, shared and everything.

Then today happened because Joy wasn't wrong about us being slammed, and I want a Valium to take the edge off. Maybe even a Percocet for my lower back pain. Geez, I hope I'm not getting another ruptured cyst. It's happened before, so the question is… why freakin' not today?

I glance toward the door, straightening my shoulders and chanting, "Couple more hours."

I swing the door open, only to have the packed diner burst upon me. There isn't an empty seat in the place. I glance over at the *Avengers* table—all our tables have movie themes—and of course they need service when this is the *last* one I want to wait on.

Fucking Disciples.

A sharp pain pierces my heart just thinking about them… *Him.* Maybe that's what's making me funky today. It's not like I even want him anymore. I mean, he's happy with Julianna.

God, I need to get laid.

That's my problem.

I need to put a body between us. Meaning, I need more than my vibrator to get me off.

A guy from a group of construction workers stares up at me. "Hey, can we get our check?"

I reach into my apron for the bunch of checks inside and slap theirs on the table, not even saying thank you.

If my bestie, Charlie, wasn't home with her new baby, I would have called in sick today. As it is, I need to suck it up.

Suck it up.

Yeah, right. I'm ready to lose it. In the grand scheme of things, would a couple Valiums hurt? All it would do is help me to not murder someone.

I glance over at Joy who is like a machine. She's got a pot of coffee in one hand and in the other, she's holding a pitcher of water. She's smiling, laughing—I want to be Joy.

I take a deep breath and make my way over to *the* table.

Edge, Axel, and Ryder are talking while they wait for me. God, it's annoying how hot they are.

Edge, with his auburn hair and blue eyes, Axel looking like a male model even with his tattoos, and Ryder... Don't get me started on Ryder.

My eyes scan the table and I notice that they have their drinks already. Did Joy take their order and spare me from this nightmare?

"Hey, Cindy." Edge looks over at me.

I smile but it's forced, and I feel my left eye twitch as Ryder turns and frowns at me.

Perfect.

"Did Joy take your order?" I ask, ignoring Ryder completely as well as that fucking tingle that goes through me.

"No," they say at once.

Of course not! Life couldn't be kind to me today.

Before I can ask what they want, though, I get distracted by the next table.

A woman who looks as if she's having the same sort of day I am stands and jabs a finger in the air at her boyfriend. Not going to lie, he seems like a loser with his stupid grin, acting as if she's the crazy one...

Feel like a big man? Making your girl lose her shit? *Jerk.*

"You fucking dick. I saw the text," the woman screams, and I take another deep breath, holding up my hand at the guys in apology as I move to the couple's table.

"Hi." I give her a smile that says, "I know men suck. We're sisters in that fight," then proceed with, "You two need to take this outside." Neither acknowledge me.

Seeing the tears streaming down the poor woman's face, the urge to hug her is real because I've been there.

God, I feel her pain.

I feel it now.

The fantastic thing about being able to take my pills—I was always calm. Okay, maybe a little too calm, but at least it felt like a warm blanket cocooned me. Instead, without the pills, I have to deal with the harsh reality of the coldness in another person's eyes. I have to feel raw and vulnerable and like I could cry in sympathy for the woman whose douche boyfriend has brought her to the level where she's humiliating herself in a packed diner.

When you're high, you're numb, so all these real-life emotions just bounce off you...

Because I want to fade into those memories and I can't, not without letting Charlie and Joy down, I snap my fingers in the woman's face to draw her attention to me.

"Look, can you please take this outsid—"

And that's when the woman throws her tomato bisque all over me.

On me. Not him. Because *that* makes sense.

The boyfriend bolts up, calling her a crazy bitch while I'm standing there, drenched in goddamn bisque, and she looks surprised that I'm even here.

I stare at my hands, now dripping with soup. My uniform's covered. It's everywhere, sticky and warm and oozing...

I snag a napkin and wipe away the excess, but there's so goddamn much of it.

I can't—

"Cindy?" Ryder's voice is behind me, and my relief at his presence is better than a Valium. All I want is for him to save me from this day.

But he can't.

I'm exactly like this poor girl, screaming and throwing her soup because of a guy who hurt her. Unfortunately for me, instead of hitting the asshole boyfriend, I'm the one saturated with her grief.

"I have to get out of here. I can't breathe."

Beseechingly, I look at him, then around the diner.

Everyone's watching. My humiliation is complete.

And suddenly, I'm back in Blade's house, watching Julianna pull the trigger over and over as the man who was going to kill us falls dead to the floor.

The bisque I'm covered with is not soup; it's blood from the Russian with the blown-off face. I blink at my wet hands and fight the need to start screaming as my neck muscles tighten.

Breathe, just breathe. It's not blood, just soup.

"Fuck," Ryder hisses, seeming to sense I'm in the middle of a breakdown.

Then, he stuns me by picking me up and walking us toward the exit. That's when I cave in and burrow my face into his neck.

Why can't I kick him? Ryder's my addiction, not the freakin' pills.

"I need my purse," I sob.

He growls something under his breath that I can't understand but yells, "Someone get me her purse."

Because it's Ryder and no one says no to him, he's snatching it from the stunned busboy Manny in less than forty seconds.

I keep clinging to him while he kicks open the front door, walking us to the corner of the parking lot.

"What's going on with you?" he queries, setting me down, but I don't let go. *I can't.*

"It's been a really bad day." I sniff.

When I lift my head, my eyes connect with his honey-brown ones, but he's unaware that I'm pleading with him for... *something.*

His voice sounds distant as he says, "It happens." He removes my hands from around his neck, but instead of letting go, I cling tighter and drown in him—his eyes, his scent, his hold.

What are you doing?

The next thing I know, I'm lifting my lips to his, whispering, "Please, Ryder."

"The fuck, Cindy!" He jerks me off him. "Are you using again?"

My humiliation is complete.

What did I just do?

"No, I... No! I-I'm not. I—" I shake my head and cover my mouth with my hands.

He must see I'm mortified because he pulls me into his arms again and pats my back awkwardly.

It's beyond uncomfortable.

This is—oh, God—this is awful.

I'm never going to live this down.

"I need to go back inside," he rumbles, his voice flat.

He glances toward the windows where everyone got a prime view of my massive, humiliating fuckup.

Then, like that's not enough, I blurt out an excuse of, "It's only, I haven't gotten laid in a long time—" My eyes grow wider as those words spill free.

It's almost as if an alien has entered my body. I need to shut up, walk away. *Anything* but say that to him. What the hell is wrong with me?

"You'll find someone, Cindy. You need to believe in yourself."

He looks at my face as if trying to gauge if I'm high or not, which is insulting considering I said that I wasn't. But clearly, I'm acting like I'm high. That's how bad this situation is.

"I'm not on anything," I snap, only then realizing that my face is wet. "God, I wish I were."

I try wiping under my eyes, hoping it's bisque and not tears. I'd rather drink Liquid Plumber right now than cry in front of Ryder—he's had enough of my tears.

I'm too ashamed to look at him, but I feel him nod and walk away. Screw him.

Biting my lip, I peek up, only to see him shaking his head on the way back to the diner, as if he can't believe what just went down either.

His disbelief amplifies my mortification, and *that* is the last straw.

I'm in fucking crisis mode.

Reaching into my purse, I grab my just-in-case pill bottle. It's a security thing. If I have them with me, I don't take them. It's ridiculous, but it works for me.

Except for today…

I dump two, screw it, three Valiums and four or five Percocets into my hand.

Done.

I'm done.

2

CADE

ACUIG

THE SECOND she reaches into her purse, I know something bad is going to go down.

Call it instinct or experience, but I've got three sisters, so I know they carry around a vault in those purses. And the frantic vibes polluting the air around Isabelle "Cindy" Davis tell me whatever she's reaching for won't be pretty.

I jumped out of my ride the second I watched that mess with the biker go down.

Intel told me he's married to some chick named Julianna, and low-level whispers are floating around about how Cindy is still attached to this Ryder guy.

Guess I finally have proof that's true.

Especially the unrequited part.

The nightmare traffic doesn't help me reach her before she's popping a handful of pills and chewing them like they're candy.

Fuck.

I can't tell how many she took either—that's not good. I don't even think you're supposed to take a handful of *anything,* never mind what-ever hardcore stuff Isabelle had in those medicine bottles.

Amid my concern over what she swallowed, a woman storms out

of the diner. She's bristling as she shouts, "Cindy, please tell me my eyes were lying to me. Did you just try to kiss Ryder?"

It's the woman from the diner. Joy, I think her name is. I always sit in Isabelle's section when I eat at the diner, but I picked up the names from the staff when I could.

Isabelle lifts a hand to cover her eyes. "Not now, Joy," she snaps, trying to walk away from her.

"What are you doing?" Joy demands.

"That was a mistake—I didn't mean to do anything," she fires right back, displaying a temper she didn't blast Ryder with.

Interesting.

Finally, I cross the first two lanes and make my way to the center median. Joy's shouting loud enough for me to hear, but I have to read Isabelle's lips to make out her part of the conversation.

"You never do, Cindy. Seriously, this is crazy even for you. I thought you were doing better but after this…" She blows out a breath. "Look, we can discuss this later. We need to get back in there." She moves toward the door, only to have Isabelle call out:

"I can't go back in there."

Slowly, Joy returns to a flustered Isabelle's side, but there's rage etched into her expression. "I've been covering your ass for months and this is how you repay me? Never mind Charlie?"

"I-I'm sorry but look at me!"

Isabelle's apology is making no headway with Joy. Even as a part of me is grateful that Joy came barreling out after Isabelle took those pills, as it could have stopped her from downing more, I have to wonder… Didn't Joy see what I did?

"Sorry? You think that's enough when you have tables waiting for you?" Joy snarls. "Where's your loyalty, Cindy? Maybe that's why Ryder never—" Joy blanches, her face turning deep red as her words come screeching to a halt. Almost immediately, she rasps, "I didn't mean that."

They were just words, but Isabelle takes each one like they're a bullet to the chest.

If she looked devastated after Ryder walked away, now it seems as if she's a few minutes away from tossing herself into oncoming traffic.

"No. You meant it. You might as well finish that sentence, Joy. Maybe that's why Ryder never loved me? Because I'm, what, crazy? Irresponsible? A slut? You tell me which one—" Isabelle swallows then closes her eyes. "Look, I can't do this anymore. I have to get out of here."

On wobbly feet, she pushes off a large cement planter and walks toward her car.

At first, tension lights me up because it seems as if she's going nearer to the road. But then, when I realize she's going to drive under the influence, fury swells inside me.

She'll get herself and/or some innocent person killed, for Christ's sake.

"I swear to God, Cindy, if you fuck me over like this, we're done. Get in there and finish your shift," Joy calls out, her hands fisted as if she's stopping herself from dragging Isabelle back inside.

Isabelle only sticks her hand up, raises it over her head, and flips Joy the bird.

"Fuck you, Cindy. This is the last time you screw me over." Joy stalks off, arms flaring wide as if she's washing her hands of Isabelle before retreating to the diner.

I don't think she even realizes that though her friend was in the wrong for trying to kiss a guy who is taken, she kicked Isabelle while she was down.

The door to the diner slams shut, and it's loud enough that Isabelle hears it and freezes in place. She runs a shaky hand over her face. Her fingers retreat to waist height and she looks at them like they don't belong to her.

The sudden shift in her pallor has me ignoring the blaring horn from a pissed-off truck driver and darting across the road before—

No.

The results of my investigation into her tells me that Isabelle is irate. Erratic at most. *Not* suicidal.

Could Joy's ill-timed intervention be the straw that broke the camel's back?

Ignoring the fact I almost got my ass flattened by an eighteen-wheeler for her, I quickly run a hand through my hair and plaster on the cocky grin that's gotten me pussy since sixth grade. Then, I stroll over to the disaster that's waiting to happen.

"I refuse to feel any worse than I already do," she mumbles then looks at her hands. "This is not blood. It's soup. *Bisque*." A laugh escapes her. "Bisque. Like this place is a Michelin-starred restaurant." The laugh morphs into a sob.

"Bisque is pretty awesome. Have you ever been to Maine? The best lobster bisque comes from there, I swear," I drawl, trying to edge into this… whatever the fuck *this* is.

Rejection from an unrequited love has to hurt, but I don't think that's what's going on here.

Isabelle looks like she's having a psychotic episode or something.

Having worked adjacent to Aidan O'Donnelly Sr., the previous head of the Five Points' Mob, I know the signs, but I haven't seen Isabelle act so out of character the entire time I've been tracking her.

Isabelle blinks at me. "Who are you?"

I tip my head to the side—doesn't she recognize me from the diner? "I'm Cade."

Her eyes narrow and she huffs. "Cade. Of course, even your name's cute."

It's weird to preen that she *does* remember me, right? "Thank you. I think?"

"Not like you can take credit for it," she snipes, pointing an accusatory finger at me. It wobbles in midair. Yeah, those drugs are starting to kick in. "Your mom picked it out. Not you."

"Ma told me that my da picked it out, actually," I answer calmly, trying not to be amused even as my alarm bells are shrieking.

Whatever she swallowed, the pills are clearly hitting her system hard and fast.

Fuck.

"Ma?" Her brow furrows. "Da?"

"I'm Irish. Her boys got American-sounding names; the girls were graced with Gaelic ones."

From how she's squinting at me, I reason she understood about five percent of that. "Huh. You don't have an accent. And you don't look like Colin Firth."

"I think you mean Colin Farrell. Irish people don't tend to always look like him," I reply stoically, but the urge to snicker is growing.

Damn, she might be a train wreck, but she's a funny one.

"You're cuter than Colin." Her bleary eyes focus on me for a split second. "Where's your accent?"

"Never had one. My parents do, but Lucas says he lost his on the flight over here, and he was the only one of us technically born on Irish soil," I inform her, wondering why the fuck we're talking about this when she needs either an ER or a bed.

She lets loose a wistful sigh. "You have a brother. That must be nice." On those wobbly heels, she staggers back and crashes into a wall. "I always wanted a sister."

Cautiously, I step over to her. "I have three and trust me, they're pains."

Her smile is more genuine. "Wow. *Three*? And a brother?" She holds up a hand and shows me three fingers.

Amused, I nod. "I had two brothers." I have no idea why, but I admit, "One died."

Her mouth forms the most perfect goddamn circle I've ever seen, and the genuine sympathy in her eyes does something to me—something I can't put words to.

"I am so sorry," she whispers, her pain etching into the words, giving them an individuality that feels genuine.

It sets me on edge.

People say sorry all the time if they learn about Vinny dying, but maybe it's the drugs that are making her weepy—she sounds as if she wants to cry for me.

It's ridiculous but it makes me confess, "He died when I was sixteen. It sucked."

"Was he sick?"

I swallow. "Something like that."

"My mom died when I was fourteen," she whispers. Her gaze drifts over to the diner. "Do you think my boobs are too big?"

My eyes widen. "Excuse me?"

She cups them. In the middle of the street. A driver honks his horn at the show. I hurry nearer to give her some privacy. "My dad offered to cut them off for me."

"What in the what?" I sputter. Now, I *know* she's high. *But it gets worse.*

"He said I should look like my mom. She was perfect. Perfect, perfect, perfect," she repeats, a dull shadow drifting over her expression. "He gave me her nose too."

Somehow, I know she's not talking about genetics and the drugs have her mixing up her words.

Is her dad trying to make her look like her mom or something?

What a fucking creep.

My brain even screeches to a halt at exactly how skeevy that is.

Her father's the reason I'm here, after all.

My boss sent me to Burbank to collect Isabelle without kicking up a stink with the Disciples.

I figure that means "seduce and kidnap her."

I'm not much of a kidnapper though. A seducer, sure.

My boss, Aidan O'Donnelly Jr., head of the Irish Mob in New York, is only involved because Isabelle's father is his surgeon, and he'd pulled some wonder stunts with his knee, which meant he regained full mobility in his leg after a drive-by shooting shattered the joint years ago.

I already knew something wasn't right with the story Dr. Davis was trying to paint, but this confirms it.

According to him, the Disciples' MC is holding Isabelle against her will and she's refused his repeated attempts to bring her home. Aidan made it sound like they were a cult and she was a mindless toy they used and abused for shits and giggles.

I can say, hand on heart, that Davis didn't look beyond the surface at her relationship with the Disciples, if he even bothered to come and see for himself.

I can also say that it seems to me Isabelle has been standing on the outside looking in when she wanted the exact opposite—to be an integral cog in the machine that is the MC.

Upon seeing her relationship with the men and their partners as I scoped out the diner, Davis already proved to me that he knew fuck all about his kid. But what kind of dad wants their daughter to look like their mom to the point where they offer to "cut their tits off?"

The red flags are so large that it's a wonder I'm not draped in them.

Another sniffle reaches my ears. "You think they're too big, don't you?"

Uncomfortable when she's so clearly under the influence, I tell her the truth even as I step back. "I think you're perfect."

Her eyes round, as do her lips.

I'm not lying—she's fucking beautiful.

Her blonde hair shines in the sunlight as if it's a skein of raw silk. Her face is close to doll-like it's so pristine, and her eyes gleam better than the sapphires in my mom's engagement ring. Her lips are perfect for blow jobs, and as for those tits that she asked my opinion on? I'd bet my left ball they'd make a titty fuck feel heaven-sent.

I have no idea why Ryder didn't wife her. In my opinion, it's like looking at Jayne Mansfield reincarnated.

"You think I'm perfect." A dreamy smile crosses her mouth but it fades and immediate discomfort replaces it when the diner door opens then slams closed and a guy with red hair wearing a Disciples cut strides over to us.

"Who the fuck is this creep?"

I scowl at him. "I'm not—"

Isabelle hurls herself off the wall she was using to support her and flattens herself against me. "He's my boyfriend, Edge."

Though my brows rise, it's nothing compared to the Disciple's reaction—*disbelief*. "Yeah, right. What the fuck is going on with you? Joy is about to lose her shit in the diner because you walked out on her. Get back in there—"

"And be humiliated? Again and again?" she yells at him.

Can't Edge see that she's high? Fragile?

My arms slide around her waist as he snipes, "Looks to me like you were the one who humiliated Ryder. What the fuck is wrong with you? You know Julianna is gonna find out about that stunt you pulled—"

"Just *stop*. It didn't mean anything. Y-You need to tell Julianna that I was just…" She swallows and words fail her.

"Trying to make me jealous," I slip in.

She tenses.

Edge frowns at me.

I press a kiss on her cheek. "It worked."

Edge's confusion turns to distrust. "Who the fuck are you again?"

"He's Cade," Isabelle says promptly, snide enough that it hides the slurring of her words. "He's a regular at the diner and my boyfriend…"

"We need to get you home, Cindy," I tell her, her name feeling foreign on my lips because she's Isabelle to me. My mouth curves into a sneer as I turn to Edge. "Your friends might not see that you're not feeling great, but I do."

I start to walk her over to her car, knowing she's too high for it to register that I know which vehicle belongs to her. When Edge lets us go—the jackass should have asked to see my ID or something—I say softly, "I can drive you to your place or call you a cab. We both know you're in no state to get behind the wheel."

She stares at me with those gleaming eyes of hers and asks in a whisper, "Why did you lie for me?"

Her lashes are starting to droop.

I shrug, which jostles her. "I know what it's like to fuck up and never be able to live it down."

"I hate feeling like I'm a burden."

More internal alarms start blaring when she grows limper in my hold.

"You're not a burden." It's strange how the urge to kiss her temple is one I can't fight. "Let's get you home."

"My keys… are in… purse…," she slurs.

By the time I have her in her seat, she's passed out to the world.

Once I fasten her seat belt, I straighten, then I notice that Edge is gone. He's not even in the diner window watching us.

For a cult that's supposed to be holding her against her will, it seems to me like the opposite is true.

What else about Davis's story is bullshit?

Before I can think about it too much, my cell buzzes. When I see my older brother's name, I sigh.

> Lucas: Aidan wants an update.

> Me: I'll check in later.

> Lucas: Fine.

I roll my eyes as I sense his disapproval from the East Coast.

Fine, my ass.

Only Lucas can give a positive word such a negative intonation via text.

As I settle behind the wheel, I glance at Isabelle.

She's not the only one who fucks up and feels like a burden. That's why, even though my instincts are screaming at me that everything is wrong here, I know I *can't* fuck this up.

This initial meeting didn't go according to plan, but as I stick the key into the ignition and think about how the Disciples just alienated and isolated her all while not checking on her very high self and letting her get into a car with a stranger, I pat myself on the back for figuring out an in before I Venmo over the cash to that chick Andrea and thank her for her soup-hurling skills.

Then, of course, everything goes to shit.

Cindy vomits all over herself and... *Jesus Christ.* It's like that time my sister got high on molly at a frat party and asked me to get her to the ER "just in case," so Ma wouldn't lose another kid in a fucking hospital.

I don't allow myself to panic.

Uncaring of the drivers who honk their horns and flip me the bird, I pull a U-turn in the street and get my ass to the nearest hospital.

I'll freak the fuck out later.

3

CINDY

"GIVE HER ANOTHER BAG OF FLUIDS—"

I fade out.

"Hurry it up, dammit. She's going—"

I fade in.

"There she is…"

At the sound of someone's voice, I open my eyes and find myself staring at a stranger in a white coat. For a split second, terror floods my brain, but then I relax. It's not him, my father, but another doctor. One with silver hair.

"What happened?" I croak, trying to move my head, which kind of spins as I take in the fact that I'm not in my apartment with the hot guy…

Wait, did that happen?

"You're in the hospital." The doctor pulls out a light to shine in my eyes then looks at a nurse who is typing on a laptop. "Can you tell me your name?"

"Why?" I rasp.

My throat is killing me, and that goddamn light! *Ouch.*

"Do you know your name?"

I scowl at him. "Of course, I know my name. It's Isa—Cindy

Davis. What happened?" I try to sit up, but my head is throbbing and I'm nauseated.

"Well, Ms. Davis, it seems you overdosed." The doctor stares at me, obviously bored by my predicament. "We pumped your stomach. Can you tell me exactly what you took?"

In this, he's like my father—I'm just a piece of meat.

Still, I shake my head. "That's impossible. I only took a couple Valium…"

In my mind, I attempt to retrace my steps.

Slowly, like a breeze blowing a feather, it infiltrates my brain, and I almost roll my head over the side of the bed and throw up.

The doctor leans closer to peer at me. "Ms. Davis?"

"I'm fine, just nauseated." I groan, then I try to move my hand, but it's got the stupid IV in it. Bruises have already started to form around the injection site.

"Yes, that's normal. After this bag of fluids is done, you should be feeling much better. Do you have someone you can call to help you?" When I nod, he hums. "I'll have a nurse bring you some pamphlets on substance abuse."

"I'm not… Oh, thank you."

The nurse moves around him to hand me a bunch of fliers. "Here you go," she chirps.

"All my medication is prescribed," I say, then I stop.

I fucked up.

I didn't just take Valium; I took Percocet too.

My head pounds.

What an idiot I am. After not taking anything for months, I popped a handful of pills—God.

I'm lucky I didn't die.

"Who brought me in?"

Flashes of dimples and blue eyes that looked at me like I was beautiful filter through the fog in my head. I really hope that wasn't a drug-induced dream.

"I'm not sure, but we have your purse." The nurse smiles at me as she reaches for it on the chair and sets it next to me on the table.

"Your blood work has come in, and it looks good. I'm releasing you on the premise that you'll remain in bed until you're feeling more settled on your feet. I need you to rest today, and please make sure that you don't eat solid foods. Only thin liquids for you for the next twenty-four hours. You should, however, be feeling much better tomorrow." He reaches for the tablet from the nurse standing to his right. While he taps the screen, he shoots me a disapproving glance over his glasses. "You are, Ms. Davis, however, a lucky lady. Do you have someone who can pick you up?"

"Yes, I have friends." I clear my throat. *I hope.*

Jesus Christ, I derailed, like full-on spiraled. That mess at the diner… Oh, God. I'm lucky if I *do* have friends after that.

For a split second, I almost beg the doctor to not discharge me, but I can't hide here forever. Eventually, I'll have to face my shame. Charlie's going to kill me, and I doubt Joy will speak to me after what went down. I probably deserve it too. Now this.

What was I thinking?

"Good luck to you." The doctor's voice snaps me back to my horrible reality as he nods and walks away, handing the nurse the tablet.

A loud beep alerts the nurse that my IV is done. "Your personal effects are over there," she informs me, and I reach for my purse.

"Can I call an Uber?" I watch as she starts to remove my IV, knowing she's bound to say no, but I had to ask.

"Sorry, we need a family member or a sober friend to pick you up."

"Okay." I sigh and glance away, letting her do her thing while I go over my options.

Any angle I come at this from, everyone is going to know what happened. I need to just text Charlie. She's my bestie, and as bad as all this is, at the end of the day, it's not that big of a deal.

"Yeah, right," I mumble, digging in my purse for my phone, ignoring the numerous texts from Joy. Instead, I focus on what to text Charlie. Even after five minutes, all I can come up with is:

Me: Heyyyy.

Rolling my eyes at my stupid brain, I rub my forehead and press send, leaning onto the crappy plastic pillow.

The nurse smiles at me. "Okay, I'll be back with your discharge papers."

"Thank you. Do you need my insurance card?"

As if it weren't bad enough dreading Charlie's reply, now I'm dreading the bill. My deductible is a thousand dollars, and since I don't take money from my dad anymore, that's all on me...

"Whoever brought you in has already taken care of your bill," she informs me, but she leaves before I can question her further.

"Holy fuck," I whisper, because that has to mean the hottie *did* exist.

His suit was tailored. He had money. Does that mean the hottie paid for me?

My pulse leaps in my throat.

What was his name? I feel like he told me.

But why would a stranger pay my hospital bill?

My phone vibrates and I jump to grab it, knowing it'll be Charlie.

> Charlie: Are you okay? Where are you?

Warily, I wonder why she hasn't mentioned the drama at the diner.

> Me: I am but I had an accident.

I can barely press send. This is bad enough. Might as well try to spin it.

> Charlie: WHAT???

> Me: Long story! I'm okay, but I need you to pick me up at Cedars. They won't release me without you. I'm really sorry for the inconvenience :(

I watch as three dots appear, stop, and start again.

Charlie: On our way.

I stare at my phone for long enough that my vision turns blurry, but I can't lose it now—they won't discharge me. I've spent a lifetime and then some in and out of hospitals. I need to be at home yesterday, not just for my mental health, but I lucked out on the bill. I can't afford another night here.

Once I can think straight, I'll deal with Charlie and everything else. That's if she doesn't tear me a new one the minute she sets eyes on me.

With a sigh, I slowly stand. Although I'm slightly dizzy, all things considered, I'm doing okay. I walk over to the plastic bag on the chair that holds my clothes.

"Oh, my God." I instantly gag as I open it. Tomato bisque and puke filter up to me like toxic waste.

Biting my lower lip, I sit on the arm of the chair and breathe, preparing to text Charlie with a request for a change of clothes. That's when the nurse returns with my discharge papers.

Wanting to spare my friend the extra task, I ask, "Listen, if I give you a hundred dollars, can you get me a T-shirt from the hospital gift shop? Anything but what I was wearing will be fine." I motion to the bag, still trying not to gag.

She hesitates as I frantically reach for my purse and pull out a hundred in cash. One thing great about waitressing—you always have cash.

"I…" She studies me compassionately, but it makes me feel like a charity case. "I'll take my break now. What size?"

"Small, medium, I don't care. I can't wear what I had on. I think my skirt is fine, but if they have sweats…" I hand her the hundred then another hundred for the clothes.

"Oh, wow. That's plenty. I'll bring you change. Sign these, please. I'll be right back," she assures me, setting the papers down as I try to force a smile I'm not feeling.

What is happening to me?

My life is spiraling out of control, and I'm now reduced to bribing nurses to get me clothes because mine are not wearable. I've sunk to a new low, which almost makes me laugh—how have I gotten to this point?

"This will all pass," I tell the room like it cares. Like anyone cares.

I can't help but notice Charlie hasn't messaged me in all the time I've been gone...

Picking up the pen, I sign all the pages, flipping back and forth, hoping I can find who covered my bill, but if it *was* the cutie, he paid in cash and there's no name—*damn it.*

I set the papers down and grab the bag, dumping my clothes and shoes on the floor. "Jesus Christ!" I croak, immediately stuffing them back in.

Garbage in the sun smells better than my things.

The nurse strides in with a kind smile. "Okay, here you go." Her nose wrinkles in distaste at the stench around me.

"Please, tell me you got me some pants too?" I plead, looking at the large plastic gift bag.

"I did," she says, passing me the bag, along with my change. "Flip-flops, too."

"Thank you. And please make sure you take the hundred." I motion to the money she's trying to leave.

"No, you needed help. I'm happy I could do it for you." She nods, picking up the discharge papers and handing me my copy.

"Please." I start to untie the hospital gown from my neck. "Take the hundred. You earned it."

She hesitates but accepts the money.

"Thank you. My friend is coming for me."

"Good. I'll get a wheelchair for you and we can wait for them in the lobby."

She's barely out of the door when I pull on a black T-shirt and a pair of sweatpants, which have Los Angeles going down the right leg.

When I slip into the flip-flops and take a deep, contented breath, I'm surprised by how wonderful it feels to be out of the hospital gown.

As I walk slowly into the bathroom, my boobs jiggle. They're huge, and I desperately need a bra, but beggars can't be choosers.

Flipping on the light, I almost scream at what stares back at me.

"Christ."

Morbidly, I lean forward because I'm so pale my blue eyes look like they're about to pop out of my head, not to mention the dark circles that make me resemble a zombie.

My blonde hair is ratted and crunchy from puke, I guess.

But I look as bad as I feel—just turning on the faucet is a chore. After splashing cold water on my face, I pull my hair up into a messy bun using the hair band on my wrist.

A small tap makes me grab ahold of the sink. "Ms. Davis?"

"Yes?" I call out.

"Your friends are here. I have the wheelchair when you're ready."

Knowing better than to try to argue with her that I can walk, I accept that, with how beat up I feel, maybe the wheelchair is not such a bad idea.

"Okay, I'm ready."

I turn off the light, grab my purse, and sink into the chair, noticing this is a different nurse. The woman goes to grab the disgusting bag of puke-covered clothes.

"Can you just burn those?"

"Um, sure." She puts them in the garbage while rolling me out. "Are you feeling okay?"

"Yes, just tired…"

We turn the corner as Charlie and David walk toward me, and my heart sinks at their expressions.

Charlie, beautiful, reasonable Charlie, looks ready to kill me, but that's nothing compared to her husband David, or Poet—that's what the Disciples call him.

Rubbing my forehead as they both catch up to me, I mutter under my breath, "Perfect."

"Oh, my God." Golden eyes take in my appearance. "What the hell happened?"

"It was just a little slipup. You out of everyone should be sympath—"

"Cindy, not one fucking word," David snaps. "Do you have any idea how worried Charlie's been? Fucking overdosing? And don't give me any excuses. I've used them all myself."

"David, please, I'll handle this." Charlie puts her hand on his chest, which must calm him. He glares at me but stays silent as we exit into the large lobby.

"I'll leave you here, Ms. Davis," the nurse says awkwardly, and mostly I'm just glad she isn't sticking around to witness this conversation.

"Look, Cindy, I love you. You're my best friend and we will do whatever you need to get you help. We're here for you—"

David's silver eyes pierce me with their disdain as he butts in, "This codependent thing you've got going on with my wife stops now."

Why didn't I call my other best friend, Doug? I can see that even Eve, the queen of the Disciples, would have been better than Charlie and David. What was I thinking?

"I'm not making excuses. I'm so sorry I texted you," I whisper, feeling guilty for worrying her and wasting their time and just, God, everything.

And while I feel like the worst friend in the world, and Charlie *does* look worried, I can't help but feel resentful too. I mean, as many times as she forgave David and he was on heroin…

When Charlie just stays silent, making me feel even worse, my voice cracks as I say, "I needed help."

David, his eyes narrowed on me like I'm a criminal, runs a hand through his light honey-wheat hair. "You're fired. Charlie doesn't have the guts to do it, but she can't be in ten places at once. She trusted you with the diner, and this is the last time you fuck her and Joy over."

I had one slipup in months, and he's firing me?

I open my mouth to defend myself but… I know he's right. In the past, I was a little unreliable, but that's the past. I've gotten help. I'm mostly off the pills…

I don't know where to look so I stare into the distance.

"David, we can talk about this tomorrow. I'm tired. Let's just take her home—"

I don't hear any more of what Charlie is saying, or what she *isn't* saying—there's no defense coming my way from her corner—because the room around me fades when my eyes connect with his.

He's here.

For me.

My heart skips a beat when his gaze caresses my face then shifts to David as if he wants to put a bullet in his head. Suddenly, this doesn't matter…

I might look like shit but my life is crashing around my feet, and I don't know how or why, but the most beautiful man I've ever seen is fucking here and suddenly, it's easier to take a deep breath. It's easier to ignore my best friend. It's easier to forget I just lost my job.

Golden brown hair, stark brows, glassy blue eyes, and dimples that make me melt.

God, he's gorgeous, yet it's more than that.

It's his mouth—quick to grin—in a strong, stubbled jaw that has my heart fluttering. It's in how he moves, as if he owns the place, dominating the air around him until it vibrates with his power that settles in me. That makes *me* feel stronger. It's in the way he looks in a suit.

It's his command and his control and…

That's when I remember—*Cade*.

Cade's here and suddenly, the rest of the world can go to hell.

4

CADE

"SORRY IF WE'RE boring you, Cindy."

Isabelle's eyes are locked on mine and I'm glad. Glad because those eyes of hers are beautiful even though she looks like she's been to hell and back. Glad because if she's staring at me, she isn't staring at her so-called friends. *Friends who just fucking fired her.*

"Back off, man," I rumble as I dive into a confrontation that is none of my business, but no way in hell am I going to let this jackass annihilate Isabelle after what she's been through. "She was discharged like five seconds ago. You giving her shit isn't going to—"

"Who the fuck are you?"

Confused, Charlie, Cindy's boss, mutters, "He's a regular at the diner, David. Take it easy, sweetheart."

Finally, I glance away from Isabelle and stare at the Disciple I know is called Poet. His top lip curls in a sneer at my dead-eyed stare.

Ignoring his woman, I drawl, "I'm her fucking boyfriend."

"Wait, you're dating this guy, Cindy?" Charlie gasps, looks from me to Cindy, her expression loaded with disbelief.

Not letting Isabelle argue with me, I move over to her and carefully help her out of the wheelchair. I haul her into my side even though she struggles. I know it has nothing to do with my support or her not wanting my help and everything to do with her smelling sour, of sickness and hospitals. But the moment I realize she's shivering, and her goddamn *friends* didn't notice, is the moment I tuck her tighter into my hold. Questionable "perfume" be damned.

Dragging off my jacket, I tuck her inside it while I glower at Poet and Charlie. "Don't you care that she's shivering when you're firing her *in the lobby of a goddamn ER*? Talk about kicking a woman when she's fucking down."

Charlie tugs on her husband's arm. I have to hand it to her—she seems genuinely distressed. *Now.* After I snapped at her. But better late than fucking never. It's enough that I lessen my glare and pin it solely on her dickwad husband, who might be defending his woman, and that deserves a round of fucking applause, but not when Isabelle's been through hell in the past twelve hours.

Still, she disappoints me by muttering, "Let it go, David. Things have been hard for Cindy lately."

"They've been hard for everyone, Charlie, and Cindy knows this."

"I didn't mean to be a burden," Isabelle snaps.

Charlie's gaze softens but Poet grates out, "That's your problem, Cindy. You don't think before you act. You just do things and everyone else has to deal with the consequences. You said you'd stopped using, but here we are—"

"I'm getting you out of here," I tell Isabelle, not even looking at the prick as I interrupt his diatribe.

"Wait! You can't just leave," Charlie cries. "I don't even know this guy other than what he orders at the diner!"

Isabelle studies me for the longest moment. I have no idea what she's thinking, but I know she's snuggling into me. I know she's stopped shivering. I know—

Goddammit.

Train wrecks.

What is it with me and disasters waiting to happen?

Fuck. My. Life.

The moment I set eyes on her a month ago, when I first showed up at the diner, I accepted she'd likely be a problem, but when she presses her hand to my abs for balance, the heat from that innocent touch surges through me like an inferno.

She stares at me for so fucking long that I'm not even sure if she remembers the half-baked story we concocted while she was high.

Then, not looking at either of her friends, she whispers, "We've been dating on the down-low."

"So "down-low" that you didn't even know he was waiting for you here at the ER? That you called us first and wasted our goddamn time trekking through L.A. traffic to bring you home?"

Every word Poet uttered before I started holding her triggered the tiniest of flinches out of her. Now, she doesn't even cringe as she turns to him and says, "I wanted my family around me. Is that so wrong?"

Because I know our relationship is fake, I'm well aware that I gave her the strength to utter those words. Words I don't think she'd have said otherwise.

The bastard deserves the guilt trip too. This was clearly a cry for help, but he's so busy tearing her a new one, he doesn't care.

Poet's jaw clenches. "Selfish junk—"

"David!" Charlie hisses.

"I'm not!" Isabelle shrieks. "Charlie is my family. I wasn't thinking though. You're right. I'm sorry I wanted my best friend close when I just got out of the ER." Bitterness weighs down each word.

"Cindy," Charlie says on a sigh as Poet reaches over to rub one of her shoulders.

I get that he's trying to protect his woman, but treating Isabelle like shit isn't going to happen on my watch.

I don't even care that she and I aren't dating. If someone spoke to my sisters like he did, I'd beat their ass.

"Just...thanks for coming, Charlie. I'm sorry I hauled you over here for no reason. If you need me for a last-minute shift or whatever, just text." Stiffly, she turns to the woman's husband and as cool as you like, her gaze withering, drawls, "David."

Like a queen, she lifts her chin and urges me to move past him.

That has to be the most regal put down I've ever fucking seen.

My God, she's glorious.

Even in this state.

As we step down the hall, she whispers guiltily, "I just gaslit them."

Not liking how wooden she sounds, I rumble, "You overdosed and the only thing he could do is fire you." When she just bites her lip, I prompt her, "Isabelle?"

Immediately, she stops walking. More tension invades her frame now than it did during that conversation with Poet.

"What is it?" I ask. "What's wrong?"

She swallows. "How do you know my full name?"

Fuck. No one calls her Isabelle around here. I don't see her that way in my head so it's jarring.

The lie comes too easily. "I saw it on your chart."

I'm getting too good at this subterfuge BS because she takes that as read. "Oh. Of course. Anyway, David didn't fire me. He's being protective of Charlie, that's all. He's just... He's, well, *David*. Disciples protect their women," she says wistfully, but her tension fades as her hand reaches for mine. Squeezing it, she whispers, "I can't believe you waited for me. I must have been here for hours by now."

"Nine," I admit ruefully.

She blinks at me, and if this were a manga comic, there'd be hearts popping out of her eyes. "You didn't have to do that. And you didn't have to pay my bill either."

I get the feeling she doesn't know if it's me for sure so I focus on the doors up ahead. "I wasn't about to leave you here on your own."

"The bill—it isn't right that..." She sighs. "I have insurance."

"It's fine."

She only took those goddamn pills because I engineered the whole mess with that couple arguing at the diner. The least I could do was cover the bill. *Not that I can tell her that.*

Jesus, I'm a piece of shit.

Her brow is furrowed and I reach over to rub it gently. "It's nothing I can't afford."

It's not a lie.

I'm earning the big bucks now that I've been promoted to the boss's crew. Dropping twenty grand eats into my savings but I'll recoup it soon enough.

"Well, I can't pay you back right now." She looks so earnest that I could kiss her. "But I will. I swear."

"I didn't ask you to." I smile down at her and take in her exhaustion. "Let's get you home."

"Why are you being so kind to me?" She swallows. "For all you know, I'm a horrible person. My friend's husband might be right about me. I did drag my BFF down here when she has two kids at home; one's even a newborn. She probably had to call Doug and Robert to watch them. God, I didn't even think of that—"

I tug her off to the side before we reach the front entrance and place my thumb on her chin. "Hospitals don't allow patients to be released without a friend or family member escorting them. What were you supposed to do? You didn't know I was waiting," I point out. "And they wouldn't let me in because I'm not your next of kin."

She bites her lip. "I should have called someone else."

"Someone else who'd yell at you?" I shrug wearily, unable to deny that I'm starting to feel the exhaustion of a long-ass day loaded with worry and stress.

Guilt and shame for yet another fuckup have been haunting my every step since the nurses wheeled her into the ER and refused to give me any updates. They took my fucking money, though.

Assholes.

I'd been so scared that she'd die—and not because Aidan Jr. would have killed me for the mistake, either.

"They don't all yell at me," is her meek response.

"I was crossing the street when I saw that other waitress screaming at you. Then that biker guy did, and now this other asswipe just talked to you like crap too."

"You're sweet, but I might have deserved it." She sighs.

I shake my head. "You deserve to be treated with kindness."

Her eyes go big and round as if that's a revelation. "Why did you say you were my boyfriend?"

I shoot her a cocky smile as I tug her into moving. I'm not sure why Poet and Charlie haven't passed us yet, but I don't feel like getting into it with them again.

"What do you know about visualization?" I ask.

Her shocked laughter lights me up.

I am so fucked.

"Visualization? Are you an actor or something?"

She has no idea.

"Something like that." I wink at her.

"So you visualize something and, what, it manifests?"

I tighten my arm around her waist. "From where I'm standing, it works."

She blushes and says shyly, "Thank you for coming to my rescue back there, Cade."

I lead us toward the front entrance. "You're welcome, Belle."

She tenses a little. "No one calls me Belle."

I squeeze her again. "They do now."

5

CADE

ONCE WE LEAVE the hospital and she's given me her address, she's quiet.

I mean, I'm a fucking stranger who waded into her life with bullshit and lies. A stranger who she's only letting in because her people have screwed her over... So, I don't blame her for the quiet time and just leave her alone to come to terms with how differently things could have been if I hadn't gone over the speed limit to get her to the ER.

It's a lesson she needs to remember. A lesson that I'm relieved I was there to help teach because, fuck, the idea of her getting hurt over something I helped orchestrate...?

After Vinny?

Shaking my head at my thoughts, I drive her home, grateful that I got the car detailed while she was being treated because no one needs to come face-to-face with yesterday's vomit.

During the journey, Belle proves she has no street smarts, either that or she's too sick to care because she doesn't seem to realize that she could be putting herself in danger... Maybe her instincts tell her that I'm safe?

Her instincts are wrong.

I'm here to topple her world upside down, and fuck, if that's not making me feel like a real piece of shit.

"I hate my job," I mutter under my breath, too quiet for her to hear anyway, but especially inaudible with the radio on low.

My hands grip the steering wheel, making my knuckles ache with the tension. It doesn't help. Pain never does—I learned that the hard way with Vinny. Shot up forty pounds of pure muscle when I started working out to take my mind off shit.

Got me laid, but it didn't heal my fucking soul or ease my grief.

Finally, we make it back to her place, and that's when I realize she was sleeping all along.

Cursing under my breath, I get out and, feeling awkward as hell, go through her purse for her keys. Picking through the collection of pom poms, a pepper spray can on a key ring, and a rape whistle—all pink— I find the one for the front entrance, then I haul her into my arms and carefully carry her to the door.

No one spots us, so no one questions what I'm doing with their unconscious neighbor—I'm almost relieved about that. This does *not* look good from the outside nosing in.

It takes some juggling to find the key to her apartment, but I get her through the door with Belle only mumbling about room service. The critique on my skills as a porter/server makes me grin as I wend a path through her chic living room—definitely bought with Daddy's dough —and into the bedroom.

That's when my tone shifts. "Belle?" I don't let her fall back asleep once her eyes open into slithers.

"What?" she mumbles.

"You need to shower and change."

Her eyes open wider. Then, she whispers, sounding horrified and, to be honest, faintly high, "Do I stink?"

My lips curve but I give her the truth, hoping vanity will keep her awake. "You don't smell fresh."

It works, but her reaction is so immediate that I almost drop the hold I have on her, from her being practically in a coma in my arms to full on drama queen—Jesus, it's a wonder she doesn't give me whiplash.

"I STINK," she shrieks, "and you're cute and oh, my God, I don't always smell of vomit," she promises.

Her legs are shaky, a lesson she learns when she tries to toe out of her sweats, seeming not to care that I'm standing right in front of her when she starts undressing.

Propping her up, I drawl, "Belle, calm down. No one smells or looks good when they just had their stomach pumped."

Then, of course, I'm reminded that in the history of humanity, telling a woman to calm down never works…

"Why do you have to be so pretty?" Her eyes are big and wide as she stares at me.

I hide a grin. "I mean, it takes one to know one?"

She heaves a sigh. "And he's charming too."

"Do you want me to help you into the shower?" I arch a brow. "My ma raised a gentleman. I won't look." *Unless asked.*

Biting her lip, she peeks at me then at the bathroom door. "Would you mind?"

"Wouldn't have asked if I did." I don't know what makes me do it, the gesture is fucking insane to me, but I press a kiss to her forehead. "Let's get you cleaned up, hmm?"

Another sigh spills from those pouty lips, then she surprises me by tapping me on the nose and declaring, "One day, I'll be more than happy to have you watch me when I shower."

Shuffling her into the bathroom, I snort. "Good to know, princess. Good to know."

6

CINDY/BELLE

WHAT IS THAT NOISE?

I roll over and blink my eyes open. The morning sun spills in, casting a slight glare off my balcony doors that's hell on my headache.

When I realize I'm alone, I sit up and instantly look for him.

"Cade?" Is that my voice? Ugh.

I reach over to the spot next to me on the bed—it's cold.

My phone vibrates on the nightstand, not only an annoying reminder that I will eventually have to deal with all my crap but the reason behind my waking up earlier than I'd have preferred.

Glaring at it, I toss the covers off and marvel at what a good night's sleep can accomplish. I still feel the aftereffects of yesterday, but at least I feel like a real person again.

I stand and stretch then grimace when my phone stops and starts up on a loop.

With a sigh, I grab it, unable to keep from smiling because as fucked up as yesterday was, Cade's defense of me was amazing, and it gave me the guts to stick it to David.

How Cade appeared out of nowhere like my knight in shining armor, standing up for me… so fucking hot. And that look on David's face, *ha*.

My phone vibrates in my hand—Charlie.

Okay, I need to do some damage control this morning. Not that I want to get ahead of myself, but if this feeling that I'm having for Cade is real, I don't want David alienating the club against him.

"Cade?" I call out again.

He wouldn't have left, right?

I mean, I know I passed out after I took a shower. My stomach flutters at how protective, almost loving he was when he brought me home. He didn't let me do a thing, even started the shower for me then wrapped me in my towel and tucked me into bed.

I kinda hoped he'd sleep beside me, but apparently he's more of a gentleman than I am a lady.

Prince fucking Charming.

"Stop it. You barely know him, and nobody can be that perfect." Trying to stop this excitement I'm having just thinking about him is impossible. Until my stupid phone sours my mood.

"Hey."

"I swear to God, Cindy, I've been calling and texting for an hour," Charlie hisses into the phone, which means she's trying to control her volume because of baby Madison.

"Sorry, I just woke up," I say, forcing myself to sound cheerful.

"It's fucking noon," she snaps then lowers her voice.

"I had my stomach pumped yesterday, Charlie," I snap right back. "Did you think that was like a day trip to the spa?"

"What the hell is happening with you? What are you doing with that man?"

"Charlie, Cade's been so kind—"

"*Kind?* Look, I'm trying to not completely lose it, Cindy, but that man said he was your boyfriend. I didn't want David to get into his face so I dropped it, but we both know that's a lie.

"Do you owe him money? Is that why he was constantly coming in? How can I help you if you don't tell me—"

"What are you saying?" I hiss, my face heating up at her opinion of me. "That no man could actually like me without me owing them money?" I toss my hair into a haphazard bun then peek out into the living room to see if Cade stuck around.

"Well, he's not your boyfriend. And you had no idea he was waiting for you. What do you expect me to think? Just be honest. Are you in trouble?"

"Jesus Christ, Charlie! I never imagined he'd wait nine hours for me in the ER waiting room. Plus, I wanted to see my best friend—you know, *my family*?—after I had a bad day, the worst of days, even. But back to Cade—"

"Bad day?" she interrupts with a small growl. "You got that right. Cindy, you had to get your stomach pumped. You left Joy with a packed restaurant after yet another half-hour spent hiding in the restroom"—that has my face flushing with embarrassment—"*and* you fucking tried to kiss Ryder in front of everyone.

"Now you've hooked up with some stranger who was dumb enough to get in David's face and who's claiming he's your boyfriend. I just don't—"

"He *is* my boyfriend!"

"Why are you lying to me?" Her voice grows louder as I hear Madison start to fuss. "You tell me everything, and you wouldn't be trying to kiss Ryder if you were with this guy."

I close my eyes against her words. It's either that or hang up. I don't do well when cornered, but it's Charlie and I love her.

"Look, the Ryder thing was a big mistake to make Cade jealous. As for Joy, I will straighten that out—"

"Do you even hear yourself? You know what? Don't bother." She shushes Madison, who must be feeling our bad vibe since she's now crying. "Joy's not happy and I'm completely overwhelmed. I can't raise two kids, run a business, and worry about David and you at the same time. It's just too much." Her voice cracks.

"Wait," I sputter. "What are you saying?"

"I'm saying you should take some time to get yourself back on track again, go to some meetings—"

"Holy shit. Are you actually listening to David and firing me?" My mind spins.

Take some time?

How about three fucking years! How about thirty?!

I mean, I know David told me that I was fired last night, but I figured he was just being an ass. She knows I need this job. For fuck's sake, I've been there for years.

Cade was right—*they really are kicking me when I'm down.*

"No, but until I come back, you need to—"

"You're unbelievable, Charlie. I overdose and your first reaction is to kick me to the curb? You know what... I have to go."

I throw my phone on the bed like it's dipped in poison. This has to be David's doing because Charlie is my bestie... She wouldn't. *Couldn't.*

"I can't believe this," I scream, sitting down at the edge of my bed, nails digging into the sheet to steady me as I try to think... *Fired.* Okay, maybe she didn't say the word "fired" but that's what she meant.

My phone vibrates and, hoping it's Charlie, I grab it, but it's Eve so she'll be calling to tear me a new one too. I can't deal with her or any of my tribe right now. I'm sure Charlie has twisted everything, so they'll be on her side.

"I have to get out of here," I mutter under my breath, jerking to my feet as, frantically, I look around for what I need so I can leave my condo. I'd rather live in my car than spend another second in this place.

Rushing to my closet, I pull out my suitcase, screaming, "Cade?" at the top of my lungs as I rip clothes off the hangers and toss them on the bed.

Please, let him be here. Please.

"Belle?" Cade demands, bursting into my room carrying two coffees on a carton tray and a bag of something. His blue eyes are fierce as they scan the room and shift to me.

"You were right," I whisper, eyes burning as I try to stop the tears from spilling down my cheeks.

But a strange relief pounds its way through me in time to the beating of my heart—he didn't leave me; he went to get coffee.

"What happened?" he asks, his tone calmer now that he sees I'm okay.

And I am, kinda.

He has this weird aura—it's soothing. It suffuses the room with his presence, and, suddenly, my hopelessness begins to fade.

It's like he can fix everything, and that is *so* hot in the wake of all this chaos in my life.

Setting down the coffees and the bag on my dresser, he moves toward me, robbing me of my breath with every step.

"C-Charlie, she f-fired m-me... kind of. After everything we've been through, it's u-unbelievable. I have to get out of here. O-Out of L.A.," I stutter. "I'm leaving."

Those strong, capable hands of his reach out to me. His fingers trail over my cheeks, cupping my face as he stares deeply into my eyes, murmuring, "Hey, just breathe. You can get through anything, can do anything."

Clinging to the dress in my hand, I swallow. "You don't know me."

He graces me with a charming grin. It's one he *knows* is charming, which should annoy me, but I don't let it. Even if I know he's trying to disarm me.

At this moment, I'll take being disarmed.

"Fuck, even when you're crying you're so beautiful, Isabelle," he murmurs, gaze drifting over my features. "And yesterday, watching you stand up for yourself was something glorious to behold. You're stronger than you realize, baby."

Rubbing away my tears with his thumb, he lowers his head to destroy me with a kiss that, until this very second, I didn't know was possible—pure feeling.

Adrenaline spikes through me as he robs me of my breath, my very soul, and I cling to him. My hands entwine in his hair and I groan, our tongues tangling as everything around us vanishes. All I feel is him and the way his mouth moves over mine in a dominant demand I can't help but submit to.

That's when he raises his head.

Jesus, he looks as if he wants to devour me, swallow me whole.

My nipples harden painfully in response when he jerks the dress from my hand and mutters, "I wanna take this off." He plucks at the tee he'd dressed me in last night.

It's crazy fast but I don't care—I nod.

He groans as he hauls it overhead, baring me to his greedy gaze. "I want your eyes on me when I fuck you, Belle," he rasps, the words sending liquid heat along my nerve endings.

His nostrils flare at my moan as he dips his head to my neck. His nose nuzzles the tender area as if he likes my scent, then his hand cups my breast, his thumb rubbing my nipple back and forth before he pinches it, causing my pussy to throb.

God, I feel so empty.

"These tits are *mine,*" he growls.

"Yes," I chant, eager desire whipping through me, taking the fear and the panic and the distress with it.

He lifts me and I wrap my legs around his waist, my hands trying to frantically unbutton his dress shirt as we both fall onto the bed. My clothes spill around us as he claims my mouth again. I don't know if it's me or him, but somehow his shirt is gone, allowing my hands access to his muscled shoulders.

God, those muscles.

When he lifts his head, I arch my back and rub my breasts against his bare chest.

"Yeah, that's it, Belle. Christ, your tits are going to fucking kill me." He grunts and I watch his biceps move while he stands to unbuckle his belt. "Open your legs," he orders.

I immediately obey, licking my lips and pushing my clothes out of the way so he can see *all* of me. His eyes stay fixated on my face, though, and with a smirk, he unzips his slacks and I snatch at the chance to see his giant cock.

"Yes," I moan as I watch his hand stroke it. "There are condoms in the nightstand to your right."

He jerks the drawer handle to retrieve protection. Then, I watch the one-man show as he rips the pouch open and slowly rolls it on his erection. I almost tell him to fuck me raw since I'm on the pill, but that'd be crazy. Right?

"So fucking beautiful." His words… It's like I've been needing to hear them my whole life. "Look at how hard I am for you, Belle. All of this is for you."

I stare at his shaft and whimper. Christ, he's big.

"Do you want it?"

"Yes," I whisper.

His smirk deepens. "Can you take every fucking inch?"

Sassily, I hook one of my legs around his hips. "Less talking, more action."

Fire lights up his eyes as he grabs my other ankle and drags me to the edge of the bed.

"More action, huh?" he drawls and wraps his fist around his cock. My mouth waters at the sight. "You like that, Belle? Or did you have a different 'action' in mind?"

"Fuck me, Cade. Please," I plead.

"I like hearing those words on your lips. Say it again. Beg me for my dick, my beautiful Belle."

That filthy mouth is going to kill me.

My eyes flutter closed.

"Eyes on me," he grunts immediately, but he's nearer. His cock is so close to where it needs to be—I can feel it when it slaps against my inner thigh.

They pop open as I plead, "Please, Cade. I want your dick. I want it inside me. I want you to fill me. I need you—"

He thrusts inside me.

Hard.

Deep.

My hands grab a hold of my sheets, clothes, whatever. I can barely remember my name. It feels so good as he pulls out and slams into me again.

"That's it, Belle, taking me like a good girl. How does my cock feel inside you?" He spreads my legs wider, watching his cock slide in and out, and his finger traces over my sex, collecting my juices so he can rub my clit.

"P-Perfect," I stutter.

His lips twitch and his eyes lock onto mine. "Tell me what you need, Belle."

Blankly, I stare at him, unsure of what to say, then he pulls out and I hear myself scream as he rubs the tip of his dick back and forth over my swollen clit.

The words come to me in an instant. "You. *I need you.*" It's not a lie. God, I feel feverish.

He crawls on top of me then, when his lips brush mine, he rumbles, "I'm right here. Words, Belle. Words. Do you want me inside you again?"

My nails dig into his chest. "Yes. Please…" I pant as he fills me, claiming my body as his. That's when I start to chant, "Yes," over and over as he picks up speed.

He grabs my hand from his chest and pins it overhead while he fucks me. "I need more than 'yes,' Belle, or I'm going to stop again."

This is fucking torment. "I-I need your cock. I need you to fuck me." I moan because hearing myself talk like this makes me feel a certain kind of crazy. "Oh, God, I'm…" I can barely form words while he pounds into me. It feels so good I can't think.

The moment my eyes close, he stops. As I shriek, he growls, "Eyes, Belle. I want to see you come undone, beautiful."

They pop open and he grunts into my lips as my pussy latches onto his cock and I start to contract and pulse around him.

"Yeah, that's it, come all over my dick," he hisses. "Jesus Christ, Belle, your cunt is fucking heaven. You feel so good, so goddamn good."

And I'm gone, splintering into a million pieces. I think I'm screaming, maybe even crying as I have the most intense orgasm of my life. Black dots appear in my vision, and I dig my nails into his back as if that can keep him inside me forever.

Because this is something I can't live without. *This* is almost cathartic.

"Cade," I whimper while he keeps fucking me, every single cell in my body alive. I'm sensitive but spread my legs wider so his cock can go deeper.

I can't get enough. I can't, I just can't, and then—

"Fuck, Belle. You're going to make me come. Do you want that, baby? Do you want my cum?"

"Yes," I beg. "Please, give it to me."

His hands grab mine and he pins them on either side of my head, then he thrusts deeper, harder, *faster.* Our gazes are locked together and I swear I can see the moment it hits him, when pleasure overtakes everything else. His thrusts slow as he strains, his fingers tightening around mine, then he stills. His pupils morph into pinpricks and, for a second, I don't breathe, only feel as his body jerks and his cock pulses his release deep inside me.

God, I wish he weren't wearing a condom.

Then, my thoughts fade and I'm floating… almost weightless. The ecstasy, the sheer delirium that strikes me like a lightning bolt to the nervous system is like nothing I've ever experienced before.

As I come down, Cade starts peppering little kisses all over my face.

"Holy fuck," I whisper into his lips, not moving. "That was…"

He braces himself on his elbows and I can feel his eyes caress my face.

"Cade?" I whisper, looking at him at long last, not even knowing what I want him to say but knowing that I don't want this to end.

"You were beautiful before to me, but now, you're just a wet fucking dream come to life." His fingers, sticky from when he touched my clit, stroke over my jaw. His lips brush mine as my heart skips. "I'm never gonna get the sight of you out of my head when you let go, Belle."

"I'm hardly beautiful right now," I whisper into his mouth.

His eyes continue to hold mine until a spark of something, regret, or maybe pain, coalesces into being. It's gone so fast I'm not even sure I saw anything as he lowers his lips to my neck, mumbling, "Where do you want to go?"

7

CADE

ACUIG

I'm an asshole.

I admit it.

Not only because I fucked her when I shouldn't have, but the question I just asked her makes me one.

Am I the asshole because I'm trying to trap my mark into heading to New York so I don't have to kidnap her?

She stares at me, those eyes of hers starry, and because I'm feeling guilty, I lower my head and suck on her nipple.

She has the best tits.

The best.

They're not fake, either. They're all natural. And they're so fucking gorgeous that I can feel my dick hardening again.

Jesus Christ, I'm too goddamn old for a recovery time this fast, but my dick does *not* agree with Belle's cunt in its horizon.

As I suck the nipple, raking my teeth over the tip, I watch her eyes flutter.

Smirking to myself, I pull away, satisfied when her pussy clenches down on me. "Well?"

"Well?" Her breathy question tells me she's on cloud nine right now.

For that matter, so am I.

I can't stop myself from thrusting into her. My cock's still hard enough to hit all her notes, something that's proven when she cries out, head falling back as I reach down and press my thumb to her clit.

Then the goddamn condom gets in the way.

Fuck.

I pull out, grab the condom, toss it on the floor, and then just stare down at her.

"You're so fucking wet for me, Belle," I breathe, looming above her for a second before I let the tip of my tongue travel over her tits and toward her throat.

"I'm clean, Belle."

"M-Me too."

"Then, no rubber?"

Her tits heave as she sighs. "Okay. I'm protected from pregnancy," she assures me while squirming against me as I seek out tender areas on her throat like I'm digging for gold.

Her hands grab at me as I find the sensitive skin between neck and shoulder, and she shudders as I slide my fingers through the delicious mess we made together before I thrust home. I continue my slow thrusts, still making this all about her as I suckle the flesh hard.

I want her marked.

A woman like Belle needs marking.

She needs the visual reminder that she's been claimed.

And the rest of the world—i.e., those fucking Disciples—needs to know to back the fuck off.

"What are you doing to me, Cade?" she whimpers as her hips rock up, her legs spreading as she grinds back into me. "I just haven't felt like this in…" Her hand flops against her face as she starts to cry.

I nuzzle my nose against her cheek. "Those good tears, baby?"

The "s" is sibilant on: "Yes." Her moans are a symphony I don't want to live without. "Please," she sobs as I find her clit again and, with my lubricated fingers, work her higher than before. She's a decibel below screeching as her nails tear into my back and she cries, "Don't stop. God, don't. Please. Don't."

I'll take it.

Hell, I'll take *more*.

I want to sear this bone-deep pleasure into her soul, make everything right in her fucking world...

Only, she isn't mine to keep.

Not yet.

If I can get her to New York, I just know Aidan will let me have her.

If she wants to be mine...

Christ, this is crazy, but she makes me crazy, and with how good this feels, I don't care either.

The thought has me doubling down, grinding back as she continues seeking release. Not only because it's way too fucking soon to be thinking shit like that, but because I still have a job to do.

When she hits the spot, her scream is so loud that if I were another man, I'd worry about her neighbors thinking something shady was going on in here.

But instead, my grin's cocky as she clamps down on me, drawing my own release out from under my control, making me roar with it. As I press my forehead to hers for those last thrusts, I get to watch as she comes, and comes, *and comes*.

When she goes limp beneath me, however, my cockiness fades away.

My mind takes me back to her car yesterday when she passed out... and to the shower late last night.

But when I'm reminded that I'm a moron for fucking her, not only because of my real role here but because she OD'd yesterday, her eyelashes flutter again.

When she looks up at me, there's still a haze, as if she's not focusing well, but then her spaghetti arms loop around my neck and she hauls me down, mumbling, "Never, ever, ever have I come like that—"

She's tiny, and I'm a heavy motherfucker, so I roll us over so I'm beneath her. Cupping the back of her head, I nuzzle my face against her throat, on the other side this time, and I find the same spot and tease it with my tongue.

"Mmpff," she rumbles, little shivers rushing through her as she lies on top of me.

Everyone's got a happy spot—seems like I've found two of hers.

A soft, keening noise escapes her as I continue marking her.

When I retreat and position myself so I'm more comfortable, I whisper, "So, my Belle, where are we going?"

When she settles her head on my chest, her arms tangle around me. She's uber clingy but I love clingy chicks, and feeling her tits smashed up against me makes it ten times fucking better that she's like an octopus.

"You want to come with me?" she whispers.

Hell, it's so soft that I almost don't hear her.

"Why not?"

It's a blasé response, but it's the only way I can make this make sense.

She can't think I'm too eager. Who picks up their life on a whim for the waitress who always remembers your order and puked on your Brioni shoes after you rushed her to the ER?

"Why not?" she repeats, her confusion clear. It has her peering at me like I'm from Mars. "Your life is here."

"I'm a New Yorker." I wink at her. "Can't you tell from the accent?"

Her lips twitch, but a slither of fear seeps into her eyes. "I did recognize it. Whereabouts are you from?"

"Hell's Kitchen. You ever been there?"

She shakes her head.

"Best place on earth. People call my neighborhood hell. Ha. They've never been to L.A. before."

My joke makes the remnants of fear in her eyes drift away. "You don't like it here? Is that why…"

"Why I feel like picking up and taking off for parts unknown?" I shrug—pretending to be nonchalant is hard when so much is riding on this. "I guess."

"What about work?"

This is where shit gets dicey.

With a lie incoming, I smooth my hand over her hip. Letting it follow the line of her thigh, I trickle my fingers inward, dragging one down to her pussy.

She's soaked with my cum and hers, and I take full advantage of this position by coating the digit in it and finding her clit.

As I stroke her there, hitting differently from this other angle, her eyes widen and I say, "I'm a digital nomad."

"A—" She releases a sharp breath. "What's that?" Her hips start rocking.

"It means my computer is my office and I can work wherever I want. I've been in L.A. for a couple months now, working on a deal with a local company," I lie, "but it finalized yesterday. Why do you think I looked so fly in my suit?" I grin. "I was coming in to celebrate with my favorite waitress at my favorite diner."

Her soft chuckle develops into a moan. "Don't you have a boss?"

"Not in the traditional sense. I'm a free agent again," I inform her, hoping she's registering this.

Her eyes are blurry. "As of yesterday?"

"Uh-huh," I murmur, reaching up to kiss her now that I know she's listening.

As my tongue finds hers, I carry on, plaguing her with pleasure, rubbing her clit until she's riding my hand.

Then I stop. As she shrieks at me, confused need filtering through her, I twist us around so that I can sink down, down. My cum coats her cunt and I let my tongue swirl through her folds before I hunt for her clit. A soft gasp escapes her when I hit *the* spot again, and once I find it with my tongue, I don't let it go until *she* lets go.

I keep stroking her clit until her thighs are clenching around my head to the point of pain. Lapping at the sensitive nub, I wait for her to shudder and release me from her hold then, nuzzling her with my nose, I investigate further, shuffling deeper between her legs until I let my cum drip onto my tongue, then I surge higher, grabbing her thighs so she can hug me with them before I cup her jaw and kiss her.

I thrust my tongue between her lips. She jolts in surprise when my cum slips into her mouth, then she groans and slides her arms over my shoulders, holding me close, not pushing me away.

With the aftershocks rippling through her, I twist us over one final time so that she's blanketing me, and I start to stroke my other hand along the length of her spine, soothing her and calming her… feeling oddly content, as if I've staked a primitive claim on her.

Dumb, but I never claimed to be a genius after sex.

She nestles against me in the silence and, when I know her mind is elsewhere, I whisper temptation into her ear. "Do you know what I do when I'm trying to think about where I'm going to live next?"

She shakes her head. The soft silk should tickle but, instead, it feels like a caress.

"I go to the airport, I buy the ticket for the next available flight that has a seat, and I get my ass on board and fly wherever it takes me. That's my next office."

"Your next office?"

I hum. "I can work anywhere in the world. Why wouldn't I go exploring?"

"I can't do that," she whispers.

"Why not? You said you wanted to take off, right?"

"I can't afford a plane ticket."

I let loose a soft chuckle. "Baby, after yesterday's business deal, I can afford your airfare."

That has her head popping up. Her stare is intense as she asks, "Why would you pay for me?"

She can't know what it does to me when she looks at me like that. So suspicious and lost and broken at the same time.

Beneath it all, there's a whisper of hope and that, more than anything, catches me off guard, enough that I admit a truth to her: "It gets lonely."

Shit.

My life *is* lonely in a sense, but not because of the bullshit I'm selling her.

She blinks. "What does?"

"Going on adventures by yourself." I shoot her a sheepish grin. "I guess it's not sexy to admit that, is it?"

"I-I don't think it's…"

I arch a brow at her. "You hang around with bikers, Belle. I've seen you with them in the diner. I can't see any of them admitting that they're lonely."

"No," she agrees slowly. "But that… doesn't make it a bad thing. It's not a crime to have feelings." Her tone grows firmer. "I don't want to be cut off from someone I like. There's nothing wrong with being vulnerable." Her brow puckers. "And let's face it, you've seen me in some very vulnerable states over the past twenty-four hours, so, I guess, thank you for being open with me."

I gently push her hair aside and let my thumb stroke along the sensitive curve of her throat. Damn, my marks look good on her.

Too fucking good.

"I wouldn't offer if I couldn't afford it," I tempt.

She bites her lip. "I'll have to pay my way when we get wherever we're going."

I tug her lip free then swoop in and nip it with my teeth. "What if I keep you busy doing other things?" I growl, chuckling as she shrieks out a laugh when I twist us over so I'm looming above her again.

"What kind of other things?" she teases, still laughing as I nuzzle my nose down her throat.

"Things that I know you can handle."

"Such as?"

"Things that come in multiples."

Her hand rakes through my hair as she encourages me to look at her. "Multiples?"

"You came three times, didn't you?"

Her cheeks burn a hot red. "I-I did."

I can tell immediately that she's never gotten off that many times before. Especially when I take into consideration her earlier, "Never, ever, ever..."

"Think you can take that on the regular?" I rasp.

Her lips part, stars back in her eyes, sure, but more because she's loving the idea of getting off so many times.

"How regular?" she whispers.

"Every night too much?" I joke.

Her fingers cup the nape of my neck, but the stars have disappeared, replaced with an unexpected seriousness. "I'm not a whore—"

Whatever the hell I thought she'd say, it wasn't that.

I gape at her.

I know I am.

I don't bother stopping.

That's when she starts laughing again. "Okay, I can see that wasn't where your mind was at. But I had to check."

"Belle, since when do johns get their hookers off? Or care about their pleasure?"

She shrugs a shoulder. "Well, I had to check."

"I don't think you're a prostitute!" I hiss. "Jesus, I was just trying to be spontaneous."

It's ridiculous, considering my reasons for being here, but that she even thought it pisses me off.

Goddammit, how low is her opinion of herself that she'd immediately go there?

As I make to roll off the bed, her hand grabs mine and with surprising strength, she hauls me back onto the mattress.

When she clambers onto my lap, straddling me, her arms everywhere like the octopus I compared her to earlier, I allow her to bury her face in my throat and to hug me as she mumbles frantically in my ear, "I'm sorry! I didn't mean to be ungrateful."

Still scowling, I grab her chin and urge her to look at me. "You didn't sound ungrateful. That isn't why I'm mad." And it isn't. "Belle, it pissed me off that you would think *I'd* think so little of you." I cup her nape and urge her mouth onto mine. Just as she starts to moan, and just as my cock starts to twitch for round three, I pull back so I can stare her straight in the eye. And even though I'm a deceitful piece of shit, I've never meant anything more than my next words: "You're a fucking queen and you don't even know it. That hurts me. It fucking hurts."

Her bottom lip quivers. That's my initial warning. Then she's on me again, urging our mouths into a fiery collision, one hand sliding between us as she grabs my cock and doesn't stop jerking me off until I'm hard.

She isn't the only one capable of the impossible when we're together—my cock's reacting like I'm taking blue pills whenever it's near her hand, her mouth, that fucking pussy...

When she slides me inside her, her cunt clamping down on me, our mutual releases easing my path in a way that's heaven-sent, our eyes are locked onto each other's.

That's when I accept the inevitable—*I'm in big trouble.*

8

CINDY/BELLE

"YOU'RE BAD FOR MY EGO."

My eyes flare in concern. "What?!"

"Whoa, calm down. I was only teasing." He hands me a coffee. "You take it stronger than me, which is saying something." His head tilts to the side. "You're jumpy."

"No, I'm not," I counter with a huff. "I just need a caffeine fix."

That answer seems to satisfy him, and he leaves me to drink my joe without a murmur. The moment he's sitting down, though, he drapes his arm around the back of the uncomfortable chair outside a boarding gate in LAX where we're waiting to be called for a plane to New York.

New York.

What the fuck am I doing? I glance over at his beautiful face and my heart kind of leaps in my throat. *This* is what I'm doing. As in him —I'm doing him—completely letting multiple orgasms and a hot man prompt me to forget that I'm about to board a plane to the one place where I do not go.

New fucking York.

Casting him a look, I fight the need to reciprocate when he shoots me a smile.

I swear this man is something else.

It was only when we used my car to get to the airport that I learned he'd taken it to be detailed as, during my "episode," I'd vomited all over the interior.

Who did that for someone? Especially after paying for my ER bill.

Something about the genuineness of his smile, about his earnestness, about his many past kindnesses makes me feel like I'm in a safe enough space to blurt out, "I can't go to New York, Cade."

It might have been fate that had us rolling up and grabbing the next available flight out of LAX, which was to the Big Apple, but I don't care.

I. Can't. Do. It.

He arches a brow at me. "You got something against the best pizza in the world?"

I don't laugh. "I wanted to get away from L.A., not go to New York." I cross my legs then frown at the two women sitting across from us who are staring at him. "Good pizza or not."

"You gonna tell me why you've had a change of heart?" His hand brushes my hair off my shoulder as his blue eyes caress my face. As I start to drown in them, he rumbles, "I want to take you to all my favorite spots. Don't you want to *come* with me?"

He did not just...

He shoots me a cocky grin.

He did.

Any other time, I'd have laughed, but I just can't right now.

When I don't smile in return, his demeanor changes, concern shifting into his expression. "Tell me why?" His voice sounds smooth, as if he's trying to calm me. *Nothing could calm me down at this moment.*

I look around the massive, crowded terminal of loud, aggravated travelers and wish I could shrink into myself and disappear.

Then, one of those women opposite us tosses her hair as she studies him. Cade's a typical man, though, so he doesn't notice.

But I do.

"I hate it there," I say, aware that I sound sulky.

He frowns and I almost attempt to smooth his grimace away

because all that worry belongs to *me*. Not those bitches drooling over him. "Tell me why, Belle."

"Because," I snap, looking down at my hands and then over at the women who are not even pretending they're not watching us.

"Belle, I just spent fifteen hundred dollars on tickets. I need more than a *because*." He cocks his head at me. "Come on, sweetheart. How can I fix this if I don't know what's going on?"

"Look, my friend, Antoinette, was raised there and her father killed her mother, and I just… It has always been a place I don't want to go." I lick my glossed-up lips. "I should have told you earlier, but you distracted me—"

"Hold on. You don't want to go because *a friend* had a tragedy there?" He looks at me like he knows I'm lying, but what am I going to say?

I can't go, sorry, but my insane father lives there and I've spent the last ten years running away from him? Um, no.

"Yes."

His eyes narrow and he takes his arm away as he studies the travelers passing us by—he knows I'm lying.

"I… It's just, can't we go somewhere else?"

I should have stopped him sooner. When he was buying the tickets, I should have spoken up, but I'd panicked. He'd seemed so set on the idea and I didn't want to disappoint him. I thought I could do it, but I just don't think that I can.

"The truth is, beautiful, it was a wise move for me to go back to New York," he admits. "Whether you come with me or not, I have to return. I'd prefer it if you were on my arm." He turns to me, and everything about his vibe is different. Even his voice has changed. As I swallow and recross my legs, a small ripple of excitement goes through me. "If I could switch up the end destination, I would, but I have business to attend to, and I want you to meet my family…" His hand brushes my neck as a shiver goes through me. "Don't you want to meet them too? I know it's fast, but we've got something good going on, don't we?"

"I just…" I shoot him a nervous glance. "I said yes impulsively. It's something I'm working on." Then, I lean into his space. "You really think we've got something good going on?"

His grin has those dimples flashing—*I am such a sucker for them.* "You know it. Rarely say what I don't mean. Life's simpler that way and things are already crazy in my world."

I can feel myself leaning into his space as his grin shifts into a lazy smile that gives my stomach butterflies and makes my pussy wet. That's when I remember I'm in the most public of spaces.

No touching the dirty-talking businessman, Cindy.

Down, girl.

Shaking my head, I study my heeled pumps.

This guy's dangerous because he's disarming. He never says what I think he will. Has anyone ever been that candid with me before? Absently, my mind drifts to our conversation about loneliness. He was right in that Ryder would have preferred to swallow a bullet than talk about his emotions with me.

God, it's no wonder Cade is like a breath of fresh air.

"Come with me, Belle. I promise it will be fun."

His hand, which is on my nape, tightens, and I blink into his clear blue eyes. When he squeezes a second then rubs his thumb down the back, only stopping when he moves it in a circle over the top of my spine, I can feel myself melt into him.

"Fine," I whisper, and I'm glad I made the decision because his eyes change, shift with his relief.

Relief.

Because he wants to be with me.

Me!

God, could I have found a man who is gorgeous, smart, and wants me even though he's seen only the worst of me? Why does it make me want him to see the best?

"That's my girl." I shiver again when he whispers in my ear, "I know something that can help you relax before we get to the Big Apple. I also know how to make you like the city... Let's board," he declares with a wink.

When he stands and holds out his hand for me, I stare into those wicked blue eyes that are making me do crazy things, but I place mine in his and grab my purse.

That's when one of those bitches opposite us giggles. It's one of those flirty laughs that every woman recognizes but no man does.

I shoot them a nasty look, even though Cade doesn't even appear to notice them.

I've always had a slight jealousy problem, but with Cade, I'm ready to scratch these women's eyes out if they don't back off. Geez, can't they see he's taken when he's been touching my face the way he has? Can't they see how he's marked my throat?

My death stare works because they both look away.

Either that or they realize Cade is a lost cause because he's too busy snatching my purse and carrying it for me in a way that's no good for the leather but is so chivalrous that I melt.

My knees feel weak as I straighten up and walk toward the gate.

There are close to two million people in Manhattan, I reassure myself, and I won't run into my father in Hell's Kitchen, that's for sure. He barely leaves Fifth Avenue—I doubt the years have made him less of a pretentious asshole than before.

Cade's hand squeezes mine, returning my attention to him.

It centers me, *grounds* me.

Helps me accept that I need to just go with the flow and see where all this takes me. The sex is off the charts, but I think the reason I'm not running in the other direction is because of how he touches me, how he looks at me as if I'm his and his alone.

It's too soon. *I know that.* But I can't find it in me to care because it's so good to feel cherished. Protected. *Safe.*

"You do know I have to come back in a week or so," I mutter, my tone thick with stupid emotions while I unashamedly cling to his hand as he walks us to the attendant and goes through the motions of getting us onboard.

He hums his understanding then smiles politely at the attendant, who immediately blushes and returns the smile.

I want to kick her with my heel. Although, being dragged away by security *would* be a way to get out of going to New York...

"God, does every woman just throw themselves at you?" I hiss as he walks us onto the plane.

"Look at you, getting all possessive," he croons.

I scowl. "Whatever."

Laughing, he stops us at the business class section. "I like it."

"You would," I say, unable to stop myself from laughing too.

He's like the bubbles in champagne—hard to be around without feeling happy. Which, for me, is saying something.

Speaking of...

"Would you like some champagne?" the flight attendant asks as we take our seats.

"Please," Cade answers. "And a blanket, also."

"Of course."

As I buckle the seat belt and look out the window, she disappears to get our drinks. It's only then that I smell her perfume.

Is that...?

It is.

Opium.

And even though I don't want to remember, the scent takes me back against my will.

"There you go, my beautiful princess."

Laughing, my mom places the plastic gold tiara on my head.

She's wearing one too, and it's sparkling like the bright sun as the candles on my birthday cake make pretty rainbows from the gems on the table.

"Make a wish and remember to make it a good one—you're only ten once." *She smiles in encouragement and, feeling safe because* he *is on a business trip, I close my eyes and nod. My tiara immediately starts to slide off my head and we both reach for it, laughing.*

Her laughter is so rare that it prompts me to whisper, "This is the best birthday ever, Mom."

He's *not here. That's why.*

Her blue eyes fill with tears of pained understanding. She sniffles but her voice cracks as she urges, "Make a good wish, my princess."

The pain in those words makes my stomach hurt.

"It's okay, Mom," I try to reassure her, but it's not. We both try to pretend that it is, but that doesn't change the fact that we live in constant fear.

"Make a wish," she orders, leaning forward. I smell the wonderful scent that only she has… and close my eyes.

I wish for Father to die and for me and Mom to run far, far away…

I open my eyes and blow out the candles.

As the room goes black, she claps. "Was it a good wish?"

"It was the best wish ever," I crow, only to scream as the lights switch on, and suddenly, the perfect day is forever ruined.

The monster has returned.

My father stands in the doorway, staring at both of us, hatred and disgust in his eyes. "What the hell is going on in here?" he demands. "Cake?" he sneers, motioning with his hand at the table as he enters the kitchen.

I shuffle nearer to Mom, knowing I'll need to protect her.

"And ice cream?" His words are loaded with disbelief. "You want to make my daughter fat. You want her to be as fucking revolting as you are."

That's when he backhands my mother, my beautiful mother who is so picture perfect it's wrong.

With a sharp cry, she shields her head with her arms, protecting herself on the table, knowing that he won't stop with just the one hit.

"Daddy… please, no!" I scream. "I'll be good. I won't eat the cake…"

He ignores me and punches her again.

"How many times? No cake ever!"

"I promise! I-I won't eat it!"

"Here we are. Anything else?"

The flight attendant's polite words have me jumping as she hands Cade the champagne, some kind of cloth, and a blanket.

He looks over at me, his blue eyes searching mine. "Isabelle?"

"Sorry, just… planes always make me jumpy." I smile, but it's forced, and his frown deepens.

"Here, drink."

He hands me the champagne and puts the blanket around my legs. I never use these blankets. You never know who had them before, but right now, I couldn't care less.

What's wrong with me? Thinking I can be a normal person and go to New York and not have the ghosts of my past haunt me is a pipe dream. A mistake. But... it's not like I'm a prisoner.

I can leave anytime.

Anytime.

I repeat the word like it's a mantra.

Deciding that I need to relax, I take a deep gulp of the bubbly liquid, then finish off the glass.

Leaning my head back against the rest, I try not to have an anxiety attack.

"I'm right here. You need to trust me, Isabelle." His gravelly voice is at my ear. "Do you think you can trust me?"

Opening my eyes, I fall straight into his. I know it's cliché, but the color reminds me of the ocean in Santorini. At least, from what I've seen in pictures.

Nothing could possibly be wrong with the world when I'm drowning in his eyes.

"I think I can," I whisper, voice cracking.

His smile is more tender than usual. I'm getting used to his smirks and his cocky grins, but this one is gentle. Sweet. He reaches over and strokes a finger along the arch of my cheekbone. "You don't have to worry about a mugger in New York. Or, whatever. I'll keep you safe. You know that, right?"

A mugger?

Oh. Crap. He's talking about my bullshit excuse for not wanting to come here.

I swallow and croak out a teasing, "You're going to be my bodyguard?"

He's back to being cocky again, and it helps me feel more normal. "You know it. No one'll get to my girl when I'm around."

My lips curve. "Your girl?"

He winks. "On my arm, aren't you?"

I bite my lip as I feel him take the glass from me. Then his warm hand travels up my thigh, making me grateful for the skirt I'm wearing.

At first, I'm sure I'm mistaking his intentions, then there's no mistaking anything when he reaches my inner thighs and aims ever higher.

"Cade," I mutter, glancing around and seeing that everyone is preparing for takeoff. Flight attendants are doing a last check, the couple on the other side already have their eyes closed—the man might even be asleep…

Can we do this?

God.

"Shh," he chides, moving into me, somehow taking up all the room, swallowing up the air, acting like a wall of muscle that separates me from the rest of the cabin.

A part of me wants to argue when his fingers dance over my G-string, but then, I think about slowing down my overactive brain, about wanting to forget, about not wanting to be alone, and this suddenly feels like the most perfect way possible to get me out of my head.

"Open your legs," he whispers, then he brushes his lips over my mouth. "Come on, beautiful. You know you want to. Let me thank you for taking this trip with me. Keeping me company…"

When he phrases it like that, he totally owes me.

My legs drift apart while he watches my face.

More magic happens—I'm wet. I swear it's like I'm under his spell.

He strokes his fingers over my slit, which has me arching my hips back in surprise at how good that feels.

When the digits are slick enough, he rubs my clit in the middle of a crowded flight, forcing a hiss out of me as I roll my pelvis, seeking out the pleasure he's giving me.

"Yeah, that's it. Rock those hips, baby. God, you're already so wet and swollen. Fuck, I wish I could taste you. I'd eat you out and take all those worries away, but instead, I'm going to let my fingers do the talking." His lips brush over my earlobe. "Now, stay quiet, and I'm going to make sure you know how grateful I am for you facing your fears."

"This is… I mean, anyone can…," I mutter without any conviction, closing my eyes and biting my lower lip so I don't moan out loud.

As he caresses my clit, a shudder works through me.

How does he know exactly where to stroke and how fast?

Then, he switches things up. The butt of his hand grinds against my clit, and as he works that, he thrusts two fingers inside my hot, needy pussy, causing me to swallow back a gasp as he fills me.

"You like me fingering this beautiful cunt," he says softly before challenging me. "Tell me I'm lying, naughty girl."

I shiver as I feel myself getting wetter. Jesus, he's absolutely filthy, and, I'm definitely not going to lie—I like it a lot.

"I love it," I rasp, spreading my legs as wide as I can within the confines of my skirt. "I-I need to come, Cade. Please, can I?"

He growls under his breath. "Gonna need to hear you say that again, beautiful."

As his hand retreats, I mewl, "Don't stop, Cade, please." My head arches back and he nuzzles into me there, his tongue finding my throbbing pulse and sucking hard enough to leave yet another mark on me. "God, that feels so good, Cade. Please, don't stop," I whimper. "Never stop!"

"You're so ready, aren't you, baby?" he whispers against my throat, which is when I see the flight attendant over his shoulder. She's getting ready for takeoff and has a flush on her cheeks—oh, fuck, she knows what we're doing.

For the first time all day, however, there's a woman who doesn't try to get his attention as she rushes by.

It's so wrong, but I know I'm going to come.

"Oh, my God," I keen, staring straight ahead at the gray seat in front of me as he keeps finger fucking me. When I try to spread my legs wider, I *feel* him smile.

Pulling his fingers out, he rubs my slick wetness back and forth on my swollen clit until I hiss, "Cade," and dig my nails into the armrest and his leg.

Then, he's shifting, forehead pressing into mine as he growls, "Look at me."

My eyes dart to his. This is when I forfeit the battle.

"Cade." I'm not even sure I said that out loud as my pussy tightens. "Cade…" My mouth trembles. "I-I—"

"Yeah, baby, I'm here." He rubs faster, the motion slick because of how wet I am, and that's it.

I'm gone.

Orbiting over into bliss as my core quivers and pulses.

Wave after wave of intense pleasure makes my eyes flutter back into my head. I don't care if I make a noise; I'm lost to what he's given me, unashamed and free from thoughts of the past, just focused on this bliss.

I bite my lip so hard I taste blood as I try to stay quiet and breathe. My fingers are numb from digging into the padded armrest but what a way to go.

"So good, Belle." He sounds pleased and pats my sensitive pussy, then he smiles as he brings his hand out from under the blanket. "Hmm, let's have a taste…"

Turning, he relaxes into his seat and brings his wet fingers to his mouth. My cheeks tinge with pink as he makes a show of sucking on one digit, and then the other, like he just ate something delicious and he's savoring the taste.

"Better than champagne," he croons before he uses the damp washcloth that the flight attendant left with the drinks earlier.

A cough makes me come back to reality. That and my ears are clogged up with the pressure shift in the cabin from the plane lifting off the runway.

Oh, God, I climaxed so hard that I didn't know we took off!

Cade smiles then leans over to kiss me, and my whole body relaxes.

"Better?" he asks, his lips brushing mine again. "Where's your head at?"

"So much better," I say, dazed as I rest my cheek on his shoulder. "And on you."

He hums. "That's what I like to hear. Close your eyes and get some sleep, baby. You're not gonna get much of that tonight." His hand caresses my hair and I sigh, vaguely hearing the captain announce the seat belt sign is about to be turned off.

Obeying his order isn't hard when my eyes refuse to stay open. "MmmKay, I'll take a little nap."

As always when I'm on the brink of sleep, my mind runs with a checklist: I need to call Doug and have him water my plants and get my mail while I'm gone, and Charlie... I hate the way that ended. I need to call her and make up, but I'll deal with all this tomorrow.

I'm drifting, loving this feeling of having him with me.

Secure.

Maybe I was overreacting about New York? Because this feels right. *He* feels right. Maybe the city where I was born will feel right, too, if he's by my side?

Like he heard my thoughts, he presses a kiss to my forehead, whispering, "I've got you, Belle."

Maybe I'm just a hopeless romantic, a sucker for love, but I believe him. Nothing bad is going to happen in New York. Not when I'm with Cade.

9

CADE

ACUIG

She's naive.

A train wreck.

Bad for me but so good when she comes.

So responsive.

So willing…

"My beautiful Belle," I drawl as I swipe my thumb over my bottom lip, watching her sleep, specifically angled in my seat so that I can study her as she leans against the window, her head tipped down, a demure cast to her features that reels me in like I'm not the one holding the fishing rod.

An angel?

No.

She's too willing to be corrupted for that.

Reaching for the whiskey I ordered, I take a deep sip and then sigh as it sinks into my veins. I let my eyes close and tilt my head back against the headrest, trying to figure out my next move.

For a moment there, back in the departure lounge, I thought I fucked up by buying those tickets to New York, where fate had been on my side when I'd made our reservations—not that I'd been overly worried when New York was LAX's most popular destination. Still, she'd been an inch away from tucking tail and returning to Burbank.

Worse than that was the fear I'd seen in her eyes.

I've seen her drugged, dazed, pleasure-drunk, delirious, and destructive, but that fear... I hated it.

Fear doesn't look good on anyone, but it's even worse on her.

She's flighty. Ethereal. Not an angel, but a fairy. Yeah, a fairy. Well, if Tinkerbell packed spiked Louboutins for an adventure, that is.

My lips twitch at the thought as the urge to protect her, even from her goddamn self, fills me.

"Daddy, please, no. I'll be good! I won't eat the cake," she whispers, jolting me in my seat.

I'm not averse to being called Daddy in bed, but this is different.

She's deeply asleep, her eyes fluttering behind closed lids, so I know she's dreaming. Or, should I say, dealing with a nightmare.

"I won't eat the cake. I won't." She whimpers the plea, the words all the more impactful because of the softness of her voice.

I've had nightmares like that. You could be shouting to the heavens that you didn't want something in that dream state but, in reality, all you're doing is moaning and crying and whining.

I've done my fair share of that.

When your brother dies and it's partially your fault, you get handed a lot of bad dreams as a punishment.

Tears fall from behind those closed lashes, and I watch as they roll over her cheeks. Should I wake her? I hesitate until the soft keening sound she releases next has me placing my hand on her knee. Gently, I stroke her thigh then lean over her, chanting her name as I press a kiss to her temple.

She stirs, faster than I expected, and her eyes are drenched when they open.

She might be impulsive and it's a trait she might believe we share, but some of my impulsiveness is an act to get her ass back to the city. Only, I can't stop myself from blurting out, "Are you Antoinette?" When Belle freezes, I reach up and tug on a soft blonde curl that's clinging to her damp forehead. "Or, I guess, is that story you told me actually yours?

"You don't know me, honey. This is a crazy thing we're doing together, and I'm all for that—*carpe diem*, you get me? But that's the best part. We can share shit because opening up to a stranger is easy as hell."

Belle surprises me by snagging the whiskey glass from my grip and placing it to her lips. "I'll tell if you tell." When she sinks back a finger of the good stuff without a cough, I know this isn't her first time with hard liquor.

Still, that childish deal of hers has my lips quirking at the corners. "On a level of one, trauma, and ten, a day at Disney, how bad is the story we're sharing?"

Her pupils dilate. "Bad. One."

Slowly, I nod. "Okay. One."

I release a breath, reach for my glass again, sink the last gulp back, then hit the button to call the flight attendant over. I don't start speaking until I've asked for two more glasses and we've got them sitting on the trays in front of us.

"Are you scared?" she whispers.

I cast her a surprised glance. "Of what I'm about to tell you? No. Ashamed, yes." Sucking in a breath, I confess, "My brother and I used to joyride when we were younger. We'd jack cars and drive around our neighborhood. At first. Then, we started getting cocky. Too fucking cocky for our own good." I sip at the whiskey when I want nothing more than to drown in it. "I liked breaking into the alarms, especially of the top-end rides, but Vinny loved street racing. We used to egg each other on. It was dumb. So fucking dumb."

Her voice is a whisper. "He died during a race?"

"He did. The car burst into flames when he crashed into the side of a building." I can still see the blaze when I close my eyes.

The heat is as raging as the grief I feel at his loss.

I figure it'll be eternal.

Pretty fitting considering I'm Catholic.

"You blame yourself?"

"How can I not? He was only using that car because I'd cracked the alarm." My fingers tighten around the glass. "I as good as killed him."

"He didn't have to race that day," she points out softly, her gaze downturned.

"Vinny and me," I mutter, "we were too alike. My older brother—"

"Lucas, right?"

I blink. "You remember that?"

She shrugs. "Sure."

"Well, Lucas is the good son. He's the eldest and he always does everything right and never misbehaves and always got great grades. Our, I mean his, boss"—Jesus, I almost fucked up there—"trusts him with shit he trusts no one else with. He's responsible. It's how he is."

"Sounds like a stick-in-the-mud," she mumbles, making me snicker.

"Nah, he's good people. He just had a lot to live up to. Our father died when Lucas was nineteen. That's a messed-up time for a dad to die, you know? There's never a great moment, don't get me wrong, but for Lucas, he had to become the man of the house and he took it seriously."

"How old were you?"

"Fifteen."

"And Vinny?"

"Sixteen," I choke out.

"Wow, you were close in age, weren't you?" Her hand has settled on my thigh, and this time, she's the one offering comfort. "You were probably more like best friends than brothers."

I gulp. "Yeah. I fucking miss him, you know? Kills me that he's dead because of shit I helped him do. We just… didn't care. Da died, Ma was sobbing all the time, barely getting out of bed, and our sisters were like ghosts who'd turn into poltergeists at the drop of a hat." I release a breath. "It's no excuse, but we wanted to escape. We wanted to change the pace. We got what we wanted.

"Within two years, my ma buried her husband and then her son." My mouth tightens. "That's on me."

She nuzzles into my side. A part of me tenses, waiting for the condolences everyone offers, but instead, she whispers, "Life sucks," and my relief is real because I hate condolences. They're bullshit words that mean dick and only make me feel worse.

Not that her sincerity did the other day… Something deep inside of me, something dark, registers that she's different, but I shrug it aside.

"It fucking does," I concur and take a deep sip of my whiskey, wishing I had a pack of cigarettes on me even though I quit seven years ago.

Nothing takes the ache away, but nothing tastes better than a dose of nicotine when you've had your feet kicked out from under you.

"I guess it's my turn," she whispers when silence falls between us.

I stare down into the amber liquid. "I guess it is."

"My father killed my mom. When I tried to tell people, he had me committed." She sucks in a breath. "He was on the board of that hospital, so I spent years doped up. It was only when this new doctor got hired on and he questioned my meds that I managed to sober up and get out." I can tell she's gnawing on the inside of her cheek. "He still kept a watch on me. Probably has eyes on me now."

God, how right she is. "Is he how you got the Valium and Percocet?"

"An old 'script,' yeah." Her jaw works, so I know there's more of a story than that, but I don't push.

"Is he in prison now?" I ask, though I already know the answer.

"No." She releases a soft scoff. "He's too powerful for that."

"Is he in organized crime?"

"No. He's… He's a doctor."

"Jesus."

A sigh drifts from her lips. "Yeah."

"How did he get away with it?"

"He has a lot of friends in high places because of his practice. H-He, I guess the only way to describe it is that he collects favors. That's why he didn't get arrested. I don't think the cops even did more than a preliminary investigation into him.

"He does a lot of pro bono corrective surgery for police officers who get injured in the line of duty. It means he has the NYPD in his pocket too." She laughs, but it sounds shaky. "I-I know I sound like a conspiracy nutcase."

My nostrils flare.

Didn't Davis do that with Aidan O'Donnelly Jr.? Collect a favor?

My boss's knee was shattered during a drive-by. For years, he lived with a shitty replacement joint, got hooked on pain meds in the process, then visited Davis, got his fucked-up knee healed, and as a "thank you," I'm here, bringing the bastard's daughter home to him.

My free hand balls into a fist. "Aside from…" Jesus. *Everything?* "Did he… abuse you?"

Belle peers at me. "You believe me?"

"Why would you lie to a stranger?"

A gleam appears in her eyes—it's a mixture of relief and sorrow. "Yeah, why would I?" It's rhetorical. The gleam fades. "He didn't hurt me physically."

The way she pronounces "physically" clues me into the many and varied ways a person can be hurt.

You don't have to beat the shit out of someone to fuck them up —that crap about cutting her tits off? Who said that to their daughter?

I stare at her. "You were dreaming before I woke you up, Belle. I heard you say something in your sleep. Something about promising you wouldn't eat the cake."

"He wanted me to be a certain weight." Belle rubs at her temples. "Every Monday at four-fifty, he'd wake me up and tell me to use the bathroom. Then, I'd go to his office in a bikini and he'd make me get weighed.

"I-I don't think it was sexual. He never touched me, but he used to look at me like I was a doll, I guess. A doll he wanted to shape."

Shaking her head, she continues, "I'd get measured—waist, hips, thighs, and chest—and if I gained weight, I was only allowed to eat dinner for a week."

My brow furrows. "That's sick."

"He's a sick man." Her gaze turns distant and her fingertip drifts around the rim of her glass. "He wants me to look like her. He killed her, but he wants me to be like a living shrine to her memory. It's crazy but then, *he's* crazy, isn't he?"

When she shudders, I say, "You should have told me, Belle. I wouldn't have made you come back to New York."

God, I genuinely mean that.

I'm so fucked.

She shakes her head, utterly unaware that I'm in over my goddamn head here. "The city is a big place and, as you said, you want me to meet your family. Aren't you lucky I don't want you to meet mine?"

Though I snort, my nails are digging into my palms.

I don't give a shit if I give Lucas a heart attack over this situation— over my dead body am I letting Aidan make her go home to her father.

Unable to stop myself, I slip my hand behind her nape and draw her into me. The whiskey sloshes in both our glasses, but I ignore that and only still once her forehead is pressed against mine.

"I might be a stranger, Belle, but while you're in the city and you're with me, you're safe from him. I promise."

She swallows. "Thanks, Cade." Her fingers whisper up and along my arm. "You're a good man."

I'm not.

If she finds out the truth, she'll soon change her mind, but she *won't* find out.

I pull back so I can press a kiss on her forehead. "How do you feel about getting something to eat to soak up the whiskey?"

Her gaze drifts to mine. I've no idea what she's looking for, but when she graces me with a nod, it's inexplicable how I feel like I've won gold at the Olympics.

10

BELLE

"How's the club sandwich?" Cade questions as he stretches his arms across the back of the booth. "Does it taste as good as you?"

Eyes greedily taking in his biceps, I almost don't hear him then I blush. "It's delicious."

"Hmm, I beg to disagree. Lemme taste?"

Biting my lip, I pass him the snack and watch as he takes a huge bite. Then, he's shaking his head. "Good, but you're a ten and that's a five."

Unable to help myself, I smirk as I dunk a fry in ranch dressing. Offering it to him, I arch a brow. He takes it directly from my hand but doesn't stop with the fry, no. He licks the tips of my fingers and sends a shiver down my spine.

He grins as his eyes dip to my lips. "Six. But not as good as that pretty pussy of yours." He watches me eat because he finished a while back, then when I've only got a sip of whiskey left, he asks, "Done?"

"With the food, yes." I grin. "Want to go dancing?"

His shocked expression has me snorting, but the snort morphs into laughter at his next declaration:

"I'm Irish. We drink, no dancing. Plus, we have our suitcases," he argues as he leans forward, reaching for his wallet with a shake of his head. "Maybe we didn't need those last two shots of Jameson."

"Are you kidding? I haven't had anything but Jack Daniels and tequila in years. Come on, Cade. We're in Manhattan. Let's go club-bing." I reach over and run my nails up his forearm.

His lips twitch. "Get those claws back in, minx. In fact, you just gave me an idea. I think we need to get a hotel room."

Doris, our waitress, passes by, and he hands her his card.

After years of waiting tables, I know it says a lot about a guy how he treats his server—Cade is literally a fucking dream date.

It almost distracts me from what he says.

"Wait. We're not going to your place?"

Cade's right. I probably didn't need that extra shot of whiskey—*it's harder than usual to focus.*

"Not tonight," he answers, signing the credit card receipt when Doris drops it off with a friendly smile that doesn't make my claws come out.

Still, it's *interesting* that he wants to use a hotel tonight. Ever since we landed in New York, Cade has been in zero hurry to get home. Case in point: the impromptu shots.

He stands and puts his wallet in his back pocket, inadvertently granting me a direct look at his cock. "Ready?"

I blink.

Ready to crawl across the table and suck on his dick? Sure.

I think, from his arched brow, he knows exactly where my mind's gone. He rounds the table, holds out his hand, and daintily, I slip my fingers into his clasp. As I stand, his arm instantly drapes over my shoulder. With his free hand, he wheels both our carry-ons as we walk out of the deli together... *like a real couple.*

Manhattan hits me in the face almost immediately—things haven't changed. I've been gone almost ten years but people are still going at warp speed, horns blaring, lights blinking, and steam from the subway simmering in the air.

Happy that I'm with him, I snuggle in Cade's arms as we proceed down the street.

"How are you doing, baby?" he asks, making me melt deeper into him as he presses a kiss to my forehead.

"I don't even know why I was worried about coming back here. Look at all this," I declare, motioning with my hands at everyone speedwalking past us. "I mean, it's fabulous. Isn't it fabulous? Don't you think so?"

That's when he chuckles. "Oh, yeah, it's *fabulous*, but know what's better? A bed. We need to get you in one."

His cute dimples flash and almost make me stumble as I whine, "Cade, we just got into the city that never sleeps." I bat my eyelashes at him. "Let's get one more drink. We don't have to dance…" I spin around, pulling my hand from his so I can spin in a circle all while his lips start to twitch.

"Good thing seeing as I don't dance. Remember?" he drawls, making me pout.

"Look at all these bars…" That's when I see it. "Oh, my God." I break free and run toward the blinking light of a strip club. *"This* is what we're doing," I squeal, nodding eagerly as he saunters up to me, then he has me bursting into laughter when he grabs me by the hips and pushes me against the brick wall.

"You want to go into a strip club?" His mouth hovers over mine. "Instead of going back to a hotel room?"

Lifting my lips to touch his, I feel my heart race as he rocks his dick into my stomach. "Umm, yeah."

"You ever been inside a strip club?"

"No, but I've always wanted to go. One of my friends taught me how to strip. She worked at The Pussycat in L.A. for a hot minu—"

And suddenly, our mouths are colliding and all thoughts of strip clubs fade as our tongues entwine.

Groaning, I melt into him, letting him deepen the kiss as my head swims, and he steals the breath from my lungs better than two fingers of whiskey could.

What is it about this man that makes me feel *everything*? That makes me forget the world?

When he raises his head, his eyes are narrowed upon mine. "One drink." He scans the area. "You stay close to me or your ass will regret it later."

Shocked into stillness by his delicious threat, I gape at him.

"Understood? Belle!"

I swallow and quickly agree, "Yes, I understand." Is it bad that I'm almost tempted to misbehave...?

Taking my hand, we walk over to the bouncer who's sitting on a chair.

"Hey, man." The bouncer nods and lets us in, not even asking for ID. My arms pebble with goosebumps because that's weird. I mean, does he know Cade? I guess he could be a regular...

"Do you know that bouncer?" I yell over "Pour Some Sugar on Me." The smell of stale alcohol and smoke makes me wrinkle my nose as Cade's hand squeezes mine tight.

"No," he answers, but he's lying. I might be under the influence, but that bouncer definitely knew Cade.

"What do you do again?" I shout over the music then almost run into his back as he stops and looks down at me, cocking his head as if he's going to say something but instead guides me to a table by the stage.

"Cade?"

"I told you already," he answers calmly, holding out the chair for me to sit.

Wait, what did he say he did...? Something weird. My drunk brain isn't firing on all cylinders, though, so I don't remember.

A waitress in black walks up. "What can I get you?" She smiles and I can tell she has no idea who Cade is because a guy this fine in a place like this? They'd be drooling over him and going the extra mile to get great tips.

God, maybe he didn't know the bouncer and I'm being paranoid after spending years with the Disciples. Those guys are ridiculous when it comes to stuff like this. You can't even enjoy an impromptu dinner without having everyone in the restaurant checked out.

Yeah, that has to be it. I'm overly sensitive.

"Isabelle?"

I blink. "Um, let's see. I think we need two shots of Jameson and two root beer chasers." The waitress nods, writing it on a napkin, then swishes away, which is when I take a moment to study the seedy club.

It's a small venue, with only the one stage, a bar, and a few booths and tables.

"Root beer chasers?" Cade questions with a laugh, lifting an eyebrow and placing a possessive hand on the back of my chair.

"I love root beer," I tell him simply.

A glance at the stage reveals a woman twirling around a pole. She's got a heavy tan and is wearing what appears to be a silver bikini— either that or it's aluminum foil.

The place isn't full, and besides the stripper and waitress, I'm the only woman here. When I look at Cade, who's wearing a big grin like he can read my mind, I wrinkle my nose.

"Not what you expected?" he teases.

"Not really. When I mentioned 'stripper,' I was thinking…"

The waitress comes back, interrupting us as she sets down the shots and the root beers.

"I need a private room." He hands her a hundred.

"Of course, room three is available." Her eyes widen when he hands her another hundred. "Can you look after our suitcases?"

"Sure. I'll put them behind the bar."

"Thanks," he says with a suave smile that has the other woman looking like a deer in headlights. She flushes as she shoots me a look then scurries away, wheeling our suitcases with her.

Yeah, *scurry off.*

Still, not even my jealousy can get rid of the excitement that's throbbing through my words as I demand, "What are we doing?"

"You'll see. Here," he orders, handing me the shot. "To you, beautiful." He clinks the glasses and before I can say anything else, he shoots his back without even a shudder. I follow, feeling the pleasantly warm sting down to my stomach as I grab my root beer chaser. "Let's go."

He reaches for my arm as I notice the stripper on stage swaying back and forth with her top off. Not going to lie, I'm disappointed with this performance—*anyone* could do that. Would it be bad to boo? That I don't know tells me I'm beyond under the influence.

Cade walks us toward what looks like a black brick wall. He stops when another bouncer appears and opens a door for us. A ripple of excitement flutters inside me, warming up my cheeks as I step into the small room. It has a mirror on two sides, a chair, and a disco ball hanging from the ceiling.

Cade sits in the chair and pulls me onto his lap. "I figured that you were expecting something more like this." His lips are at my ear as the door opens, and a brunette walks in wearing a sparkly pink dress with slits up both sides.

I wrap my arms around his neck and squirm on his lap. "Yes!" *Something more enticing than a skewered baked potato on a rotisserie spit.*

"Oh!" She looks at Cade, then me. "Hey."

"Hi." I smile at her, even though that weird feeling comes back.

I swear to God, her eyes lit up like she's either seen Cade before or she knows him... Maybe he *is* a regular here?

I'm not sure I prefer that option, though.

Cade tips his chin up in greeting, but that's it.

"Do you have a song you like?" Her voice breaks me out of my paranoia and has me focusing on her as she licks her gooey lips. She runs her long, pointy nails through her hair, preening...

For Cade.

My jealousy starts to flare.

"Do we?" Cade questions, his smirk deepening when he sees how flustered I am.

Well, I can't deny that I didn't expect a private dance! Especially one with a stripper whose both hot and interested in my man.

"Um, yes. *Yes, we do.* Please, play, 'Kiss Me More' by Doja Cat."

Cade's arms tighten around me as liquid heat travels from his hands to my core, making me squirm on his knee. I can feel his erection...

No sex in front of the stripper—*bad Cindy.*

"That's the song you want?" he growls in my ear before lightly biting the lobe.

I shiver as the stripper types the song title into her phone.

"You want me to get another chair? I can give you both a dance." Her eyes travel up and down my body.

"Nah, darlin', she's fine on my lap," Cade informs her. Then, in my ear, he whispers, "I've got my show right here."

The shivers that whisper down my spine are more of a thrill than when the song's beat spills from the speakers. I'm pretty sure that I can feel the bass in my core, and when he presses a hand to my stomach, it's as if he squeezes a groan out of me.

When she starts to sway, Cade wraps his hand around my throat. "You like watching her dance, beautiful?" He angles my head so that he can brush my lips with his. "Well?"

We both peek at her as she grinds to the melody but, again, she's not that interesting.

Especially when Cade wraps his hand around my ponytail and uses it to bring my mouth down to his. I taste the alcohol, the root beer, but most of all, I taste him, and suddenly all I want is to get out of here. Get a hotel room and fuck him for days because this man is just it for me.

Why did I decide this was a good idea again?

"Hello?" The stripper's voice is petulant, loaded with aggravation. It kind of reminds me of an annoying teacher I once had. "Do you guys want me to leave?"

I lightly bite his bottom lip and reluctantly turn away to watch her, seeing as he dropped a couple hundred bucks on this.

She's no Antoinette since all she's doing is rolling her hips. But come on, how many strippers are actual prima ballerinas? I mean, Antoinette can extend her leg straight up; she can do things normal people can't. So, I'm giving this chick a break on her average-at-best moves as she unsnaps her top and shoves her fake breasts in my face.

I blink at her large dusky nipples as she tries to straddle us. "Wow."

Not only is it awkward, but Cade's fingers suddenly clamp down on my arm.

"Okay. We're done," he snaps, stunning the hell out of me as he surges to his feet, taking me with him.

For some reason, his beautiful face is twisted in anger… Oh, my God, is Cade jealous of the stripper? Or just mad at her getting into my personal space?

Either way, it's kinda cute.

Even though I'm still raw from our last conversation, I can't wait to tell Charlie—she'll crack up.

"Wait." I hold up my hand, grab my purse, and pull out a handful of ones. "I've always wanted to do this." I smirk as I put a dollar in her bottoms and then one on the other side, snapping the side of her G-string when I'm done.

Cade grunts at my antics but doesn't stop me, just hands the stripper a wad of cash with an expression that makes him look like he sucked on five limes. But to me, he only orders, "Hotel, now." He steers me by gripping my hip as we make our way outside.

The urge to laugh fills me again, and I don't think my chest has ever felt this light.

He wants me.

Is this what happiness feels like?

Holy fuck, that's what this is. It's not the booze; it's Cade. I can't remember the last time I felt… *this… if ever.*

I gaze at his face, which is still showing his aggravation as he clicks his fingers at the waitress. It's the rudest I've seen him act with servers, but I'm okay with it because it's nice to know that I'm not the only jealous one between us. Our suitcases are in his hand again within a couple minutes and shortly, we're outside and he's whistling for a cab.

He's also still aggravated which is cute as fuck, something that has nothing to do with the snow that's starting to fall, either.

"Cade?" I rasp, grabbing a hold of his shirt as a cab pulls up.

"Yeah?"

"You make me happy," I say, not even caring if he says it back. After that fit of pique in there, I know we've got the same vibes going on even if he can't admit it because he's a *man* and men are slow on the uptake.

His hand clamps down on mine as he stares into my eyes. Right there, deep in their center, there's an incandescence that makes me grin back at him.

All he says is, "Let's go, Isabelle," but I *know* he feels it.

I make him happy too.

"The Ritz," he orders the cab driver, dragging me onto his lap and burying his nose in my neck. His fingers tighten on my hip while he caresses my hair with the other. Then, he stuns me by showing more emotional range than a piece of Laffy Taffy by growling, "You're mine, Isabelle. No one is taking you away from me. Do you hear me?"

Suddenly, I know this isn't *just* how it feels to be happy.

This is what home feels like too…

11

CADE

MY PLANS GET DERAILED thanks to a pile-up on East Twelfth that not even my cab driver, a seasoned pro at this game, can get us around.

When I see the first street that isn't a one-way, I request, "Take us down there, please. We'll get out at West Forty-Seventh."

I receive a grunt as an answer, but Belle, who's been all over me like jelly on a PB&J since she had too much whiskey on the flight, chuckles. "You changed your mind about going to a hotel?"

"Baby, the only place I'm taking you is bed." My lips curve when she wriggles on my lap. "*But,* there's a pileup, and that's going to slow me down from getting you horizontal."

Heat flashes in her eyes. "You were jealous of that stripper."

Which means she's not against me being possessive. I'm not surprised, not when I think about how she turns into a green-eyed monster if a woman starts trying to flirt with me.

I don't point that out, though, just reason, "She was shoving her tits in your face."

"Isn't that her job?"

"Nah, she was into you." I know Jemima from school. She's all about the pussy. A love we both share.

"You don't know that," she teases, her leg kicking up and over my knee so that, in a couple of seconds, she's straddling me on the back seat.

The cab driver's done this longer than Santa's been living at the North Pole, so he isn't shocked at what goes down in his back seat, but...

I don't like it.

I don't want him seeing her.

She's got a short skirt on. In the rearview mirror, maybe she's flashing her ass or something.

It's weird—caring.

I'm not used to it, and I don't like it. Not at all.

But she's making me think crazy shit. Making me do even crazier shit. Hell, maybe her type of crazy is contagious?

What was that about when we got in the damn car—calling her mine? That wasn't me. I don't get possessive. Not like Lucas.

Not like my da.

As if to fight the thought, my fingers tighten of their own volition around her waist, digging into her soft curves.

"You were jealous," she whispers. "Say it."

I want to argue that I wasn't, but my dick isn't in agreement. When her pussy is as close to it as it is right now, no way in fuck is my cock going to jeopardize any potential action.

I might be acting nuts, but I'm not a goddamn fool.

I squeeze her again. "Like you weren't in the airport."

Her eyes light up. "You liked it."

"I did." Again, fucking strange.

With the "crazy" contagion obviously having infected me by this point, I have to admit that, for the first time in a long while, I'm enjoying myself.

Shit has been serious with the Five Points for too long, what with the old boss, Aidan Sr., getting shot in that graveyard, and then everything that's gone down with those secret society motherfuckers, the New World Sparrows, never mind those *Éire le chéile go deo* bastards who are affiliated with the IRA...

Brothers in the Five Points were revealed to be traitors, and some of the top brass even got involved in a mutiny against the O'Donnellys —going so far as to kidnap my boss and his wife. Throw in a bad allergic reaction to a fucking insect bite that sent me to the brink of death...

Yeah, all work, a hospital stay, and no play makes Cade a very dull boy.

The car swerves, taking us down a side street, and I see we're nearer to our destination than I thought.

When we tumble from the cab a few seconds later, me grabbing our suitcases before the driver takes off, I'm faced with the prospect of heading home or going to Lucas's, which isn't far away.

Home means she'll inadvertently meet one of my sisters because they're incapable of staying out of my place.

If we go to Lucas's, I know he'll be working because he's a Type-A workaholic so we'll miss him, but Ma checks in every day to make sure he's eating, and with how my head's feeling—and Belle's won't be much better—I could imagine waking up and finding her making us breakfast.

Is my ma the only woman who makes breakfast for one of her son's one-night stands she'll never see again?

I don't know if it's an Irish thing, a Catholic thing, or a "Patricia" thing.

My nose crinkles as I think about which of the women in my family I'd prefer to deal with.

Just as I'm about to make a decision, my cell buzzes.

> Lucas: Why aren't you answering your damn phone?

I squint at the screen and realize there are a couple of missed calls from him.

Shit.

Because I don't want to deal with him, I decide against Lucas's place. With my luck, he'd come back tonight.

Decision made, I take us to my home, which is a few doors down.

My father built our building back in the eighties. I don't even want to know how he got this piece of turf out of the O'Donnellys' clutches, but he achieved a miracle and earned enough money through his position with the Five Points to have this place constructed.

Ever since, we've been living here. Well, apart from Lucas who moved out when he got a promotion as captain of Aidan Jr.'s crew.

The Five Points' legit front is Acuig Corp, and a swanky loft in one of Acuig's skyscrapers came as part of the deal.

I'd prefer to live here than handle the extra responsibility.

Sure, his place is worth a couple of million, but it's a few floors below Aidan's apartment, which means he's always on the job and never in that million-dollar "promotion perk."

Fuck that.

Our building is long and thin because Da thought ahead—all his kids have a duplex so they can have kids too.

That means even Vinny has one.

I ride past it every night in the elevator, knowing that I helped take away his future.

We always dreamed of the day when we could live in our own apartments. We told each other we'd watch games at his place because he'd have the big TV, but because I was on the top floor, meaning the one farthest from Da, I'd have the better sound system for parties.

Shit like that mattered when you were a teenager.

You didn't think you'd die in an illegal street race.

You just thought you'd live forever.

"Hey." Belle's soft voice has me blinking at her. Her hand cups my jaw, making me realize it's still snowing. As I stare at her, I watch a snowflake fall onto her cheekbone as she asks, "What's going on? Are you okay?"

I swallow. "Nothing."

"Nothing?" She squints at me. "I may be very drunk right now, but I know something's wrong."

"I was thinking about Vinny, that's all. Stupid shit. Nothing important. Come on, let's go back to my place. I don't want to deal with my sisters, but it's better than being stuck in traffic for an hour."

"We could go to a nearer hotel than the Ritz," she offers, making me smile.

"Only the best for my Belle."

My cheeks flush at how dumb that sounded, but Belle doesn't think it does. Not from the way she plasters herself against me, her lips smacking onto mine, tongue thrusting deep like she wants inside me—now. Snow be damned.

She makes me forget, and I didn't realize how badly I needed that.

Unfortunately for me, she doesn't just make me forget about my brother, but my sisters too.

As I half drag her down the street, pulling our baggage in between kisses, finally making it to my building, my hands juggling between the curve of her ass and the key I'm trying to get out of my pocket, the door pushes open before I can do dick.

I only know because gravity has us tumbling backward, and as I've pinned Belle to the door, we go flying.

Straight into the street where one of the railings outside keeps us upright.

Barely.

"Cade!" Kitty shrieks. "What the fuck are you doing creeping around the front door?"

Jesus fuck, of course it had to be Kitty.

Not Neev or Róisín.

Nope, Kitty.

God fucking hates me.

"You moron," Kitty snarls when I don't answer. "What the fuck were you thinking?"

I scowl at her. "Do you have to be so goddamn loud, Kitty? What is it with your voice box? Do you have a loudspeaker installed in there?"

Belle blinks at me, then at Kitty. "Wh—"

"My sister," I grumble. "Catriona Caitlin. Kitty for short."

My sister is the perfect cat.

She's a pain in my ass, quick to swipe out with her claws, always lands on her feet (hallways not included), and she has nine lives, meaning there's no chance of ever escaping her.

I scrub a hand over my face. "This is Isabelle."

Kitty sniffs at me, but to Belle, she's pretty polite. "Isabelle, it's a pleasure to meet you. What someone as beautiful as yourself is doing with a pig like Cade is beyond me—"

"And I wonder why I'd have preferred to stay at a hotel tonight," I gripe. "You're so great for my ego—"

A chuckle escapes Belle but she stifles it by slapping a hand over her mouth when I gawk at her.

Whose side is she on here?

Ignoring her, Kitty drawls, "You've got the charm of a swine, Cade. What can I say? I call it how I see it."

"I know you do. That's your problem, Kitty," I snipe. "Why are you sneaking out at one in the morning, anyway? I bet Ma would love to hear about that."

"Just like she'd love to hear about Belle, I'm sure," she growls.

Belle's face whips from side to side as my sister and I serve each other several doses of shade. I can tell by the glee in her eyes that she loves it. I would have known, without a damn investigation into her, that she doesn't have any brothers or sisters because a kid who didn't grow up with siblings is the only type of person who can appreciate a spat like this.

Family—you've gotta fucking love them.

"I'm sure she would. Belle, do you like crepes? Ma makes the best crepes. She'll probably cook for you in the morning anyway," I say dismissively.

"You want Ma to meet her?" Kitty squawks. "You and Lucas always complain about how she—"

Before she can blurt out the truth about how Ma cooks for our one-night stands, I snap, "It's weird, but not this time. I figure Ma will like Belle and vice versa."

Kitty blinks at me while Belle blushes. It'd be cute if it didn't make me want to fuck her, but I've already been cock-blocked by a front door and my sister—it isn't safe to get a boner now.

"I thought you were in L.A.—"

"Well, you can see that I'm not." A thought occurs to me. "But if Lucas comes around, tell him you didn't see me."

A catlike smile curves my sister's lips. "I'll tell him those *exact* words, I promise."

That smile tells me I've fucked up somewhere, but that's when this two-act play turns into a Broadway production. A door down the hall opens and my ma calls out, "Cade, is that you?"

"Jesus fuck," I mutter, unsure if this could get much worse, unless… "Is Lucas having a late dinner with her too?"

"Nah," Kitty says with a smirk. "You missed him."

Thank God for small mercies.

Still, I'm a momma's boy and I ain't ashamed to admit it. Lucas got tough because Da whipped him into shape. Me, I got whipped by a rolling pin and a towel around the head.

Shooting a look at Belle, I grace her with a grin. "I know this is early, but… want to meet my ma?"

12

BELLE

"Wait. Your mom?" I blink at him, but he's as cocky—read unhelpful—as ever.

His grin widens. "Yeah."

His sister ducks between us, staring at her brother like he's grown a second head.

"Are you crazy? You can't take Isabelle to meet Ma right now." Kitty crosses her arms as he frowns at her. "No offense, Isabelle, but you're covered in snow!"

"Since when do I listen to you, Kitty?" he retorts, not letting me answer.

Deciding to wade in before this becomes a sibling battleground, I smile kindly at Kitty. "I think you're right, Kitty—"

"Ha, just took someone with a lick of sense to realize it."

"—maybe meeting your mom in the morning would be better." Snuggling into his side, I try to distract Cade. "Take me to your apartment? I'm starting to feel cold."

He shoots me a concerned look then starts to run his hands up and down my back—

"Holy fuck, Cade. Down, boy." Kitty's loud voice makes us both look over at her as she holds up a hand, steps around our suitcases, and walks toward the door. "Sorry," she says around a snicker. "I, just, I mean, wow, Cade. At least let me leave before you start getting boners in front of me."

When she winks at me then, with another laugh, walks out the door, I realize that she reminds me of Dolly, one of my besties back in L.A.—zero filter.

"Nice to meet you, Kitty," I say to her retreating back, surprised to find that I mean it.

Cade scowls at her as the door shuts behind her. "Okay, Ma's tomorrow's problem." He rubs my cheek with his thumb. "Just give me two minutes so she isn't standing on her doorstep for too long."

I watch him leave, studying his ass, which is impossibly hotter thanks to my beer goggles. The man's practically edible when you're stone-cold sober. Now, I want to eat him up more than I needed that club sandwich earlier.

I blink when he returns—he really meant it when he said two minutes. Without a word, he takes my hand, grabs our baggage, and walks me down the hallway toward the elevator.

As we climb in, I ask, "So everyone has a place in the building?"

"Yeah."

My hand tightens on his as the elevator doors open. "I love that."

"Yeah, it's... interesting. Sorry about Kitty. She's... Kitty. More attitude than sense," he grumbles, swinging open the front door, and for a second, with the whiskey bringing a foggy clarity to everything, I'm homesick for my friends—we all have more attitude than sense. But they're not just friends, they're my family like Kitty's his, and I just upped and left them. *I suck.*

"You're lucky to have her, Cade. You never have to apologize for family. Not to me, anyway."

And I mean that.

I always wanted a brother or sister because it was so lonely growing up in our giant townhouse, which was not kid-friendly, and after my mom died...

No.

I push all these thoughts away, refusing to go dark tonight. We're having too much fun to wreck it with things I can't change.

"Ready?" Cade pushes me up against a wall and then flips on the lights as his lips dip down to mine for a kiss. "Or do you want a shower first to warm up?"

Not needing to answer, I shoot him a teasing smile as I wrap my hands in his thick hair, silently accepting that I need him more than he can ever know to take my ghosts away. It's one of the reasons I came.

Closing my eyes, I let my body respond to his hands and tongue and just feel him. Inhaling through my nose, I smell the lingering notes of his aftershave as his mouth moves to my neck and I moan out loud.

"Fuck." He pulls back, his blue eyes fierce as my breath stutters. "Unzip me," he growls, and a shiver of excitement snakes up my spine.

"Yes, sir," I tease.

My hands deftly unbutton him and slowly ease the zipper down. He cages me in, planting an arm on either side of me, but, smiling, I drop to my knees, taking his pants with me.

"Mmm, have I told you how much I love your cock?" I croon.

As I look up at him, my hand strokes his velvety hard erection. Loving being at the center of his attention as he watches me with narrowed eyes, I flick my tongue over the tip, which is already leaking.

I suckle it, tonguing the slit until he's hissing. Then, letting spit trickle down his length, I slurp around his shaft so that, when he's nice and wet, I can lean forward and take him deeper into my mouth, sliding lower and lower until he's almost in my throat.

"Jesus Christ," he rumbles, grabbing a hold of my hair and tilting my head back. "That's it, take my cock, Belle. Take every fucking inch. I know you can do it. Such a good girl." He groans when I reach for his balls. As I hold them in my fist, I start swallowing around him, and that has him growling, "Your cunt is wet, isn't it, Belle? It turns you on to choke on my dick, doesn't it?"

When I mewl, he moans and starts to rock his hips, thrusting deeper into my throat. My eyes start to water as my gag reflex kicks in, but God, my core is close to meltdown as my pussy pulses in response to his loss of control.

"Fuck, next time, I'm going to bury my face in your cunt as you suck me off, Belle. So I *know* you're enjoying it." He grunts, thrusting back and forth while keeping his hands on the wall.

My other hand clutches his ass, encouraging him to go deeper while I relax my throat to take more of him. Saliva drips down my chin, ropes of it making his passage easier as he fucks my face.

"Jesus Christ," he snarls, hips snapping faster. "You're going to swallow every drop, Belle, aren't you? Like a good girl."

I release a keening sound, loving the words that drip from his lips.

He knows, too. "You like that, don't you, baby? You want to be my good girl, don't you?" His chuckle is dark, deep. God, if I touch my pussy, I just know I'll be drenched. "Do you want my cum, Belle?"

I mumble around his dick, "I need it."

"You can have it, baby. You can have it. Now, remember, swallow," he hisses, thrusting one more time, deeper than before, than ever.

As his cock hits the back of my throat, he lets go. I obey, swallowing as much of his cum as I can before it starts to spill out of the corners of my lips. God, I feel his groans in my soul. They light a fire inside me that has me wanting to please him, makes me want to hear those moans for the rest of my life.

When he retreats, I suck in a massive breath, but his thumb traces over my mouth, swiping cum and saliva along my cheeks. It's sticky and wet but I love feeling his claim on me.

"You're fucking perfect, Belle." He means it. The sentiment throbs through the words.

While I shoot him a smile, he's busy leaning over, snagging me in his arms so he can pick me up.

I try to look around at his place, but I'm kind of dizzy from being Jameson-and-dick-drunk.

I guess that's his living room? Sure, there's a couch and a large TV, but where the hell is the other stuff? Then he's kicking open a door and setting me down on a giant bed. Yet another blank canvas.

Maybe he's a minimalist. That's our first difference—I'm such a maximalist.

"Clothes off *now*," he orders and walks over to a dresser to set down his phone.

When he pulls off his T-shirt, for a moment, I simply stare and admire his gorgeous back, the way his muscles ripple as he moves...

"Belle, clothes," he demands, his voice bringing me back to the now.

In a scramble, I crawl to the edge of the bed and try not to fall over when I simultaneously drag my skirt down and step out of my wet panties.

"Everything, Belle. I want you naked on my bed," he states, his voice fading...

I twist around and find myself standing in an empty room. As I kick off my pumps then toss my shirt to the floor, I drift over to the doorway and watch him return with the suitcases.

He shucked his pants off, but his boxer briefs remain on and, sweet Lord, he belongs either in porn or a painting that I can hang on a wall, one that I'll forever jill off to.

"Cade?" My voice sounds breathy because where the hell did all the oxygen go?

Knowing what it'll do to him, I unsnap my bra, not even trying to hide that I'm staring at his thick cock, then hold out my arms for him.

"I love your tits so goddamn much." He stops in front of me, the suitcases forgotten, one hand reaching out so he can rub my hard, aching nipple with his thumb. "They're fucking beautiful."

"I used to hate them," I mumble.

He picks me up again and holds me under my thighs. My pussy rests against his lean abs, and I'm more than aware that I'm getting my slick all over him.

When he falls back on the bed, I squeal with laughter as we bounce.

"How could you ever hate these? Christ, if I were you, I'd never leave my room, just lock myself in and play with them all day," he teases, gracing me with a wicked smirk.

"If you were in my room with me, I never would," I retort, sliding my nails over his scalp then releasing a sharp cry as he scrapes his teeth over my nipple. "Anyway, my dad was embarrassed by them. He wanted my mom to get them reduced when I was eleven, but she refused." I groan as he sucks harder, and my hands tangle into his silky hair.

That's when I realize he's frozen on top of me. "What did you just say?"

I blink at him and force my brain to keep up.

Shit, now I know I've had too much to drink. That never should have slipped out. He looks like he's ready to murder someone and because I'm fucked up, I like that expression too much for my own good.

"It… Cade, it's nothing." Tenderly, I touch the frown line between his eyes. "I shouldn't have said anything. It's in the past—"

"It's *not* nothing. What kind of sick fuck is he? You were eleven." His voice becomes louder, but I put my finger on his lips.

"Stop. I don't want to…" I sigh. "I want you. I need you. Please?"

As I stroke my finger over his mouth, he seems to calm down. I can still feel his anger but my touch brings him back to me. In turn, my heart speeds up.

God, I'm falling for this guy.

Hard.

"You're right. Not tonight. I'll deal with this later."

"Let's not talk about it again," I whisper.

When his mouth latches onto my nipple, I arch up, hissing when he bites down. "Oh, God, that feels too good."

My head moves to the side so that I can watch him, but he stops and starts to move lower, coming to a halt at my belly button. His tan hand caresses my stomach as he lifts his head, and our eyes connect.

"You're so fucking beautiful, Belle. Perfect, no matter what anyone says." His voice is filled with emotion, emotion that stems from truths I shouldn't have shared.

I bite my lower lip because suddenly this night has turned heavy, thick with whatever this is between us. It's like we're in our own world, our emotions real and purely overwhelming. I know that I should be scared about how deep I'm falling, but I can't be.

"Thank you," I whisper, my eyes filling with tears at the tenderness in his voice.

Though he shakes his head at me, he rumbles, "I want to kiss and lick every inch of you."

My core clenches at the prospect of being his very own feast for one.

"Fuck, I can't get enough of you," he rumbles, dragging my legs apart before using his thumb to rub my slick clit hard before he replaces it with his mouth.

"Yes," I hiss, closing my eyes as I feel myself start to climb. My hands grab at the sheets, tearing it from the corners of the bed. "Cade…" I whimper as my body tenses.

His tongue keeps at me like it's motorized. I writhe around on the mattress, fighting his hold on me but simultaneously needing more, needing everything. I love how he's feasting on my pussy like he's getting off on my pleasure too.

"I'm gonna come…," I scream, wave after wave of ecstasy pulsing through me until he shuts me up by capturing my mouth.

That's when he thrusts into me.

In and out, he tortures me as I lift my lips to his and our eyes lock.

Time, sounds, the world itself seems almost muted. It's just his breath caressing my lips, his cock deep inside me.

"Christ, Belle. What you fucking do to me," he hisses into my mouth, almost as if he's angry. Maybe he is. Feeling so much is scary.

"I know." I understand his fear. Trying to comfort him, my hands reach up to grab his face.

Neither of us expected to feel like this. It's as if my whole life I've been waiting for this connection, for this man who makes me feel as if I'm his.

"Wrap your legs around me," he orders, grunting when I obey.

"Fuck," I cry.

He slams into me, his mouth quieting my scream as my nails dig into his back, and he picks up speed. I close my eyes and let him take everything away.

"Yeah, that's it, Belle. So fucking good. Such a beautiful girl for me. That fucking pussy of yours is like goddamn heaven," he praises, and my eyes pop open because I'm climbing again. Each hard, deep thrust has my body tightening, tensing in preparation for the blast that's about to send shockwaves throughout my nervous system.

"Cade," I whimper, vaguely understanding that I keep saying his name as I go over, splintering into a million pieces.

"Yeah, that's it. Fuck, I love your cunt milking the cum out of my cock," he growls, and I blink away the black dots dancing around the corners of my vision, needing to see him come undone. "You're so fucking beautiful, Belle. We all have a little voice in our head that we listen to too much. You should ignore yours because you're gorgeous. Absolutely fucking gorgeous." Then, his voice darkens, deepens. "I'm going to kiss and lick every inch of your pretty pussy." My core clenches at his filthy promise. "So you know I don't just say shit, I mean it. Now, spread your legs."

Much like the other morning, he doesn't seem to care that he's come inside me. That his seed must be sliding out of my pussy…

With bated breath, I wait for that first toe-curling caress. His fingers burrow into my inner thighs, pushing them wider apart so he can access every inch of me.

Then his tongue is there.

There.

"Oh, God," I scream, so hypersensitized that I'm sure I'm about to go mad with the intensity. My body bucks beneath him, hips writhing and rocking as I try to escape his caresses as well as dive into them.

As I sob, he rumbles, "Fuck, I can't get enough of you." Then, his tongue is sliding into me. I shudder, limbs locking when I realize he's tasting himself, tasting us…

My brain short-circuits while my pussy clamps down around his tongue because that's all I can do, just hold on for dear life. My feet burrow into his back as he takes me to the stars, and then and only then, does he finish. *With a noisy slurp.* I'm too far gone to care though.

Slowly, he moves higher, drifting back into my hold so that he's pressing me into the mattress again. His weight feels grounding, and after a trip around the Milky Way, it's exactly what I need to feel more like myself.

God, it's never been like this with anyone but him. Not even Ryder…

The thought scares me because this is only supposed to be a temporary thing, but nothing about it feels like it's short-term.

Fuck.

"What are you thinking about?"

"Just…" How to answer? "Odds."

"Odds?"

I hum. "What are the odds that we'd hook up?"

He cocks his head at me then slowly tumbles onto his back, tossing an arm over his eyes as he does.

"Odds have a funny way of working out in someone's favor if they're willing to take the bet."

I blink at the peculiar statement, but he drops his arm and reaches for me.

Eager to stay close to him, I rest my head on his chest, my fingers clinging to his shoulder as I snuggle into him.

"Sleep, Belle."

He kisses my forehead and I let my eyes close as I inhale his scent. Both our faces are marked with each other, and as much as we desperately need a shower, there's something comforting about it.

Something primal and primitive deep in my soul is at peace because of it.

Hearing his heartbeat, strong, powerful, I whisper, "Cade?"

"Yeah?"

"I'm glad I'm here."

His arms tighten around me but I don't realize he doesn't answer because his heartbeat against my ear has already lulled me to sleep.

13

BELLE

"What is that noise?" I mutter, burying my face in Cade's neck.

"Go away," he yells.

I groan because my head is killing me and that didn't help matters. Throw in the asshole knocking on his door and I'll be yelling next.

"Ma wants to meet Isabelle. She made breakfast." The woman's voice has my eyes popping open.

Ma.

God, he'd said it himself, hadn't he?

Ma is tomorrow's problem.

He roars, "Kitty, I swear to God—"

"Don't yell at me. But I'd get up. The eggs are getting cold." She sings the last part, obviously enjoying being our alarm clock.

"Wait. Does your family have a key?" I whisper as he sits up, his eyes caressing my face before dropping to my breasts.

"They do," he confirms, scrubbing his hands over his face as he rolls out of bed to stand. "But I'm not bothered about that. Kitty won't stop banging on the goddamn door until we're awake and out of here," he grouses. "Pain in my ass."

I'm no longer focusing on the sibling byplay. I'm too busy staring at him and his morning wood.

"Are you always hard?"

"Only when I'm around you." He grins, suddenly cheerful. "We'll say hello to my ma, eat some breakfast in her place, then come back and you can sit on my face. How about that for a to-do list?"

"Cade, Kitty might be able to hear you," I grumble, rubbing my temple where my hangover is making itself known. Absently, my eyes take in his bedroom, which is nothing more than a bed, dresser, and white walls which are total blank canvases. His floors are hardwood with no rug or even a chair. It feels like he just moved in… "I thought you lived here?"

"I do. And Kitty is the last person to worry about. Now, Ma, we might want to get dressed for that," he drawls, disappearing for a moment into the bathroom. "I'll give you a tour of my apartment later." I hear the toilet flush, then he returns, opens a dresser drawer, and retrieves a pair of jeans.

I blink at him. "Cade."

"Yeah?"

"Please tell me you washed your face." When he just winks at me, I gasp. "You get back in that bathroom and wash your face!"

"Who's going to make me?"

I gape at him then sputter, "We're going to eat breakfast with your family!"

"They're not going to sniff my face," he points out.

"I'm not sitting on it after breakfast if you're still wearing last night's…" My nose crinkles. "Ew. Go and wash it."

He mock-pouts. "You gotta ruin a good thing."

I snort then ask, "Um, where's my bag?"

"I'll get it." He jerks on his jeans, not bothering to button them, so I get to feast my eyes on his delicious eight-pack before he disappears again then returns with my baggage. "You okay?" He looks at me and lifts my suitcase onto the bed. "Sore?"

That arched brow makes me flush. "A little. Mostly, I'm just hungover. Last night was…" I hesitate, though I'm smiling as I unzip my carry-on. "I don't know. Last night was—"

"Incredible," he finishes for me, and my cheeks flush.

"Really?" My eyes dart to his for confirmation.

"Really." His thumb caresses my lips as my smile widens. "Get dressed. I want you to meet my ma because she's going to love you."

He means it. And he's not pushing me away or trying to back down from the intensity of the last few days. Man, this could be one of the best mornings of my life.

"Okay, I need a shower and so do you," I retort, quickly unzipping my bag and pulling out some white jeans and a cute, cropped pink shirt.

I wear a lot of pastels, but pink is my favorite. It just makes me happy, like everything is rosy. I smile at how ridiculous it is, but it's true.

"Babe, we're just going for breakfast. Besides, I like the smell of us fucking on you," he admits with zero shame as he pulls on a black T-shirt and reaches for his phone.

"Cade, I have to take a shower." I laugh. "I'll be super fast."

Before he can stop me, I run toward his bathroom, which is much like his bedroom—completely empty. The white tile walls and floor look clean, but other than some black towels, along with his toothbrush and toothpaste, that's all I see.

My feet are freezing on the floor as it doesn't have a rug. I'm almost tempted to tell him I can go shopping with him for *things*, but it's too soon for that.

Shoving aside the strange vibe of the empty space, I'm in and out of the bathroom in five minutes, a new record for me. Hell, I barely even put any makeup on.

"Belle, you ready?" Cade asks, walking in as I walk out.

"Give me five minutes." I arch onto tiptoe upon his approach and rub my nose along his jawline. "You smell of sex. My pussy, to be precise. Clean up."

He's mock-pouting again as I watch him wash up. Once he's

covered and he can't back out, I retreat to the bedroom and drag on my clothes.

When he next leaves the bathroom, he's swiping a towel over his face.

"How do I look?" I ask, smiling up at him as I step back and twirl.

"Stunning." He grabs my hand and butterflies flutter in my stomach. "Fucking beautiful. What color is that?"

"Pink?" I drawl with a laugh.

"Nah, it's purple."

"Purple?!" I stare down at my blouse. "Are you color-blind?"

"You got me seeing stars, baby girl. Black is white and gold is silver."

I hoot out a laugh. "So corny."

"Got you going, though, didn't I?" he teases. "Need to make sure you're nice and calm. Ma's super chill. You don't have to worry about her. Now, my sister is another matter entirely."

"Um, so what is your ma's name?" I ask, but despite his pep talk, I am nervous.

The one thing I have is perfect manners so it's ridiculous to feel anxious. It's not like I was raised without them, but I'm pretty damn sure that I'm falling in love with this guy. I want his mom to like me.

"Patricia. Don't call her Mrs. Frasier, she always says that's my grandmother. You can call her Ma," he says with a wink while leading me to the elevator, holding out his arm to let me inside first.

"Cade, I can't call her ma," I retort.

"Sure you can! Everyone does. Ma's... *Ma.*"

I huff at that, but the elevator doors open, letting in the sounds of laughter and voices, which get even louder as we approach an open front door.

"Christ," he groans the second he hears them.

"What? What's wrong?" I ask quickly before I can start panicking.

"Nothing. It sounds like my other sisters are here too," he complains before pulling me into the apartment with him, which is when the entire room goes silent.

Everyone stares and looks at us and then explodes with all of them greeting him.

"Ma, please," he moans with a laugh as a small woman with blonde hair in a bun and a trim figure smothers Cade's cheeks with kisses and holds him tight to her chest. I know they saw each other last night, but it's as if she hasn't seen him in months.

I'm happy for him; really, I am. But for a split second, pain fills me. I miss my mom. Even though I try hard to push the grief away, it never goes anywhere. It's always there, hanging around. Seeing this, his mom being so affectionate, just throws me for a moment.

"You were gone too long," she chides, slapping his side playfully as, chuckling, he drapes an arm around her. Which is when the other two women I haven't met yet move in for a hug.

The only one who is ignoring Cade is Kitty. She's sitting on the couch, dressed in the same clothes as last night, sipping coffee or tea, and wearing dark sunglasses as if the morning light is too much for her as well.

Damn, rushing around this morning made me forget my shades. Talk about a rookie move.

"Ma, Neev, Róisín, I want you to meet Isabelle." He removes his arm from around his mother to beckon me toward him.

"Isabelle. Yes, Kitty told us all about you. I'm Patricia. So nice to meet you." She takes my arm and leads me into another room.

Unlike her son's condo, hers has actual furniture: yellow walls, a big red couch, tons of family pictures everywhere in a multitude of different frames, and a brick fireplace in the corner.

"Nice to meet you, Mrs. Frasier," I say shyly.

But she tuts. "None of that Mrs. stuff. Call me Patricia." We walk into a big open room where there's a giant table and floor-to-ceiling windows. A large island is the only thing that separates it from the kitchen. "You must be starving," she declares. "It's already ten AM."

God, it feels as if it's five in the morning, and with the time difference, it *is* seven. Throw in the jet lag, the alcohol, and the late night, it's small wonder I feel like shit.

"You have a beautiful home," I offer instead, smiling nervously as she takes in my appearance.

What she has to say is a curveball, for sure. "You aren't from here."

"No, not anymore. But I was born here before I moved to the West Coast." I smile again and change the subject. "I just think it's wonderful that you all live here... together," I say, looking at the food she's prepared. "And that smells delicious." I motion to the large platter of eggs, bacon, and what looks like sausages, along with some toast and jam.

"Well, good, I hope you're hungry. I thought my other son was coming over also, but he has to work apparently." She looks over at Cade, who is now moving to my side. "Where is that boy?"

"Like I'd know. You know Lucas. Busy, busy, busy," he mocks.

"He's a workaholic." Kitty huffs, then she puts her sunglasses on top of her head so he can see her roll her eyes at him as she sits down at the long table.

"All my boys do is work," Patricia agrees with a sigh as she goes to grab a stainless-steel pot of coffee and pours some into a cup. "Would you like cream or sugar?"

"Both, thank you."

Cade slides his arm around me, kisses the top of my nose, then pulls out a chair for me. When I look at him, I know I'm blushing at his gentlemanly moves.

"I told you," Kitty mocks, smirking at her sisters' and mother's shocked expressions.

Patricia recovers enough to set the coffee cup in front of me, but I can see her curiosity is eating at her. "So, you two met where?" she inquires, studying Cade, who holds up a finger because his phone is ringing.

"I've got to take this, Ma." He caresses my cheek and I kind of melt into his hand before he turns and walks toward the living room area. That's when all eyes are on me.

I'd be nervous, but it's uncanny how much they look alike.

Damn, Ma and Pa Frasier had the best gene pool.

"So?" Patricia sits at the head of the table while Neev and Róisín cluster around Kitty and me. "Where did you meet?" Patricia prompts.

"Um, well, it's kind of sweet." I take a sip of the coffee, needing to think exactly how much I want to tell them.

I can hardly say, *Oh, you know, we bonded when your son saved me from OD'ing and paid my ER bill. We haven't left each other's sides since...*

"I was working." I glance at each of the pretty faces and wonder if Neev and Róisín are twins. *Focus, Isabelle.* "I'm a waitress at this great diner in Burbank, and Cade was kind of a regular—"

When his sisters start hurling questions at me, Patricia holds up a hand. "Girls, please." Patricia surprises me by reaching over to pat mine as if she's silently giving me her strength, maybe even support. "Sorry, I know we're loud. You don't have any siblings, do you?"

The kindness in her voice makes tears gather in my throat. "No," I croak. "I don't."

Why do I want to run all of a sudden? It's a standard question but somehow, she makes me feel like I need a hug. I'm about to ask her where her bathroom is when Cade walks back into the room, his blue eyes focused on me, then his mom. He must sense something is wrong because he walks straight over and rubs my shoulders when his ma lets go of my hand.

"What'd I miss? Did you tell them how I was so enchanted by your beauty I came in to your diner every day, using the excuse of wanting a burger?" He flashes everyone at the table a dimpled smile as he sits next to me.

I nod but only rasp, "Yes."

Conversation flickers around me but I retreat until—

"Isabelle?"

I almost jump at Cade's voice. "Sorry, what?" Embarrassed, I mumble, "I think I need more coffee." I take a deep sip and almost choke on the hot brew.

"I'll answer for her, Raisin—"

"Stop it with the Raisin, Cade!" Róisín argues.

"*Raisin*," he snipes, wrapping a possessive arm around my shoulders. "I hope Belle wants to stay for a long time."

My eyes flare wide at that. "Oh, well, I own a condo and I have friends. I needed to get away, and Cade lives here so, I mean, you, I-I have a job and..." Knowing Cade will be no help as he obviously wants me to stay, which is actually nice to know, I still feel like I'm in the hot seat. Desperately, I stare beseechingly at Kitty, as if she can help me, and surprisingly she does.

"You are never gonna guess who I ran into last night!" she bursts out. "I can't believe I forgot to tell you—"

Just like that, all the blue eyes that were staring at me turn to her as she rambles on about someone named Stan who is so smokin' hot he's on fire.

"Cade, honey? I need a word with you," Patricia murmurs, smiling at me as she stands and walks toward the hallway, not allowing Cade to refuse. "Make yourself at home, Isabelle," she calls over her shoulder.

Cade leans down to give me a quick kiss. "Be right back."

As he follows his mom, I realize I'm left with three women I know nothing about. Yet, how they're gossiping and laughing makes me feel at home.

Standing, I fetch the coffee pot and pour myself some more. It's only then, as I have a moment to myself, away from prying eyes, that I realize how expensive the kitchen is.

From the massive stove to the industrial-sized refrigerator, the elegant cabinets and the marble counters that are loaded down with more gadgets than a QVC demo... Then, of course, there's the fact the family owns the whole building.

What is it he does again?

14

CADE

ACUIG

"What's wrong, Ma?" I ask the second we're back in the living room.

She folds her arms across her chest, which never bodes well, and muses, "She's very nervous."

"She didn't think she'd be meeting the full Frasier clan this morning. It's intimidating as hell, wouldn't you say?"

"Language," she grumbles, her toe tapping against the floor.

I roll my eyes but know better than to continue in that vein. I can see the dishcloth she's got tucked into her waistband. That shit hurts even when you're in your thirties. "Well, it is. Plus, we got in late last night. We were kinda jet-lagged and had a few too many drinks. What do you expect?"

She squints at me. "What was that call about?"

I scoff because this conversation suddenly makes sense. "That's the real reason you brought me here, isn't it?"

"Can't a mother be scared for her son when he's on his first mission?"

"Mission? Ma, I'm not exactly James Bond."

"All I know is that you've been gone for weeks with barely a phone call home, and you come back in the dead of winter with a tan and a girl on your arm who looks like she's been to hell and back."

I blink at that. "She doesn't look that bad."

"She does. Of course, she's beautiful." She waves a hand. "You and your brother attract pretty girls like flies to honey. But…" Her words drift to a halt, her concern palpable.

Suddenly, I'm curious. My grandmother used to say that she had the "sight." I don't know if that's bullshit or not. What I do know is that Da used to come back flush from a win at the racetrack because of Ma's insight.

"But what, Ma?" I prompt.

Her hand scrubs up and down her arm like she's cold, but she keeps her rooms overheated—it's her one indulgence. "She's been hurt."

"Hasn't everyone?"

Her lips tighten. "I suppose. Don't be mean to her, Cade. It wouldn't be kind to kick a girl when she's down."

"I don't intend to kick her," I grumble, taking offense at that last comment. "Did you and Da teach us to raise a hand to a woman?"

"Words and actions hurt as much as a fist to the face." She steps over to me and presses a kiss on my cheek. "It's good to have you home, son."

"It's good to be back actually."

That wasn't a lie.

I have a lot of responsibilities in New York now, which I haven't liked so much, but in all honesty, I've missed home and my family.

Even Kitty.

Not Lucas, though. I didn't have a chance to miss him with how fucking often he called to moan at me for taking too long to bring Belle back to the city.

"What made you come here with her, son?" she inquires, her brow puckering. "Is it serious?"

Ignoring that last question, I answer, "Because this is my home and I didn't feel like staying in a hotel." It's not a total lie. This isn't the first time I've brought a hookup home and she's never given me the third degree like this before. Or the woman either.

Why is Belle different?

Is it because *I'm* different around her?

"There's more to this than meets the eye."

My mouth opens to deny it, but I realize that'd be gaslighting her. Instead, I duck my head and mumble, "It's work-related."

Her gaze turns knowing, like that's enough to confirm her suspicions. "Will it hurt that poor girl even more?"

"I don't intend on hurting her."

"That didn't answer my question."

I sigh. "I'm going to work on making sure she isn't hurt."

"Better answer."

"Don't tell Lucas I'm here, Ma."

Her eyes narrow. "Why not?"

"Because if he knows I'm here, then I have to act, and I don't want to yet."

"Why not? Have you gotten her into trouble?"

The question makes my lips twitch. "No, Ma. She isn't pregnant."

"Praise Jesus for small mercies," she retorts. "You boys will be the death of me. What, with Lucas working all hours and you deciding to drop off the face of the earth for weeks on end! Why can't you be like my girls? That's what I want to know."

I don't answer that. Don't tell her that "her girls" are not only as bad as "her boys," but her girls also get to have more of a chance at leading a normal life than Lucas or I.

We had two options when we were eighteen—join the Army or the Irish Mob.

At least with the mob, you get to wear slick suits and earn expensive condos as bonuses.

Not wanting to upset her, I slide my arm around her shoulder and drag her into me for a hug. "You wouldn't know what to do with yourself if you weren't worrying about Lucas and me."

She rolls her eyes. "I'll tell my doctor that when he adjusts my blood pressure medication, shall I? You think you kissed the Blarney Stone, that's your trouble, but you forget only your da knew how to activate it in me. I've got a monitor for your nonsense."

My lips twitch even as I ask, "How is your heart?"

"Beating just fine, thank you very much. Not that you help my blood pressure stay low."

A raucous wave of laughter sounds from down the hall.

"Sounds like Belle is fitting in just fine," I tease, though I admit I'm surprised.

Clan Frasier isn't particularly inclusive. Whenever I've brought a girlfriend around for dinner in the past, my sisters have always grilled them. That's why I groaned when I heard them cackling like a bunch of witches.

"Kitty told Róisín and Neev that you were chivalrous last night. So they're curious."

What? "I wasn't."

Ma arches a brow at me.

I scowl. "I was being polite."

"Well, what does it say about you when your sisters think that means you're two steps away from proposing because you're nice to a girl you brought home!"

"You say that like I'm mean—"

"You've gone through this neighborhood like the measles," she grumbles, making my lips twitch again—I'm not dumb enough to smile. "I can barely open my curtains now without another mother glaring at me wherever I turn. Especially when you've never given even the glimpse of a wedding ring to their poor daughters."

"I'm not that bad!" I argue. And *poor daughters,* my ass. I offer complete satisfaction, three orgasms per fuck—what more can a woman ask for?

"You are. The Lord made you pretty, son." She pats my cheek. "It's a curse you have to bear."

My eyes ache with the need to roll them. "I think I deal well with the disadvantage, Ma."

Another wave of laughter sounds from the dining room and she mutters, "They'd better not be telling her about Stan's penis."

That has me gaping at her. "Stan's dick? Why the hell would they be telling her about that? And how do you know about it?" *Who the fuck even is Stan?*

She sniffs. "It's something that happened at the hospital." Then, she hurries back down the hall, and, hell, I scurry after her.

"—helicopter—"

That's all I hear, and it's all I need to hear before I growl, "Catriona Frasier!" I don't care that I've made her jump.

"God, you sound like Da when you use that tone," she clips at me.

"Imagine if he'd heard you talking about—"

"Helicopters?" Belle inserts, her brow furrowed in faux confusion. "What's wrong with talking about helicopters, Cade?"

I glower at her. "You're siding with them?"

Her grin is mischievous and she knows it. Kitty holds up her hand so they can high-five one another. "Women have to stick together so we can headbutt the patriarchy en masse," my sister informs me. "And this was a beautiful helicopter. The best in the—"

"I'm not the patriarchy and I don't need to hear about another guy's—"

"Cade!" Ma bleats before I can swear.

Kitty just sniffs. "You would say that, wouldn't you?"

"Less of the feminism at the table, Kitty. I don't want you getting into a debate with your brother again," Ma grouses as she butters a slice of toast. "It took two days for that migraine to go. Why the good Lord blessed me with six children and made them louder than freight trains, I don't know."

"Why was this Stan guy doing helicopters with his dick anyway?" I demand, taking a seat next to Belle once more.

"Cade Shaun Frasier!" Ma cries. "You can't be talking about that at the dinner table!"

The girls cascade into laughter, but it's Belle's who makes something weird ping in my chest.

I already know she's been hurt—didn't need my ma or her "sight" to tell me that.

I have no desire to break her heart. No desire at all. But is it already out of my control?

After placing a few sausage links on my plate, along with some bacon, two eggs, and a mountain of toast, I eat with one hand and keep the other planted on Belle's lap, our hands tangled together.

If we were at a restaurant, I'd have probably let my fingers do some flirting, but Ma will serve me up on the table if there's any funny business going on between us and, oddly enough, I'm more than happy for her to just hang out with my sisters, who aren't being their usual pain-in-the-ass selves around her. Me? Sure. But with her, they're being nice.

As they joke and tease each other like they've been friends for decades, Clan Frasier's females drawing her deeper into the conversation, which is more G-rated now that Ma's around, I'm hit with a strange truth—she fits in with my family.

Whether that's a good thing or a bad thing, I'm not sure yet, but whatever it is, it puts a smile on my face.

15

CADE

ACUIG

"WHY DO you give Kitty such a hard time?"

The question has my brows arching. "You want to talk about my sister? Right now?"

She chuckles, and the soft sound has me grinning even as I tuck her closer to me. Gravity has only just left my dick out in the cold so, Kitty? Definitely not my conversational topic of choice.

"I just wondered," she murmurs.

"Wonder another time when we're not both lying in the wet spot."

With a snort, she buries her face in my throat. "She's a great sister."

"She's a great pain in my ass."

"She loves you."

"And I love her." My lips twitch. "We just give each other shit. It's what we do."

"Why do you think she wanted to be a nurse?"

"You mean, aside from her *caring* and *compassionate* nature?"

She snickers. "She doesn't have the kind of personality for it, does she?"

"No, but she's damn good at her job." I know I sound proud. Hell, *I am*. "She's the first and only one of us to go to college."

"What made her want to take that route?"

"Neev got high on molly when she was in high school. We tried to keep it from Ma at the time because she'd, *we'd*," I correct, my voice suddenly thick with the emotions of years past, "just lost Vinny. I think it hit home with her how important nurses are, you know?"

"Yeah, they are. And they get none of the glamorous jobs either."

"No, they don't."

"I can imagine she's terrifying when she's working, but I bet she's the one you want to be at your bedside in a crisis."

I hum. "Ma got sick last year. Had some issues with her stomach. No one bosses her around. You've seen that already—"

"Kitty did?" she inquires.

"Yup. She got her straightened out, told her the new order of how things would work since she was in charge now—"

"Bet Patricia *loved* that," she teases.

"Oh, about as much as you'd expect. She said she got better just to take Little Ms. Dictator off her high horse. But Ma was proud too. We're a pretty healthy family all things considered, so we never had much of a chance to see her work. Until then.

"She made Nurse Ratched look friendly, let me tell you, but I'm sure that none of us have been sick since so we don't need to have her look after us." When she laughs, I grin and press a kiss to her nose. "You like her, don't you?"

She hitches a shoulder, but her words are shy as she mumbles, "I like them all. They're cool."

My grin widens as I stare into space. "Yeah. They are. Still pains in the ass though."

"Of course." Her sigh is wistful. "I always wanted a brother or a sister. Then, as I got older, I stopped…"

At her silence, I prompt, "Why?"

"Because if I were the older sibling, then I'd have to protect them. And if they were the older sibling, they'd have to protect me. Better for only one of us to deal with that."

Guilt spears me yet again. It makes me drag her deeper into my hold, a move she facilitates, clinging to me as much as I cling to her.

"I bet you'd have made a great big sister," I say to distract her, even as I feel the ticking clock making its endless goddamn countdown.

The question is—how do I protect her from Aidan Jr. and his skewed fucking morals?

I don't know. I really don't. If I did, I'd have dealt with this by now. But Aidan's... *Aidan*. Dr. Davis did him a favor, and the Five Points always repay their debts.

Belle is a debt.

So, how the fuck do I keep her safe?

"You don't know that," she chides, bringing me back to the conversation.

I blink at nothing. "Seen you with my sisters."

"That doesn't mean anything."

"You fit right in."

Her chuckle is low. "They make it easy to fit in."

We stay in, don't go out... That's an option. Then, I keep her busy in bed to distract from the fact she's in the city that never sleeps and I don't let her leave the fucking apartment...

That might work.

She's easy to distract, and she *does* like my family. I get it, they're awesome, but she looks at them through the hazy lens of someone who didn't have to put up with them her whole life.

I'll take it though. If it'll keep her safe.

Hugging her tighter to me, I mutter, "They like you."

A soft whisper of tension flutters through her. "You don't know that."

"I do. I do know," I argue, then I press a kiss to her forehead. "I like you too."

This time, she giggles. It's childish and buoyant and it makes my grin turn dopey. "I'm glad you do," she whispers, nestling into me in a way that feels right and natural and perfect, and yawns at the same time.

She drifts off then, starts to fall asleep.

I don't.

My eyes are wide open as I stare out the window at the building across the street, trying to devise ways of keeping her home, of avoiding Lucas, of keeping under the radar.

God, I should never have brought her to the city.

Ever.

I squeeze her tighter in my embrace.

"I'll keep you safe, Isabelle," I whisper. "I promise."

My mind shifts to something my da had once told me.

"Frasier men never make a promise they can't keep, Cade. You remember that, do you hear me? It's a matter of honor."

Throat thickening at the memory, I have to wonder if salvaging my honor is an impossible feat.

Da would have said I lost it when Vinny died.

I'm thinking it happened the morning I convinced her to return to the one place she feared the most, the place that had once been her home.

Closing my eyes, I repeat, "I'll keep you safe, Isabelle. I promise."

It doesn't soothe her, but it soothes me.

The promise is struck and, like Da said, a Frasier man never makes a promise he can't keep...

16

CADE
FOUR DAYS LATER

The TV might be on, and a home reno show might be trying to teach us how to properly caulk a bathroom, but neither Belle nor I are interested in learning that particular lesson.

Nuzzling my face into her throat, I nip the area between her neck and shoulder as I slowly finger fuck her. The butt of my hand grinds on her clit and she melts into me, arms and legs trembling as I keep edging her.

Her legs are spread thanks to how I hooked her knees over mine, and I've got access to all that honey between her thighs.

Slick digits sliding over her clit, I rumble in her ear, "So fucking wet for me, Belle. I bet I could just do this"—I make a come-hither motion with my fingers—"and you'd be ready for me to fuck you. Always so hungry for my cock, aren't you, baby?"

She arches into me, her ass grinding against my dick, soft moans whispering from her lips.

With a grunt, I stop moving my fingers. "That ain't an answer. What are you hungry for, Belle?"

Her whimper has me hiding a groan, especially when she reaches up and palms one of her tits.

Those fucking bad boys are my kryptonite. I've titty fucked them twice now and made her eat dinner with them drenched in my cum.

It's worth it just to see those pretty cheeks of hers glowing red.

"Your cock." She breathes her answer, the words dragged out by how heavily she's panting.

"Where do you like it?" I tease, spreading my fingers wider in her channel. Her hiss lets me know how that feels and it also tells me she isn't focusing on my questions. I tsk. "You're not concentrating, Belle."

I grind my hand into her clit, listening to her heavy groan.

"E-Everywhere," she whimpers.

"But where's best?" I taunt.

"My pussy," she rasps as I pull back, gifting her with a soft rub of her clit with my drenched hand.

"Do you like it when I fill you up?"

Her ass shimmies against my dick. I slap her cunt with my fingers to prompt her to answer.

"I love it," she cries.

"I'm going to make you walk around the city one day with my cum dripping out of you," I whisper in her ear.

"W-Why?"

I shrug. "So you're all slick and warm and so I can bend you over and fuck you wherever I want. Don't you like the sound of that?"

She groans again as I reach for one of her tits.

"Well? You're not being very good today, Belle," I chide. "Not answering my questions…"

"You're asking too many!" she says with a pout that makes me grab her chin, tilt her head to the side, and devour her lips.

As I thrust my tongue into her mouth, I let my fingers slide in deep again. This time, I don't stop until my knuckles are at her slit. Her moans and whimpers egg me on, but she's not ready for more yet.

She might have been if my cum was lubing her up…

Making a mental note to try that tomorrow, I focus on that soft, spongy pad at the front wall of her pussy.

When Ma told me everyone was out of the apartment today on errands, I knew I had to make her scream. She'd gone all quiet since Róisín told her over dinner two nights ago that she could hear us fucking.

Breaking Belle's sudden nervousness has been on my agenda ever since. And seeing as that agenda involves nothing more than getting inside her pussy as often as I can, whether it's with my tongue, fingers, or dick, my failure to make her chill out has led to drastic measures.

Drawing my fingers down, I palpate them, making sure her clit gets some love too. I thrust my tongue into her mouth, forcing her to focus on me and nothing else.

Her legs clutch at mine, thighs tightening as she tries to close them. Her hips rear up, pumping the air as she seeks the pleasure I'm forcing on her while also trying to avoid it.

Is it wrong to want to break her with pleasure?

To make her crave this?

Crave me?

I don't have a clue what's going on between us. It feels really deep, really fast, but I know I'm only putting off the inevitable. Maybe Savannah, Aidan's wife, can help me protect her—

She rips her mouth from mine and shrieks, "Stop, Cade, stop. I-I can't. I can't!"

My mind is back on her—one hundred percent.

"You can, Belle, you can," I rumble. "Let it come. I want you to pass out from coming so hard. Can't you do that for me, baby? I want you to scream so loud the taxi drivers outside can hear you."

"No, no, no," she chants, her fingers trying to pry at mine, but I'm relentless.

I trail my tongue over her earlobe and whisper, "I'm going to ruin you, Isabelle. I'm going to make you want me forever." At her whimper, I continue, "I'm not going to stop until you scream with pleasure."

Her cunt ripples around my fingers.

"If you're thinking of other people, then you're not focusing hard enough. I want your screams, baby. They're mine. All mine."

She releases a loud gasp and grinds back into me, my words breaking through the wall Róisín thoughtlessly crafted with her teasing.

"This slick pussy is so hungry for me, Belle," I whisper, loving the gasps she releases. "It's all mine too, isn't it? Are you going to gush for me? I bet you will."

"Oh, God, Cade, I c-can't."

Smugly, I smile. "You can. I'm not gonna stop until this pussy recognizes only me in the future—"

That's when she breaks.

Her cunt turns into a vise around my hand and she screams herself hoarse, back arching, shoulders digging into me as she soars so hard she forgets about everything else that's going on, forgets about fighting the pleasure, and takes what I want her to have.

Everything.

I smirk as she rides my hand, focused on herself, greedy for all of it.

That's when the knock sounds at the door.

Fuck.

A horrified gasp escapes her as her befuddled mind registers what's happening, but I don't let her go. My arm clamps around her waist and my fingers stay deep inside her. She keeps on pulsing around me, her body torn between what I've made her feel and what's happening.

"Stay right where you are," I growl.

"No! Oh, my God, someone heard us, heard me—"

When she starts sobbing, I kiss her, nuzzle into her to comfort her, wanting to shoot whoever knocked on the goddamn door when they had to hear I was otherwise engaged.

"I'm at home. I'm over twenty-one. And we're both consenting adults. We've done nothing wrong, Belle," I retort.

"I-I'm too noisy," she whispers, and that breaks my fucking heart.

Is there nothing she thinks she does right?

There's another knock that has her jerking like she's been stung with a cattle prod.

I don't give a shit that one of my sisters is standing outside the door. I cup her chin and whisper, "You're fucking perfect, Belle. I love that you scream. I love that I know I'm fucking you exactly how you want me to. I never wonder if you're enjoying yourself because you tell me. Loud and clear. You let me know, and I love that. I don't want you to stop—"

"But, your sisters—"

I shrug. "Maybe I should get my place soundproofed if they can hear us."

Her mouth forms a perfect circle that gives my dick ideas we don't have time to carry out. "That's insane."

I shoot her a wink. "Maybe I'm insane about you."

"Cade, for fuck's sake. Open the damn door!"

My tension is immediate.

Lucas.

Shit.

Because we're as close as can be, she senses my tension and rasps, "What's wrong? Who is it? Is that Lucas?"

I'm fucked.

Literally fucked.

There's no way this is going to end well, but it has to. I have to make this right because as dumb as I sounded before, I was speaking the truth.

I *am* wild about her.

Knowing my time is running out, I gently run my thumb along her chin and mumble, "Belle, I want you to know—"

"Cade! I need to speak with you. It's urgent!"

I ignore him. "—that I will never let anyone hurt you. Not even my brother. Do you hear me?"

"Why would you..." She stiffens. "Do you think Lucas will hurt me?"

My mouth tightens. Because he could. Just not physically. "There's shit you don't know about me. I can explain, but you need to listen to me, okay?"

"What's going on?" she demands worriedly, all that beautiful languor from her orgasm having faded into dust.

I'm a dumb fuck is what's going on.

I press a kiss on her cheek. "I need to speak with Lucas. Wait for me and I'll come back and explain everything."

"You're scaring me, Cade. What's to explain?"

When Lucas's fist bangs on the door again, I know I've run out of time. Explaining this will take too long, especially if I don't want her to hate me in the aftermath. I have to get out of here, make sure she doesn't overhear what I have to say to my brother. Then I can fix things.

Lifting her off my lap, I shake my head. "I'll make this right, princess."

"Cade!" she cries, but I ignore her, shove the hand that's coated in her pussy juices into the pocket of my jeans, and aim for the door. I open it but before Lucas can push his way in, I rush forward into the hallway and snarl, "Not here. Vinny's."

Vinny's place is mostly empty. Some of it's a shrine, some of it's the overflow from our apartments, but the door is always open.

Not letting him argue, I run downstairs and wait for Lucas to join me in the living room our brother never got to enjoy.

"Why the hell did you bring me in here?"

Lucas hates reminders of the past.

Me, I'm different. I like to rip at a scab to make sure it never closes. That's what Vinny is to me now. A wound that will never heal.

"I need privacy."

"Yeah, I heard," he snaps, earning a glower from me. "You're supposed to be in L.A."

"I came back a few days ago."

"I know. Róisín told me by accident that you'd gotten together with some Belle chick and were keeping her awake at night. Why didn't you tell me you fucked up, Cade? I can't fix your mistakes if you don't warn—"

That immediately makes me scowl. "I didn't fuck up."

"You did. You're here, aren't you? Not in California where you're supposed to be. And Cindy goddamn Davis sure as hell isn't here, is she?"

His sneer makes me want to punch him. "I didn't fuck up, and I don't always need you to fix my mistakes, damn it."

"That you're here without Cindy Davis says otherwise," he repeats. More annoying than anything is that he doesn't sound smug, just resigned. "If I'm wrong, explain what's going on." When he folds his arms over his chest, he looks so much like Da that it makes me turn away again.

My past is littered with the fallout from one major fuckup, but Lucas and Da always acted like there was nothing I ever did right, and they never let me forget what I did.

As much shit as my sisters give me, it's because they're pains in the ass and not because they hold Vinny's passing against me. Not even Ma does.

Just Lucas and Da.

I tip my chin up. "Whatever Davis told Aidan was a lie."

He didn't expect to hear that. His shoulders drop in surprise. "What?"

"I'm telling you, Davis is a liar. Cindy"—God, it's so strange calling her that when she's Belle to me now—"wasn't being held against her will by the Disciples."

"Davis said they kept her hooked on prescription meds and that was why she hung around, working her ass off at that diner until all hours—"

"She worked there because she wanted to and I saw her prescription meds. They had Davis's name on the label—he prescribed them to her as her doctor."

Lucas jerks back. "What?"

"I'm telling you he's a liar. He abused her, Lucas." I grit my teeth. "I'm not letting her go back to him."

He stares at me for a handful of seconds. "You're not letting her go back to him," he repeats as if I've suddenly broken into French. "What makes you think you have a choice in this? You're my brother, and you're only a part of Aidan's crew because of that—"

"Nice to know how you feel about me, Lucas," I snap.

He shrugs. "You know it's true. Your head's never in the game, Cade. When Aidan drew you into this, I knew you'd fuck up sooner or later. Why do you think I've been riding your ass hard about it? Trying to keep you on the straight and narrow—" He breaks off then slaps his palm against his forehead. "Isabelle. Belle. Please tell me that the broad you were just fucking isn't Cindy Davis?"

I lift my chin and retort, "I wasn't fucking her."

He knows me too well and reads between the lines with ease. "Sure sounded like you were to me, what with how she was wailing like a banshee."

That's when I hit him.

It doesn't even register that I'm close enough to smack him until my fist meets his cheekbone and he's falling back on his ass, my attack unexpected enough that he's not prepared for it.

When he surges forward, arms curving around my legs to haul me to the floor, I let him because I want to have an excuse for beating the fuck out of him.

I land heavily on my hip, but I don't care. I'm straight into the fight, ready and raring to goddamn go.

"Decades of you talking down to me," I snap, ramming my fist into his face. "Decades of you thinking—"

Fuck.

He gets me in the gut. Once. Twice. A third time.

"You're the one who's a mess, Cade. You can't do anything right, you asswipe—" That's when I grab his hand and jerk it backward, oddly satisfied when I hear a hard crack.

When he snarls in pain, I shove him away only so that I have enough room to hit him. "I made one fucking mistake and you condemned me for it forever."

"You killed Vinny. That wasn't just a mistake, Cade," he roars. Even with his sprained wrist, he's strong enough to fight back. "And you're doing it again. I can't believe you fucked her!"

"I think I love her, Lucas!"

My declaration freezes him in place. His snarl of exasperation twists into a bitter laugh that hurts to hear. "Of course, you think that. Why wouldn't you?" he scoffs. Then, he's shaking his head and getting up off the floor, using his good hand to stand tall. Cradling his bad wrist against his chest, he clips, "Unless you've got evidence that Davis is a liar, Aidan won't want to hear it. He's doing this as a favor. Saving some poor bitch from her fate tied to an MC that's got her imprisoned—"

"I'm telling you that's not how it was. She ran away from her dad! They gave her shelter."

"No proof, no truth," he dismisses, his cool demeanor frustrating me as nothing else can.

"You're a fucking disgrace," I bite off. "You want to send a woman back to her abuser. How the hell would you feel if Róisín, Kitty, or Neev were in a similar situation? Wouldn't you hope that someone could help them?"

That's when my words hit home—his shoulders slump. Thank Christ.

Lucas, as much as we don't always get along, is a good guy. Too good. That he was being callous tells me one thing and one thing alone —he didn't believe me.

Me. Not Belle.

He thought I was selling him a story to cover up my inability to bring Cindy to New York without drawing the attention of the Disciples and triggering some kind of war over her.

He rubs at his eyes, his fatigue clear. "If you think she's in danger from Davis, you need to get her to tell Aidan that."

I swallow. After all, that's not as easy as it sounds. Not when she thinks I'm a nomadic businessman.

"Fine," I rumble. "I'll call him later."

"You'd better. And before he finds out for himself that you're in the city and didn't check in with him first."

I grant him a brisk nod then watch as he storms out of Vinny's place without a backward look, sprained wrist cradled against his chest.

Slowly, I release a breath.

It's time to share everything with Belle. No more holding back. These feelings I've got for her might be tossed down the trash chute by the time I've finished, but at least I won't have broken my promise to her.

She'll be safe from Davis.

Even if she was only ever in danger from him in the first place because of me.

Grimacing at the thought, I limp out of Vinny's apartment. My hip's aching like a fucker from where I landed when Lucas dragged me down so I hobble as I climb the stairs.

Heading inside my apartment, I look at the sofa, expecting to see her there, the throw blanket tucked around her. Only, she isn't. The TV's still on though. With a frown, I switch off the unit and head to the bedroom, but that's empty too.

It's only after I check the bathroom and kitchen that I realize what's happened.

She's gone.

Fuck.

17

BELLE

"WHAT'S WRONG? Who is it? Is that Lucas?"

"Cade! I need to speak with you. It's urgent!"

The loud pounding of a fist on the door makes my heart skip a beat as anxiety crowds me. I know the last four days have felt like a bubble, us just getting to know one another, hanging out with his family, fucking as if our lives depend on it. Only, I can't help but feel as if that bubble is about to be popped.

"—that I will never let anyone hurt you. Not even my brother. Do you hear me?" Cade grabs my chin, forcing me to look at him, and I nod like a bobblehead.

"Why would you... Do you think Lucas will hurt me?"

And his beautiful crystal-blue eyes change. The pupils dilate. As his nostrils flare, he states, "There's shit you don't know about me. I can explain, but you need to listen to me, okay?"

"What's going on?" I warble, panic setting in. As if he knows I'm two seconds away from freaking out, Cade kisses my cheek, but for the first time, it doesn't soothe me. "I need to speak with Lucas. Wait for me and I'll come back and explain everything."

That's when I want to burst into tears or throw the remote at the TV —what the hell is he hiding?

"You're scaring me, Cade. What's to explain?" A loud bang makes me jump as Cade removes me from his legs and stands.

"I'll make this right, princess."

"Cade!"

As he walks to the door, I hear him spit at Lucas, "Not here. Vinny's." And then he's gone and I want to throw up.

No answer.

"What the fuck just happened?" I mutter to myself, bewildered and —*stupid, stupid, stupid, Cindy*—feeling oddly betrayed.

When I reach for the jeans he tossed on the floor earlier, I growl under my breath when I realize I'm shaking.

"Stop it!" I snap at myself before I tug on my tee and, after reaching for my phone, head out of the apartment.

Vinny's—I heard him say that was where he was heading. That's how bad this is—he went to his dead brother's apartment.

"Come back and explain everything to me? Fuck that," I whisper, bolting down the stairs. I need the truth, not Cade trying to sugarcoat whatever it is that I know involves me.

"You're supposed to be in L.A.," Lucas states, his voice grim with his annoyance.

"I came back a few days ago," Cade snaps.

More like a week.

"I know. Róisín told me by accident that you'd gotten together with some Belle chick and were keeping her awake at night. Why didn't you tell me you fucked up, Cade? I can't fix your mistakes if you don't warn—"

"I didn't fuck up." Cade's answer is like a knife that's been inserted into my chest. He was "sent" to L.A. *Who is he?*

"You did. You're here, aren't you? Not in California where you're *supposed* to be. And Cindy goddamn Davis sure as hell isn't here, is she?"

How does Lucas know my name when Cade introduced me to his family as Belle? When his sisters call me Isabelle most of the time?

Calm, just be calm, I chant in my head. Maybe Lucas is his business partner or—

"I didn't fuck up, and I don't always need you to fix my mistakes, damn it."

"That you're here without Cindy Davis says otherwise. If I'm wrong, explain what's going on."

Heart breaking, I swallow back bile as Cade counters, "Whatever Davis told Aidan was a lie."

Davis.

Father.

And there it is.

I've been played by a devil with piercing blue eyes and dimples that turned my head.

He was sent by my father to bring me back to New York and, like a fucking pathetic loser, I let him. I followed him because he made me think I was special.

Staggering against the wall, I allow it to support me as Lucas demands, "What?"

Cade retorts, "I'm telling you, Davis is a liar. Cindy wasn't being held against her will by the Disciples."

I cover my trembling mouth, the urge to speak to Charlie strong. As is the urge to run. To get back to L.A. To have the Disciples hide me. I'll take anything but staying here, listening to the man who *lied* to me, who made me feel like he was falling for me all so he could deliver me to my death.

"Davis said that they kept her hooked on prescription meds and that was why she hung around, working her ass off at that diner until all hours—" Lucas's voice makes me lift my head as my nails dig painfully into the wall.

"She worked there because she wanted to and I saw her prescription meds. They had Davis's name on the label—he prescribed them to her as her doctor."

"What?"

"I'm telling you he's a liar. He abused her, Lucas. I'm not letting her go back to him."

Suddenly, I'm dizzy enough that I might pass out. Did Cade just say he's keeping me? That he *won't* let my father have me?

What's happening? He's defending me to Lucas, but he's the one who brought me here in the first place!

"You're not letting her go back to him," Lucas repeats. "What makes you think you have a choice in this? You're my brother, and you're only a part of Aidan's crew because of that—"

"Nice to know how you feel about me, Lucas."

"You know it's true," Lucas retorts. "Your head's never in the game, Cade. When Aidan drew you into this, I knew you'd fuck up sooner or later.

"Why do you think I've been riding your ass hard about it? Trying to keep you on the straight and narrow—" He pauses. Hisses beneath his breath. "*Isabelle*. Belle. Please tell me that the broad you were just fucking isn't Cindy Davis?"

"I wasn't fucking her."

"Sure sounded like you were to me, what with how she was wailing like a banshee."

Holy shit, are they fighting?

I finally make myself move and open the door, only to see Cade hit Lucas in the face. Gasping, I cover my mouth as Lucas attacks in turn and Cade goes down. I want to break them up but I don't have a chance of stopping them.

"Decades of you talking down to me. Decades of you thinking —oof."

I hear someone grunt.

"You're the one who's a mess, Cade. You can't do anything right, you asswipe—"

A hard crack ricochets from the room.

There's a snarl of pain and Cade is hissing, "I made one fucking mistake and you condemned me for it forever."

"You killed Vinny. That wasn't just a mistake, Cade," he roars. "And you're doing it again. I can't believe you fucked her!"

"I think I love her, Lucas!" And that makes my heart literally freeze in my chest.

Those words are suddenly on repeat in my head—*I think I love her...*

"Of course, you think that. Why wouldn't you? Unless you've got evidence that Davis is a liar, Aidan won't want to hear it. He's doing this as a favor. Saving some poor bitch from her fate tied to an MC that's got her imprisoned—"

And that's when my mind taps out. My body takes over.

I turn and force myself to move.

Run.

Running is the one thing I can do. I've done it before and made it, and I can do it again. I head toward the elevator then rush into the entrance hall, not caring if anyone sees me. All I know is I need to get away.

"Isabelle? You okay?" I vaguely hear Kitty calling after me as I burst onto the sidewalk.

Run. My legs must be obeying because I'm out of breath when I finally stop. Looking back to see if anyone has followed me, I see that I'm alone.

Despair makes the tears finally fall as I lean my back against the brick wall in the alley and cover my face with my hands as I try to figure out what my plan is.

It boils down to one thing. Well, one person.

Charlie.

I need Charlie.

I jerk my phone out of my back pocket, trying to catch my breath as I tap her name.

"Cindy?" Her voice is loud. Bewildered. "Thank God! Where the fuck have you been?"

I start sobbing, then I hear someone start laughing and jolt when I see a couple of old men are sitting on a bench, watching me like I'm an afternoon matinee at the cinema.

Snarling under my breath, I push myself off the wall and head deeper down the alley, wrinkling my nose at the stench of garbage and the rats that don't even try to hide from me.

"I'm sorry I worried—"

"Worried us? We thought you were fucking dead, Cindy! Jesus Christ! I've had David checking the morgues—"

"Charlie, listen, I'm in trouble. I…"

How many times am I going to do this?

Depend on other people to save me from problems I get myself into?

The words stick in my craw and my voice trails away to nothing.

"What? Where are you? You're scaring me."

The last thing I want is to frighten her, and her words prompt me to admit, "I'm in New York."

Waiting to hear her scream or lecture, I'm surprised when she says, "Go on."

"Remember that guy?"

"The stalker from the diner, the one who got in David's face? Yes, I remember him." Her voice is dryer than the Mojave.

"Yeah, well, he's not a stalker." I start to defend him then I realize what I'm doing. "He's not a stalker. I *wish* he were because he was sent to bring me back to my father." I choke on the *father* part.

"Fuck." She sighs, and suddenly, I hear Eve in the background, demanding to talk to me.

"Wait, Charlie, don't put Eve on—"

"Cindy," Eve snaps.

The last thing I need is a tough talk from her. "Put Charlie back on!"

"No. You walk all over her. We got Antoinette to get Axel to break into your place, Cindy. Do you realize what you've put us through?"

"I get it. I suck. I'm sorry but I wasn't in the best place—"

"You think we don't have problems too?"

"Eve, I really don't need a lecture. I need help."

"What's happened?" Her voice is strong and sure, and it makes me straighten my shoulders back and start to walk away from this pit of an alley.

I inhale and slowly exhale, then I tell her everything.

Him luring me here to bring me to my father and, finally, that he thinks he might be falling in love with me. She stays quiet as I vomit it out.

"So, you don't know who he works for?"

"Maybe the mob," I whisper.

"Christ, Cindy." She sounds more exasperated than stressed. But then, there's a reason Eve is such a badass. She came from the streets and did the unthinkable—brought the mighty Blade McCormick, President of the Disciples, to his knees.

She's cunning, smart, and fierce, and she's also loyal to a fault. Seriously, if Eve loves you, she'll take a bullet for you. She's also honest. So damn honest it hurts.

I wish I had some of her guts.

"What makes you think it's the mob?"

"He said something about taking me to 'Aidan,' and Cade was sent to get me. Normal people don't do that."

"Isn't there an Aidan who runs the Five Points' Mob?" There's chatter in the background, and I can hear them conferencing on this.

Then, there's a shriek.

"Aidan O'Donnelly Jr., seen here with his wife, Savannah O'Donnelly, née Daniels, has long since been associated with the criminal underworld in New York City, but the police have never—" Charlie continues reading a news article that I tune out.

My heart starts to race as my head throbs, and I turn around and look down the street, just wanting to run.

I've been fucking a mobster.

I'm literally in bed with the mob.

First, an MC, now the Irish Mob? What a goddamn collection. But the Disciples are *friends*. The mob... not so much.

"Cindy?" Eve's voice jerks me from my mushrooming anxiety. The air around me is practically nuclear with the toxic levels of panic I'm exuding.

"He's going to kill me." I just don't know if I mean my father or this Aidan O'Donnelly guy. "Eve, I'm dead."

As the full magnitude of what has just been unveiled to me resonates, I start to walk down the crowded street, needing to keep moving or I don't know what I might do. This nervous energy needs to burn off because it's making me even antsier.

"He isn't going to kill you. You haven't done anything wrong." She hesitates then clears her throat. "Have you? You didn't rob a fucking bank or anything while you've been loved up with that loser?"

Before I can growl out a negative, someone yells, "Isabelle? Jesus, wait up." I spin on my heel, seeing Kitty running to me dressed in black workout gear. She grabs my arm and demands, "What's going on? You look like shit! Are you all right?"

I swallow as Eve grumbles in my ear, "Who is that?"

Ignoring her, I ask Kitty, "Is Cade in the mob?"

Kitty's eyes flare wide, then she takes an involuntary step back.

"Is he?" I demand.

Her lips part, and for the first time since I've met her, Kitty, ever confident, ever loudmouthed, hesitates.

"Is Cade in the mob?" I scream at her, just needing confirmation.

She jerks my arm. "Are you trying to get us arrested?"

"Jesus, warn a girl before you start screaming, Cindy," Eve complains, but I ignore her and take in my surroundings.

I'm at the center of everyone's attention. I'm literally starring in my own show and the sidewalk is my stage.

"We need to get you back to the house—"

"Don't touch me," I snap. "I'm not the only one whose got connections. T-They'll come for me. They won't let you hurt me."

"Listen, Belle, you really need to calm down and talk to Cade." She holds up her hands like I have a gun pointed at her. "He's an asshole but he's a great guy. I'm sure he didn't mean to upset you."

I bark out a hysterical laugh. "You think we had an argument?"

"Didn't you?"

"Who the fuck is that?" Eve snaps.

"It's Cade's sister." I turn my back on Kitty so I can focus on Eve. "I-I met his family."

"You met his family?" That revelation triggers mutters in the background. But Eve grumbles, "Well, she gave you your answer. She didn't deny it."

She hadn't.

"Come on, Belle. Cade will make things right."

"He's the one who made things wrong," I half-sob.

"You said he loves you, Cindy. You need to think about what could happen if the Disciples go to war with the Five Points. It'd be a blood bath... and I'm not going to let that happen." The finality in Eve's voice hits me hard.

All I hear is—*I'm not worth fighting for.*

"Eve—" I plead.

"No, you listen, Cindy. I love you. But you're crazy. The shit you do, the stunts you pull... You need to take responsibility for yourself. This isn't a joke. These men don't play nice. They're dangerous. Think, for fuck's sake."

"I *am* thinking. I can't go back to my father. You don't know what he is capable of—"

"You said this Cade thinks he loves you," Eve reminds me, her voice softer this time. "Why would he make you go someplace you're not safe?"

"Cade would never let anyone hurt you. Have you met him?" Kitty gently teases. "He's still feeling guilty over something that happened when he was a teenager and that had nothing to do with him. I-I don't know why you think he's going to take you to your father, but he'll never let you get hurt."

Frowning at her, I bite my lip. Eve's hard talk and Kitty's gentle reassurances are such a contrast that they spear through my panic like nothing else could.

But I barely know Kitty, and I trust Eve with my life.

"What should I do, Eve?" I whisper, voice cracking.

"Do you love him?"

"I-I thought I did. It was crazy fast, but it felt right..."

"Everything you do is crazy fast," she grumbles. "But you need to talk to him, and if he isn't the man you think he is, then *I'll* come and rescue you."

My throat closes at her words because Eve has the guts to do that.

"And the mood I'm in," she continues, "I can take on the entire mob."

I've gone from feeling like a burden to feeling loved. "Thank you,

Eve," I whisper, knowing she means it and that she probably could take on the Irish. "Tell Charlie not to worry. I-I'll check in soon."

I shoot a blind look at Kitty, who watches me slip my phone into my pocket.

"If you're really scared, I'll help you get away."

Taken aback by the offer, I mutter, "You shouldn't get involved."

She sniffs. "I'm not the kind of person who stands by and let's people get hurt, Belle. If you don't want to talk to Cade, you don't have to. You can stay with me until you find your feet. A-Are you actively in danger?"

Maybe? If my father is looking for me, if he knows I'm in the city, then yeah, I guess I am.

Weighing my options, I rasp, "Cade is the one who put me in danger."

That makes her frown. "You know, I don't think the sun shines out of his ass, Belle. So, when I say this, I mean it—Cade would never willingly do that. You might only have known him a short while, but I have no horse in this race, and I can tell you that whatever he's done to fuck this up, it's not because he wants to leverage your safety."

Am I a moron for believing her?

I rub my hands over my face, wishing that the sun were shining today instead of these miserable gray clouds. How is it only a week ago, that I was in L.A., at the diner, being jealous of Juliana? How is it that the only man I wanted to kiss me was Ryder?

Everything between Cade and me has been so fast and intense but... right. Is that a lie? Is he stringing me along? But if he was, why would he say he loved me?

None of this makes sense.

"Do you believe in God?" I ask Kitty, who laughs.

She arches a brow at me, clearly wondering where I'm going with this. "Of course not. I was raised a good Catholic girl."

Despite my situation, her words reassure me. Kitty is a "no bull-shit," "take no prisoners" kind of person and her earnestness about her brother makes me feel better.

"I was just wondering if I should pray that I'm not making a mistake."

She snorts. "He's a man. Of course, you're making a mistake. But hey, he's pretty, and I'll bet you can make him miserable enough that he begs for your forgiveness."

I gulp. "I-I don't need him to do that."

"You're too kind, Belle. Don't worry, I'll negotiate on your behalf. We'll have him on his knees in no time."

18

CADE

ACUIG

AFTER SCOPING the rest of the building, taking note that Kitty's out, waking Róisín up and growling at her for not keeping her goddamn mouth shut about Belle to Lucas, then banging on Neev's door so loud that her dog starts howling, I head to Ma's and find she isn't hiding Belle either.

What she is doing is tending to Lucas's black eye—his wrist is already isolated with bandages. Three boys and she's gotten as much experience as Kitty has with fixing up injuries from fights.

"What have I told you two boys about fighting?"

"He fucking started it. Ripping into me about all the mistakes I make—"

"The truth hurts," Lucas grouses before he jolts in surprise as Ma slaps a steak onto his bruised eye.

"Lucas, how many times do we have to talk about this? I'm starting to think you're not just stubborn, but stupid, son, and I didn't raise any fools.

"Vinny was the older of the two of them. He should have been the one talking Cade out of that nonsense, not the other way around." She tuts under her breath. "I love my boys, but if there's one thing I know about you, you're hardheaded.

"Now, tell me what's going on here. Why's everyone caterwauling like Jesus himself is rising from his grave?"

Her Irish accent is coming on strong and thick at this point, so I know there's no turning back.

Once the brogue is out to party, the next step is her fingers pinching our ears as she forces us to apologize to one another.

You wouldn't think Lucas answered only to the head of the Irish Mob and his family. Nor would you think I was on an O'Donnelly's crew.

"Cade was tasked with finding this girl in L.A.," Lucas grumbles. "He was supposed to bring her back, take her to Aidan, and then, that was it. Job done. But instead, the fucking moron starts banging her, and he tells me he's in love with her and that—"

"Wait a second. What is she, an Amazon package that's gone missing? Why did he have to bring her back? Was she lost?"

"She ran away from her dad. He was abusive, Ma. Told her she needed her tits reduced—"

"Language, Cade. But sweet Jesus, why on earth would a father say something like that to his daughter? I'd have battered your da with a frying pan for the audacity."

"It goes deeper than that, Ma. She believes he killed her mom."

"Davis told Aidan that she's dependent on prescription meds. She's not well. He thinks the Disciples are a cult."

"With a name like that…" The Catholic in her clearly disapproves of the MC's name. I snort to myself, wondering if Blade McCormick will give a damn about my little Irish ma's opinion. "We are talking about Belle, aren't we?"

"We are. She's fragile, but there's nothing wrong with her."

Uneasily, she wipes her hands on a dish towel. "Maybe that's what I can sense. Her father."

Lucas rolls his good eye—he doesn't believe in Ma's "sight." "I can tell you what I *do* know. The head of the Five Points, our boss, was so grateful to his surgeon that he offered to do him a favor—"

"If a favor is all it is, then why would Aidan be caring about his surgeon if he's a crappy daddy?"

I shoot Lucas a pointed look. "Exactly."

"Because a man like Aidan doesn't just let a favor lie."

"The O'Donnellys are many things, but they're not going to force a lass like Belle to go back to an abusive household." She plucks at her bottom lip. "I can speak with Magdalena. She can help—"

Lucas jerks upright at the mention of Aidan's mother. "Don't! She's not doing well after…"

"Aye, it's hard when you lose your husband," Ma muses. "Maybe she needs some company."

"She's sticking close to Padraig."

Her brow arches. "How close?"

"Ma, no gossiping about our boss's mother and his uncle."

She sniffs.

"Ma," I warn.

"What?"

"We know you're nose deep in the Old Wives' Club." The club of "old wives" who'd been widowed when their husbands had died in the line of Five Points' duty.

Her blush gives her away. "There's nothing wrong with getting together with women who know what you've been through—"

The outer door slams.

Not letting Ma finish her sentence, I run down the hall and toward the front door. Dragging it open, I spy Kitty and—

Thank fuck.

"Belle!"

She jerks in surprise, and when I catch sight of her tear-streaked face, guilt hits me.

I never expected to feel like this about her. She was a job, nothing more, but everything goes to shit around her—including my good intentions.

"Leave her alone, Cade. You've done enough damage," Kitty snipes at me.

I glower at her. "Don't start, Kitty. I know I fucked up but I offered to soundproof my apartment—"

"Soundproof your apartment?" Kitty shrieks, taking away my last hope that Belle *hadn't* overheard my argument with Lucas. "You think that's because you and Belle make more noise than cats in heat?

"Belle seems to think you're going to force her to visit her father or something. Why you'd do that, I don't know, and why the Five Points are involved, I don't even want to know, but she looked like she was going to have a panic attack when I found her. So you can get on your knees and beg for forgiveness!" Kitty frowns and goes on. "You're lucky I was in my running shoes and not my heels or you'd have lost her for good!"

Belle's hand snaps out and rests on Kitty's forearm. She squeezes her gently, her gaze locked on me, as she whispers, "You lied to me. You brought me here under false pretenses."

"I'll never put you in danger. I told you that upstairs and I meant it." I know my voice is flat, but maybe if I keep this free from emotion, it'll cut through her fear.

"Come with me, Belle. We'll get you some tea and I'll set you up in my spare bedroom—"

Though I scowl, I rub the back of my neck. "You can stay in Vinny's place, Belle. You don't need to stay in my apartment or Kitty's. You can have your own space."

She blinks. "Y-You're not going to make me see my dad?"

Her words hit me on the raw. "I…"

Why haven't I forced the issue with Aidan Jr.?

None of this was necessary. The moment I trusted my gut that Belle was genuinely scared of her father, I should have sorted this situation out.

But there's no denying that Aidan Jr. is, as his father used to say when I was on his guard, "an apostle short of the Last Supper."

Just last year, I watched Junior cut out the tongue of a Five Pointer who lied to him. That was nothing to watching him hang some Pointers from a fucking crane so every single one of his men could watch the traitors dance and know they'd be next if they messed up.

Not knowing what to say, only knowing that I have to act, I step forward, my hand outstretched. When she jerks back as if my touch is poisonous, I rasp, "I'll make this right, Belle."

She shakes her head. "I don't understand what's happening. W-Why would you help my father? How do you know him?"

The truth is the only way she won't run from me so I ask, "Do you know who the Five Points are?"

Her nod is hesitant.

"I'm one of them. My boss, he's the head of the Points, well, he felt like he owed your father a favor after he performed a successful reconstructive surgery on him.

"Your father told Aidan that you were being held captive by this MC in L.A. and that you were in danger and basically, he sent me in to rescue you."

"That was my home. I was safe there. I didn't need rescuing," she shrieks.

Despite the situation, I shake my head at her. "You weren't safe there, Belle. I get that I've burned a bridge with you, and I know I'll be lucky if you give me a chance to earn your forgiveness, but don't let yourself believe that you were in a good place among people who didn't care when you were mentally fragile and who fired you when you were at your lowest."

"Charlie didn't fire me," she mutters.

I shake my head at the thought of it. "I watched you overdose in front of me while Joy was yelling at you about serving your tables."

"Don't bring that up so you can use it against me. I know what Father would have told you—that I'm fragile. That I-I can't live on my own. I know I make stupid decisions! I'm looking at one at this exact moment—"

Ouch.

"Burn," Kitty mumbles under her breath.

I shoot her a glare, noticing that she isn't heading to her apartment to give us privacy. No, she might as well bring out a bowl of fucking popcorn.

"But I'm of sound mind even if I do make mistakes. I know what my father is—he's a murderer. I won't go back to him, Cade. I won't."

Raising both hands, I surrender to her. "And I'm not about to make you."

"Then what's going on? Why did you bring me to New York? What, between me getting on a plane and watching you and your brother beat the shit out of each other, has changed?"

I swallow. "You know what."

Derision stamped onto her features, Kitty snorts. "Was it love at first sight, Cade?"

My jaw clenches at her scorn. "You know what, Kitty? It was. It fucking was, okay?"

Belle gasps then whispers, "How could you do this to me, then? That's not love!"

"I'm sorry, Belle. I'm fucking sorry, and all I can do is try to make this right. Whether you take me at my word or not, I won't let your father get his hands on you. I promised you that you were safe with me and—"

"The only reason he could hurt me again is because of you. Sorry? You think my friends are bad? They've dealt with years of my drama and have loved me through it. Their lives aren't easy. Charlie's got a new baby and Joy's been carrying me for years—every friendship has ups and downs, and we've gone through a rough patch. But that's all it is.

"As for you, you started *this* with the intention of taking me back to a man who tormented me throughout my childhood, who beat my mother in front of me, who destroyed—" She pauses. Sucks in a breath. "Do you know what? You're not worth this. You're not worth wasting my words or my oxygen." Then, with that regalness I know she's capable of, she tilts her chin and condemns me, "I don't accept your apology."

When she storms toward the elevator, I close my eyes and rub them tiredly. Cade from a week ago would have blamed anyone but himself for what's gone down. The Cade of today knows *he* and he alone is the one who fucked up.

Kitty, because she likes to kick a man when he's down, steps over and punches me in the arm. "That's for manipulating her. But that was on the way to being a semi-decent apology, Cade. Keep up the good work. Six out of ten."

Glowering at her, I watch as she follows Belle to the elevator.

Massaging the back of my neck where a tension headache is building, I find my other arm being punched.

Twisting around, I grab the person's hand and find Lucas there, staring at me like I'm an alien. "You just told her you're in the mob. Are you an idiot?"

I scowl at him, but I don't get a chance to lay into him—the dishrag is already whipping through the air, and Lucas jolts as Ma clips him around the back of the head. She's better than Indiana Jones and his whip with that fucking thing, so when he hisses at the sting, I merely smirk at him.

Not for long, though, because she deals with me next.

"You don't love that girl if you treat her like she's a piece of meat to sell at the market, Cade Shaun Frasier. I thought I raised you better than this."

"I didn't take her to Aidan," I argue.

"No, instead you hole up here, get us to lie to your brother on your behalf, and bury your head in the sand."

"More like her pus—"

"Language, Lucas," Ma spits then wags her finger at me. "You're a man now, Cade, and instead, you're acting like a boy. A foolish boy, at that. You get your arse over to your boss's office and you tell him what you know.

"If you've lost that girl for good, well, I can't blame her for thinking you're an eejit, but it'll be a life lesson for you and it's one you need to learn. But don't think you can be eating any breakfast at my table until you make this right, do you hear me?"

With a sniff, she spins on her heel and retreats to her apartment, slamming the door behind her, locking it, and leaving Lucas and me standing outside in the hall as if she can't stand the sight of us any longer.

"Well, you can't speak to Aidan looking like that," he grumbles as he takes in my scuffed jeans. "You need to get changed."

Blankly, I stare at him. Then, I realize what he's actually saying. "You're going to help me with him?"

He sneers. "When don't I get you out of trouble, Cade?"

19

CADE

ACUIG

I'M NOT EXACTLY nervous when I head into the elevator and make my way to Aidan and Savannah O'Donnelly's apartment, but mostly, I'm hoping I don't fuck this up.

I didn't need my ma to make me realize that I acted like a fool. No, I only needed to look at the agony in Belle's eyes.

I did that. *Me*.

I didn't mean to. That was the last thing I intended. But fuck if that didn't happen anyway, and fuck if she ain't hurting and sobbing and terrified over a situation that I put her in.

Knocking on the door, I wait for someone to answer. Lucas, at my side, is grumbling under his breath as he checks his messages, and I stare at the door blindly, hoping to get this over with so I can go back home and tell Belle that she's safe.

She's right—I don't deserve an apology. Rectifying this mistake is the least I can do as a human goddamn being. As for earning her forgiveness? Right now, I'm at a loss. I just can't accept that she'll never—

The door swings open before my brain can start tripping over itself, and Savannah greets me. "Cade? I thought you were in L.A. You missed a great poker game last week. I bled Lucas dry."

My brother protests, "If you weren't my boss's wife, I'd accuse you of cheating."

Savannah smirks. "Those are the words of a sore loser."

"Oh, he's definitely that," I needle, enjoying the opportunity to say that without earning a punch in the process.

Laughing, Savannah waves us in. "You look like you've been fighting, Lucas. Is that a black eye?" Her brows furrow as she takes in the support bandages on his wrist. "You hurt your hand?"

He clears his throat. "It's nothing."

She hums her disbelief. "Aidan, Cade and Lucas are here!" she yells, and Aidan, wiping a towel over his face, strolls out from the gym a few minutes later. "Lucas apparently got into a fight with the invisible man."

"What are you doing back in the city, Cade?" Aidan frowns at Lucas though he takes in my brother's injuries and shoots me a knowing glance as Savannah tosses him a bottle of water from the kitchen. "Why didn't you tell me he got the girl? What's her name again?"

I clear my throat. "Cindy."

Aidan, still scowling, demands, "Where is she, then?"

Straightening my shoulders and praying that I'm not about to end the day being carved up like a turkey at Thanksgiving, I rasp, "Dr. Davis lied to you."

I chose those words very carefully.

Under his da's rule, if Aidan Sr. found out you lied to him, he'd cut off your finger. Aidan's already set the precedent that he'll slice out your tongue if you try to con him.

My statement has him standing taller. A dark scowl creases his features, and he rumbles, "Savvie, go and get some work done. You don't need to hear this."

She huffs. "Fuck off, Aidan. I want to know what's going on. I'm the one who recommended Davis to you. He still plays golf with my dad. The man fixed his knees and back more times than I can remember!" To me, she questions, "Aidan said that Dr. Davis believes his daughter was in a cult or something?"

"It isn't a cult. It's an MC," I mutter, not surprised by how much Savannah knows about the business. "And they're no better or worse than the Satan's Sinners' MC. They're sure as fuck not a cult."

"Okay, so she's in no danger?"

"No. Only from Davis himself. Cindy told me that she believes he killed her mom."

Aidan's eyes narrow as he repeats, "He killed her mom?"

"Cindy believes so."

"Did she see it with her own eyes?"

"What do you want me to do, Aidan? Get her to show you the crime scene?" Aidan's brows rise at my tone, but I'm pissed. "He abused Cindy. The shit he did to her doesn't bear repeating."

Lucas elbows me in the side. "Repeat it. Aidan needs to know he was disrespected by Davis."

I'm not happy about sharing this with him, but I do it anyway. "He used to make her strip in front of him so she could get weighed, and he controlled her food—he beat his wife and manipulated Isabelle by threatening to hurt her mother.

"After his wife was gone, Isabelle tried to tell people. He had her committed to a hospital where he made sure she was doped up." I look at Aidan and then at Savannah. "She ended up escaping and living in fear until she got with the Disciples."

Savannah's eyes turn round with horror. "Aidan, you can't give her to that bastard!"

He ignores her. "Where is she currently?"

"She's staying in the family building," Lucas answers, his tone grim.

Aidan narrows his eyes at me. "And why would she be there, Cade?"

I swallow. "I've got feelings for her, Aidan."

"Feelings? What are you? A grade-school girl? *I got feelings,*" he mocks.

My cheeks flush with heat. "What do you want me to say?"

"Maybe claim her if you want her so goddamn much." He heaves an impatient sigh. "Were you dating her on my time?"

Oh, fuck. "Jesus, no! I was trying to get close to her, trying to figure out how I could snatch her if need be.

"From the very start, I knew the doctor was lying because she was friends with the Disciples. They weren't holding her hostage and making her work so they could steal her income. They were her people. Her friends. Her fucking family." When no one speaks, I keep going. "When I saw that, I knew there'd be no getting her to leave without stirring shit, so I changed plans.

"But before I had the chance to do much of anything, she over-dosed so I..." I grimace. "I guess I manipulated the situation and wormed my way into her life—"

"Gee, you're such a gentleman, Cade," Savannah snipes, folding her arms across her chest, beyond unimpressed with my less-than-stellar moves. Who could blame her? I'm a piece of shit. "How could you treat her like that?"

Ashamed, I mutter, "I was trying to do the right thing while also trying to not get strung up by my boss."

"Aidan won't hang people unnecessarily, will you?"

He just grunts.

Reassuring.

"Within a couple days of getting on her good side, we were flying back to the city. I swear, boss."

"When did you get back?"

"Just under a week ago," I rasp.

"And you've been claiming expenses?"

"No! Do you think I have a death wish? Two of those days were the weekend," I point out, unafraid to admit that I sound desperate.

Aidan's biceps bulge as he approaches me. "If you're fucking lying, Cade, I'll make you regret it."

We're the same height, but the power Aidan has is unreal.

If I fuck this up, there's no making shit right with Belle—it's literally game over.

"I swear to God I'm not lying."

"Why didn't you bring her here now?"

"Because she won't talk to him," Lucas inserts before I can say a word.

"Serves him right." Savannah snorts. "She's got good taste then."

I scowl down at the floor rather than at her.

"Lucas," Aidan says. "Do you believe Cade?"

My older brother sighs. "I saw her talk about her father. She was terrified, Aidan. My da was quick to punish, just like yours. But none of my sisters flinched the way she did when she was talking about Davis.

"Whatever the reality of her situation when she was growing up, she fears him and does believe he's a murderer—I heard her say that. I definitely wouldn't feel comfortable leaving her with him—"

"Bet your ass you're not going to leave her with him," Savannah screeches. She storms over to Aidan's side and grabs his arm. "He lied to you, Aidan. He fucking lied. You can't let some poor woman—"

He cups her face. "You can't save everyone, Savannah." Before she can squawk her outrage, he presses a kiss to her lips. "But in this instance, you can tell this Cindy she can return to L.A. if that's what she wants, Cade."

My Adam's apple bobs at that.

The last thing I want is her on a fucking plane back to L.A., but I keep my mouth shut, lock my gaze on the floor, and await my punishment.

"You barely know her."

My brows lift at his words. "I know enough, boss."

"He thinks he loves her," Lucas scoffs.

I can feel Aidan studying me. "Davis lied to me. He disrespected me. We'll be heading into his office once I'm ready. Understood?"

Eyes flaring at the request, I take a chance. "I'd like to help, Aidan."

My boss arches a brow at me. "You'll be taking center stage, Cade. It's time you prove where your loyalties lie."

20

BELLE

FEELING HEARTSICK, I stare out the window then look down at my phone. Nothing. No phone calls, no texts, no information on how he's going to make this right... and it's been hours.

"Isabelle, come have something to eat. Don't worry about Cade. He'll fix things, you'll see," Patricia calls as she pulls some homemade scones out of the oven. "You want some tea?"

It's funny to think that this is the mom of a mobster. Tea and scones. Who'd have thought? Patricia's gone a long way to making this day better. The shock of finding out about Cade being part of the Five Points has faded, but it wasn't what he *did for a living* that bothered me. How could it when I've spent years in love with Ryder, for God's sake.

You do what you gotta do—that's my motto.

Just so long as that "gotta doing" doesn't return an abused daughter to her abuser...

"Thanks, Patricia," I say huskily as I walk over to the large table, watching as she places a scone on a dish then pats the table for me to take a seat beside her. The butter and berries smell amazing. If I wasn't completely depressed, I'd eat three of them.

"Here, this will put a smile on that pretty face." Patricia sits down as she pours the tea. "In the US, it's all about the coffee. Even my girls are hooked on it. But nothing beats a pot of tea to make the world right."

I think it'll take more than that, but I just tell her, "You know you don't have to wait on me."

"Nonsense. I'm thrilled you're here," she says briskly, but her expression is sincere.

There's something that reminds me of my mom in her eyes. Maybe it's just that "mom thing," or I'm so desperate I'm making it up, but Patricia's kindness has helped me feel less alone. No matter what happens, if Cade fixes this or doesn't, I'll always be grateful for her easing my anxiety today.

"So, tell me about L.A.?" She adds some sugar to her tea. "When did you move?"

I take a bite of the scone and groan at how good it tastes. "You're an incredible baker."

She takes a small bite of hers then watches me glance at my phone again as she murmurs, "It's one of my favorite things to do."

Still no message.

I'm putting all my faith in the man who led me into this mess. But worse than anything, I'm mostly worried about him—what if he's not able to do anything and he ends up getting hurt himself?

"Isabelle, this is all going to be okay," Patricia soothes, but her voice still makes me jump.

This woman has had six children, buried a son and husband, and still gets up and smiles and enjoys life. I've always wondered how some people seem to have a strength in them that makes them able to pick themselves up and continue, while others crumble and fall apart.

I used to think I was one of those people who fell apart, but maybe I'm not. Sure, at first, I freaked out, but now, I'm just waiting for the fallout. Then I'll adjust and overcome. Isn't that what I've always done?

"I don't mean to be such a terrible guest. I'm sorry—"

She tuts. "Drink your tea and tell me about Los Angeles. Do you see a lot of movie stars? I think I heard Kitty telling Neev that one of your friends is married to a rock star." She leans back and crosses her legs, looking genuinely interested, which of course I'm sure she's not and is only trying to distract me, but I'm grateful.

I drop a cube of sugar into my tea. "Are you familiar with a band called the Stuffed Muffins?" At the look on her face, I gather she's not. I wave my hand and take a small sip of her dark tea. I don't know what kind she brews, but it's delicious. "Anyway, Axel—he's married to my friend Antoinette—used to be, well, he still is a musician, but he's friends with Rhys Granger."

"Oh, yes, I've heard of him." And my mouth twitches because you'd have to be dead not to have heard of Rhys Granger.

"Well, I know Axel better because my best friend Charlie is married to David, and both Axel and David are part of a... motorcycle club called Disciples." I look at her to see her reaction but she just nods her head as I continue. "Yes, well, I used to hang out with them a lot." I take another sip of tea, watching her watch me.

I don't know how much she knows, but come on, her boys *are* part of the mob.

"And Charlie is the one that gave you a job in that diner?" She passes me some jam. "In Burbank, no?"

"Yes, she's my best friend. Well... all of them are really. There's Charlie, Eve, Dolly, Antoinette, Doug, and..."

My mind naturally goes to Julianna who I can't say is a friend, but that's not on her. For the first time in a while, I think about Ryder in *that* way, and I realize that all the things he used to say to me are clear.

He knew.

It's not that he didn't care about me. It's just that his heart is with someone else. Jesus, he was right about me not loving him; I loved the idea of him. I loved feeling secure, but more than that, I loved the feeling of having the Disciples as my family.

So, I tack on, "Julianna."

As she adds some jam to her scone, she asks softly, "And your family?"

I bite my lip. "*They* are my family."

"Yes, but your mother?"

My heart aches at the mere thought of her. "My mother is dead. She died when I was fourteen, killed by my father who is a deranged, murdering sicko." Venom drips from my lips and for a second, I can't believe I just said the truths I've kept locked up for so long.

Patricia doesn't flinch. Her eyes, which have always held compassion, change, and I can tell she believes me.

"You are the first person besides Cade I've admitted that to. When it first happened, I tried to run away and medicate myself so I didn't have to feel anything. Finally, I got the courage to tell someone. I reached out to one of my mom's friends." I stare down into the dark amber liquid, remembering that day like it was yesterday when the doorbell rang...

I hang back, knowing this is it, that there is a God. My monster of a father is going to be taken away. He will *pay for the pain he caused my mother.*

My hands are sweating and my throat is dry as I stare at the police officer's dark uniform. Over and over, I whisper the chant, "He can't hurt me anymore."

"Dr. Davis?" the officer addresses my father.

"Yes?" He motions for them to enter.

Rain pelts the earth behind them as Mary Ann and the cop come inside the building that has never been my home.

"Your daughter, Isabelle, shared some very damning things with Mrs. Channing. She is saying you killed your wife.

"I've questioned the coroner and he's confirmed that she died of a drug overdose and blunt force trauma when she hit the steering wheel from running into the stoplight—"

"I'm so sorry, Donald," Mary Ann blurts out, ignoring the scowling cop as she wrings her hands. "She came to me, and I had to believe her. I mean, you understand I had to at least call the police. But now, I feel just terrible..."

Hit the steering wheel from running into the stoplight?

No!

That's not true!

She died here!

I saw him inject her with drugs!

My father sighs and walks toward a tray he keeps with his whiskey on it on a side table, motioning for them to follow. "Mary Ann, thank you for caring for my Isabelle. To be honest, I'm terrified. It's like she's had a break from reality and blames me for not being there when her mother died." He puts a hand to his lips as if he can barely talk then drops it. "My daughter is a very sick girl," he continues. "Please, rest assured that I know what's happening and I'll be keeping her home and getting her the best help."

Bile surges into my throat as I watch in horror while they both apologize again for disturbing him.

Disturbing him—the murderer of my darling mama.

No. Don't leave me! *I want to scream.* You have no idea what he's going to do to me, what he's capable of...

But it's too late. They're gone.

"Isabelle?" Patricia asks softly, her kind voice making me blink at her as I bring the room back into focus.

"You have no idea what my father's capable of," I whisper as I feel myself grow cold. "I can't go back to him. He'll kill me. But before he does, he'll make me wish I were dead."

With a gentle nod, she moves over to a buffet. "You'd be surprised, dear. I can relate more than you think." She opens a drawer, retrieves a Glock, and sets it on the table with our tea and scones. "See, I don't ever leave anything to chance.

"Now, my boys are taking care of this, but I always have my gun nearby."

It looks so alien amid the trappings of afternoon tea, but I can't deny it provides me with *some* comfort.

After Charlie and Dolly's baby shower, where the Russian got past security and almost managed to murder all of us, the Disciples decided the women had to learn to shoot a gun. I can hit a target fifty yards away.

That's when my phone starts to ring, causing me to jump out of my skin, making the whole table rattle in the process. As tea sloshes everywhere, I groan. "I'm so sorry. I'm on edge and, well, you're freakin' amazing." To Cade, I half scream, "Cade? What's going on?"

"Belle..."

This is not the time to be wondering how he betrayed me but can sound so gravelly and strong and, God help me, *like the man I love.*

"What happened?" I demand. "Are you okay?"

Standing, I start pacing as Patricia pours herself a fresh cup of tea and sits back to sip it, like we're out for a picnic in the Hamptons. Not at all freaking out that my insane father called in a favor to get me back and that Cade might be forced to give me up to a murderer.

"I'm fine. I want you to go stay with Ma, okay? Until I come back. Do you hear me, Belle? No wandering around."

"I understand. I'm at your mom's anyway." I rub my hand through my hair and try to steady myself. "Did you tell Aidan everything?"

"Yes. He says you're free to return to L.A." I hear cars and horns so I know he's in the city but, and I have no idea why, his words are a cold comfort. "Everything will be over tonight. I need you to trust me. I know you're upset, and you have every right to be, but I will make it up to you. I promise.

"I'm so fucking sorry, baby. Every step of this has eaten at me, torn at my instincts, but I'm a soldier and I obey orders." He sucks in a breath. "I let you down, Belle. I know I did. I meant it when I said you were safe with me, though. No one will ever hurt you. Not even if you decide to cut and run back to L.A. I won't let Davis get his hands on you, do you hear me?"

I close my eyes at his admission of guilt, and his promises whisper reassurance through me... I haven't been safe since the day I was born.

"What about Aidan?" I ask softly, wanting to believe him, but life has taught me otherwise.

"He doesn't like being lied to, which your father did. Trust me, Isabelle. I'll make this right. I fucking swear I will," he growls.

As the line goes dead in my ear, I turn to look at Patricia, who arches a brow at me over her teacup.

"He said for me to trust him."

"And do you?" she asks, her tone neutral as she sets down her cup.

"I can't blame you, dear, if you say you don't. Cade hasn't shown you the best side of himself today, has he?"

Her candor makes it easy to admit, "Before today, I felt like everything was too perfect. Like *he* was too perfect. I think I've been waiting for it all to come crashing down around me." I take a breath. "Now that it's hit me and the worst has happened, I don't feel as scared as I thought I would. I'm literally in New York when I promised myself I'd never return. I did that because I trusted Cade. I trusted him when he said he'd never let me get hurt. I guess when I thought he was talking about muggers, he was talking about Father…"

"Cade's very protective of the women he loves," she says easily. My eyes widen at that, but she just smiles. It's a knowing smile. That "mom thing" again. "He's had his ways, and he's been looser than a whore's knickers, as my grandmother would say, not in company, mind, but I've never seen my son like he is around you with *anyone.*

"But you need to trust yourself first, Isabelle. Both of you deserve to have this if you want it, and while he's let you down, I know he'll spend the rest of his life trying to make things right if you choose to have a future together."

Her insight into her son paints the world in brighter shades— maybe things aren't so bleak?

It makes my eyes fill with tears and my heart, which has been beating in terror, suddenly slows.

"Thank you," I breathe. Like he knows, my phone starts ringing again. "Cade, I trust you."

But then, there's silence.

Cold, stark silence.

"Cade?" My blood turns cold. Teeth chattering, I stutter, "H-Hello? W-Who's there?"

Patricia's eyes connect with mine as she grabs the phone from me. "Hello? Hello? Private number." There's nothing private about it—call it instinct, or a goddamn guardian angel, but I know *who* that was. How the hell did he get my number? "This, dear," she declares, straightening her shoulders like she's preparing for war, "is exactly why I'm always ready for anything. Now, you take a seat and finish your scone. It'll settle your stomach."

For a second, I don't think I heard her right, but she pushes the plate at me and stares me down until I pick up the baked good and take a bite. I thought it'd make me puke, but it doesn't. Oddly enough, it *does* settle my stomach.

When she starts to talk about her children when they were kids, I'm able to concentrate. I do exactly what she said—I listen to her stories and finish my scone.

She's prepared. I'm not. But that's okay. The monster's out. He might know where I am, but there's a Glock set amid the crockery and I'm not a child anymore—I know how to shoot that gun and I won't miss.

I won't.

21

CADE

"SHE'S WITH MA," I tell Lucas, ducking down to stare at him through the passenger window.

He arches a brow at me. "She didn't hightail it out of there the moment you left?"

"Apparently not." I scratch my chin and blindly look ahead. *That's a good sign, right?*

In her shoes, I'd have gotten the hell out of Dodge, that's for fucking sure.

Steam eddies around the fender of Lucas's SUV as the heat clashes with the intense cold—it's almost enough to make me miss L.A., but the cold is good. It keeps me aware. Keeps my agitation contained.

From behind the wheel of our ride, Lucas checks the clock on the dash. "What do you bet they started fucking when he took off for a shower?"

My lips twitch even though the adrenaline inside me is demanding I make shit right with Belle, and that isn't going to happen if Aidan gets waylaid in the shower by his bride.

After how I spent the last few days, I empathize with the man, but now ain't the time for sex.

Antsy, I pace the sidewalk. With last night's snowfall, it's fucking frigid, but the temperature's keeping me in line as I wait for my boss to finally show up.

"You like her, don't you?"

I shoot Lucas an incredulous look. "Which part of this mess made you think I didn't?"

"I dunno. You're never serious about women."

"Neither are you."

"Yeah, but you're worse. You ain't interested in women *or* work."

"Whereas you're all about overachieving." *Suck-up.* I narrow my eyes at him and try not to find enjoyment in the bruises I landed on his face. We never fight, so that was a long time coming. I should probably feel bad but I don't. He enjoyed lighting into me as much as I did with him.

"Might as well aim high," he says dismissively, peering at the massive skyscraper beside us. "Da wanted more for us. That's why they moved here. I'm only living up to his wishes."

"Whether or not you got me the job, I'm as high in the ranks as I can be," I grumble, sensing his disapproval. "What do you want me to do, Lucas? What more can I goddamn do?"

It's not that I need his approval, but his judgmental tone is starting to piss me the fuck off.

"I guess I want what I can't have."

At his words, my head whips around so I can look at him. My nostrils flare in response because I know what he's thinking, know it even if he doesn't utter a word—he wishes I'd died. Not Vinny.

My expression flatlines. I lock down. Bitterness unfurls inside me, but I don't react. What's the point?

He *does* want what he can't have.

I'm here, Vinny ain't, and I'm tired of taking the blame for something that happened when I was a kid. I'm over knowing that my family would prefer Vinny to be the brother who survived and not me.

My hands ball into fists as I rasp, "I didn't hogtie him into the car. I didn't cuff his hands to the wheel. I didn't hold him at gunpoint. He loved it. You should have heard his laughter when he took off." I could hear it, like a ghostly whisper in the wind. That, in itself, makes me wonder if it's Vinny haunting my ass because in New York, you don't hear "whispers." It's so fucking noisy that you could miss a goddamn foghorn if you aren't concentrating. "He loved it," I repeat. "No, he didn't think it would kill him, but some people are like that, Lucas. Some people prefer to live fast and die young. That was Vinny.

"Whether you choose to believe that or not isn't down to me," I continue. "I'm telling you he wanted to be there. I'm telling you we were in that together. I ain't to blame for his death—"

I've never uttered those words out loud before.

Ever.

For a second, I simply stare at him, bewildered by the admission.

I've always blamed myself and have always felt guilt, but it wasn't my fault.

It wasn't.

I was a kid. So was he.

Kids fuck up.

We fucked up big time.

There's a strange feeling inside me. It's like I've been stabbed. As if deep down, there's a gaping wound in my soul that's just been drenched in hydrogen peroxide.

I forgive myself.

I didn't set out with that intention, just got pissed at my older brother *again*, but fuck, I do. I really goddamn do.

Lucas grits his teeth at me, and when I'm sure he's about to spew more shit to make me feel bad for still breathing, he stiffens, and his gaze dances into the distance.

At long last, Aidan Jr. has shown up at the entrance to his building.

His focus drifts over to me and then to Lucas as I open the door to the back seat for him. Once he sits down, I duck into the passenger side and Lucas heads for Davis's medical practice.

For the majority of the journey, Aidan is silent. I can hear him tapping on his cell as he conducts business, but the stillness of the car is eerie and I'm glad for it. It lets me process what's happening.

It allows me to stare blindly ahead as I liberate myself from something I did when I was too young to understand how bad the consequences could be.

Vinny's death made me hesitant. It made me quick to obey orders. It made me hate stepping out of line because when I did, major fuckups happened.

And that's why I let myself take this shit with Belle so far.

Because what I wanted and what I knew was right went against Aidan's demands.

I screwed up big time. I've potentially lost the appreciation of a good woman, the only one who's interested me in *ever*, and that's on me, sure, but it's also on how I've been responding to shit since Vinny's passing.

It's time to accept that I messed up, but so did Vinny. His death wasn't my fault, and my family had no right to make me feel as if it were. Vinny got behind the wheel. I didn't shove him in the car. He started the ignition, and I was with him for the ride.

Feeling like a weight has been lifted off my shoulders, I push back into the seat and twist around to look behind me. "Boss?"

"Yeah, Cade."

Releasing a breath, I go for broke. "Liars get punished in the Five Points."

"They do. Not sure why you're telling me something I already know, though."

"You can punish me for countermanding orders and you can punish me for not bringing her to you immediately, but I didn't lie to you."

He narrows his eyes at me. "A lie of omission is still a lie."

"If you knew Savannah was in danger and you'd been told by your boss that she wasn't and you had to reconcile how to fix things, wouldn't you—"

Aidan lifts a hand to stall me. "If I wanted you punished, I'd have your ass hauled to the cement factory and I'd deal with you there after handling Davis." He pauses then settles a glance on me that has me tensing before, eventually, continuing, "Instead, you're going to deal with Davis on my behalf because if you want her, you claim her, and you do what needs to be done to make sure she's safe. Understood?"

"Understood." I blink at him. "You're not going to punish me?"

"You've done the bare minimum during your time as a Five Pointer, Cade. You always do what you're told, so I can never reprimand you for that, but this ain't the Points my da was running. I demand loyalty from my men. I demand the truth."

I nod and remain silent.

"The moment you knew something was wrong with the narrative Davis sold me, you should have contacted me." He studies me. "That you didn't tells me we got shit to work on."

I gape at him. "What?"

"Trust is a two-way street," he retorts. "Da would have sliced your throat for disobeying, but I ain't him. I want a crew who's got my back and who knows I've got theirs in return. Otherwise, we might as well be fucking cavemen, cannibalizing our numbers from the inside out."

Exhaling, I wonder if there may be hope for me yet. Who knows?

"In the future, you come to me," he says. "You tell me. I can't scope a situation without having my eyes on the bigger picture, and you know how much I value intel."

Still bewildered, I mutter, "I know, boss."

Aidan retains so much info about the most random shit that he's pretty much a walking Wikipedia of New York crime factions.

"This is your final warning, Cade," he says. "You won't get another chance."

I tip up my chin. "I don't need one, boss. I got your back."

He grunts, stares at his cell, and starts tapping out a message. "So, you'll deal with Davis, seeing as he's your woman's problem." He flicks a final look at me. "But you make it hurt."

Gritting my teeth because I know what that means—hurt but leave alive—I nod. "I won't kill him."

Another grunt is my answer and knowing that I'm dismissed, I turn back to the traffic, making sure I keep my head turned to the side so I don't even glance in my dipshit brother's direction.

Forty minutes later, we're walking into Davis's office.

Usually, Aidan meets him for his appointments at a hospital in the city, but this place is his private surgical center and it's on the outskirts of the Upper East Side. He's been here a couple of times, but not often.

Over my time with the O'Donnellys, I've come to realize that a true measure of wealth isn't how many cars you have or where your address is or if you own a yacht—it's who your healthcare provider is.

Aidan's doctor appointments take place in hospital suites that are so fancy, I wouldn't even mind being hospitalized.

The receptionist at the front desk recognizes Aidan, and because this office is swanky as fuck, she looks like a catwalk model when she stands and greets Aidan with a polite smile. "Mr. O'Donnelly, I didn't realize you had an appointment today."

"I don't, Chantal. Is he busy?"

"No, sir. He's between appointments."

"I'm glad to hear it. I'd like you to clear the rest of Dr. Davis's appointments for the day, please. You can head out as well."

Eyes flaring wide, Chantal gulps. "I-I can't do that, sir."

"Yes, you can," he rumbles, the threat in his words making her jerk backward. "You take home his schedule and you make the cancellations on the road. Understood?" A couple hundred dollars appear in his hand and he tosses the wad on the desk.

Her mouth trembles as she darts a glance between us and then at the cash. Without another word, she twists around, grabs something from a drawer that she hauls against her chest, takes the money in a fist she shoves in her pocket, and rushes toward a door behind the reception desk.

A few moments later, she returns with a coat and purse, and without a second look, she gets the hell out of here.

Aidan waves a hand at me. "This is your show, Cade. I'd imagine you have plenty to make up for where this woman of yours is concerned. Remember—make it count."

Striding forward, I grab the door handle and push forward, ignoring Davis's, "Chantal, I told you not to disturb me!" Then, he looks away from his computer and spies me, demanding, "You work with O'Donnelly Jr., don't you?" as I slap my hands on his desk and loom over it.

"He does, Davis," Aidan answers on my behalf, strolling into the room too, my brother at his back.

"D-Do you have an appointment, Aidan?" he queries, his tone more high-pitched than usual as he shuffles his focus between us, clearly unsure of what's going on. "Do you have news about Isabelle?"

I'm not a sadist, not by any stretch of the imagination, but I appreciate his fear at this moment because I know he terrorized Belle. If the fucker can feel even a fraction of what she experienced, then I'll consider that a goal ticked off my bucket list of shit to do before I die.

"I think you know I'm not on your schedule today, Davis." Aidan wanders over to the window behind the fucker's desk and slowly pulls down the blinds.

"What are you doing? You can't—"

"Davis, you know who I am," he drawls. "You know I can do whatever the fuck I want." He leans against the side of the desk and studies the older man. I'm not surprised Davis isn't shouting and cursing—not only because he'd be a fool to piss Aidan off but because he's a bully, and they only pick on people they perceive to be weaker than themselves. Fuckers. "You should have known that I'd find out before you sent me on that fool's errand."

"Fool's errand?" He gulps. "I-I didn't send you on a fool's errand. My daughter's been missing for years—"

"Willfully," I snarl. "She wanted to get away from *you*."

Davis growls back, "That's a lie!"

"I'll tell you what's a lie," Aidan rasps. "Getting me to send one of my men to L.A. to save your daughter when she didn't need saving." He glares at Davis. "The surgery you performed on me has changed my life, Davis. I owed you one. I'd have given you any-fucking-thing you wanted, and you chose your daughter. But you lied, and there's one thing you don't do with a Five Pointer... What is that, Cade? Lucas?"

Lucas is the one who drawls, "Lie, Aidan. You never lie to the Irish Mob."

Aidan, ignoring Davis's insistence that he hasn't lied to us, speaks over the bastard, "And why is that, Cade?"

I thought about what he'd done to Cain MacMurray to show him what happened to traitors within the Five Points' fold. "You find your-self without a tongue."

Davis's Adam's apple bobs. "Y-You can't be serious. I didn't lie! This is nonsense. Isabelle is a liar. It's compulsive, borderline socio-pathic, and you fell for it! Why would I ask you for a favor that would antagonize one of the most powerful men in the city?"

His desperation leaks through each word.

"Because you're arrogant," I say simply. "And you have a sick obsession with your daughter."

I round the desk, watching him watch me, and I pull out a knife that has him rolling back in his chair so fast that he collides with the wall.

When he scrambles to his feet, I slice my hand out and cup his throat, flexing my thumb and pointer finger around his windpipe. Surging forward, I pin him to the wall, watching with satisfaction as fear leaches into his eyes.

"I wonder if Belle was as scared as you are now," I snarl in his ear, "when she realized you killed the only parent who loved her and she was left alone with you."

Davis struggles against my hold, and his legs flail as he tries to kick me. Arms wild, he's intent on escaping, so I hit him where it hurts and knee him straight in the balls then kick his legs out from under him.

As he crumples to the ground, he chokes because I'm still holding him up by his throat.

That's when I let go, long enough for him to slump but fast enough to snatch his hand. I snap his wrist, then I grab the other and pin it to the wall, thrusting my blade through the center of his palm to hold him in place, watching in satisfaction as he screams.

"My da would take a finger per lie, Davis. Unfortunately for you, sometimes you don't have to kill to devastate someone's life." He nods at me. "Cade."

Plucking another blade out of my pocket, I press the edge to his pointer finger and hold it steady. He bawls when I slide through the flesh and straight to the bone.

One by one, I rupture his livelihood, destroying fingers that have made his name, that have given him a God complex that's devastated his little girl.

With each finger I cut off, as blood spurts and coats me, I accept that he'll never know the pain he caused Belle, but that doesn't stop me from trying to dole it back at him.

When I'm done, I retreat, watching him clutch at his arm as he tries to free himself from the knife pinning him. He slides in the blood pooling around him, his arms flailing against the blood-soaked wall.

"You'll regret this," he sobs, growing weaker from pain and blood loss with each word.

"The only thing I'll regret is that I don't get to kill you. But you go anywhere near your daughter, Davis," I threaten, "and I won't just give you a matching set—I'll make sure that's the last mistake you ever make."

22

ISABELLE

IT'S BEEN hours since Cade called. Neev just left for work so only Patricia, Kitty, and I remain, but even with their encouraging smiles, I know they're getting worried.

"We need to try Cade again," I mutter, interrupting Kitty who's talking about yet another guy's dick. Not a Stan's this time, but an Andrew's. I'm not sure why she sees so many but she has a tale for each one.

"Isabelle, you need to stay calm," Patricia advises, in the process of checking on the shepherd's pies she's got cooking in the oven.

"I know something is wrong. I can feel it. He should have contacted me before now. He knows I'm scared."

"Yes, but he doesn't know about that prank call. This happens all the—" Her phone rings. "It's Lucas. Quiet," Patricia orders, wiping her hands on her pants before connecting the call. "What's happened?" She frowns. "I don't understand. How is that possible? When is he getting out?"

My eyes dart to Kitty's.

"Lucas, I don't like this. Get your brother out of there! Ask Aidan! I don't want him spending—" She rubs her head and turns toward us.

"No, no. Of course I trust you to deal with this, but do it fast. Don't keep me waiting, son."

After she disconnects the call, she sets her phone beside the Glock in the middle of the table.

"What happened?" I croak.

"Nothing, it's nothing to worry about." Patricia straightens her shoulders back and smiles, but it's forced and makes my heart pound faster than ever—I feel like I could pass out. "Cade was pulled over on the way home for a busted taillight and they're holding him because they say there's a warrant out for his arrest." Her smile is so fake it's unreal, but she plasters it on anyway and smoothes her already perfect bun in place then returns to the oven.

"What?" Kitty yells. "That's bullshit. What warrant?" She follows her mom into the kitchen as I plunk my ass down in the chair. "We'd know if there was a warrant out on him. Raisin's boyfriend would have told us."

Cade is in jail?

Unease slithers up my spine.

If he's not here and Lucas is with him and by this time, Aidan O'Donnelly could have informed my father about my presence in the city, that means we're alone. That means when Cade promised me I was safe, it's likely that I'm not.

That we're not.

"I know, Catriona, but calm down. Lucas says he's handling this and I know he'll do us proud. Cade will be home tonight. There's no need for your concern."

Kitty growls, "Did the NYPD—"

The doorbell rings, cutting her off, and all three of us look at each other.

God, it feels like a scene from *Scream.*

"Relax, both of you. Let me handle this." Patricia holds up her hands as Kitty grabs her phone, her eyes narrowing at the screen. That's when I realize they have a camera app on the door.

"I don't know who they are," she mutters, flashing me the footage on the app.

"Wait, let me see." Taking the phone, I enlarge the image and see a man in a black trench coat. "I don't know him either."

"Good, so stay here. Just wait, it'll be another of Raisin's deliveries," Patricia says with a bright, unconvincing smile. The most unconvincing part of it is that she grabs the Glock from the table and flicks the safety off then tucks it into the back of her jeans.

I can't let her endanger herself, though. I've no reason to believe those men are anyone other than well-dressed delivery guys too, but... "I think we should stay on the safe side and not answer the door until Lucas and Cade are back. Just ignore whoever that—" The doorbell rings again and then, there's the sound of loud pounding.

"FBI. Open up."

My eyes flare wide, and Kitty and Patricia gape at one another.

"Oh, God," I whisper, my heart racing so hard I'm starting to sweat.

"Relax." She looks at both of us. "I know how to handle the feds."

The feds? Where's the cozy little baker I first met? Suddenly, I'm dealing with the wife and mother of mobsters—I need some of her courage.

Apparently, Kitty does too because, her fingers flying on her cell phone, she mutters, "Ma, maybe we *should* wait for Cade and Luc—"

"No, I'll handle this, Catriona," Patricia scolds, walking out the door and into the hallway before calling back, "This is *not* my first rodeo."

"Do you have another gun?" I question Kitty, who's grabbing a bat from behind the buffet.

"No, just stay behind me," she orders, starting for the door, but I snag a hold of her arm.

"Kitty, stop. We need another gun. Trust me. I can shoot."

"If I arm you," she retorts, "and they *are* the feds, then you'll be charged for possessing an unlicensed firearm. Mom's *is* licensed"

"FBI." It's practically a scream, and both of us jolt in surprise when there's an explosive noise that feels like it tears through the house itself.

Upon running into the hallway, we're in time to see Patricia being knocked into the wall with the force of the battering ram breaching the door.

"You fucker," Kitty snarls, taking the man in black by surprise as her bat connects with his face. Her loud cursing and crazy energy that reminds me of Dolly is almost soothing as I drop to my knees beside Patricia.

"Mrs. Frasier?" I reach for her shoulders, checking her out, but I'm hoping her slurred, "It's Patricia, Belle," means she's better than she looks.

"You thought I wouldn't find you?"

The voice makes me freeze for the scantest moments, holds me paralyzed until I force myself to stir, to hunt down the gun I know Patricia put down the back of her jeans.

Inside, it's as if my very organs have been put in the deep freeze. Then, my fingers collide with the gun and I can suddenly breathe easier. I even look up, but when I do, my eyes connect with my very own boogeyman, the man I've spent my whole life running from but never really escaped...

That's when I see he has a knife to Kitty's throat as he steps over the body of "the agent" she'd been "handling."

"I'm here for *you*, my love. No one else needs to get hurt. I can slice her throat if you want..."

Bile rises in my throat as fear for Kitty throttles me.

It's been years since I've seen him. His tanned skin is waxy, and his hands are wrapped, one in a shell that's like a cast, the other in blood-soaked bandages—but it's his eyes that have my heart stuttering in my chest.

Dead.

They're dead.

How could I have forgotten? Maybe I blocked it out. Maybe I *had* to.

"Daddy," I croak, fighting my nightmares, veering away from memories of my past because if I let them, they'll swallow me whole and I'll just allow him to take me. I'll just concede to his will because that's what you have to do to survive when he's in your life.

But surviving isn't enough for me anymore.

I want to live.

"You thought you could trick me by becoming another man's whore?" he rumbles, his tone too calm, a sharp contrast to that knife he's digging into Kitty's throat. "Spreading your legs like a common tramp. What the hell is wrong with you, Isabelle? Why can't you just behave? You're exactly like your mother. As much of a slut as she was. Incapable of following orders and doing as. You're. Told."

Concerned, I dart my eyes over to Kitty. She's staring at me, not one bit of fear in her gaze. If anything, she's angry, and I know she's going to do something if I don't stop her.

She doesn't understand how fucking crazy he is—he'll happily kill her and Patricia just to get to me.

Collateral damage means nothing to him, but Cade's already lost too many people. I just can't let him lose anyone else, not for me.

"Take it easy, Daddy." I study his hands. "You're hurt. Put the knife down and I'll come with you." In my peripheral, I see blood trickle down Kitty's throat.

Is that from the knife or his bloody hand? His bandages are drenched.

"*Hurt?* He butchered me, broke *me!*" he roars, and I flinch, waiting for him to drop her, waiting for his fist to collide with my face, seeing him in my mind's eye leaning over my mother as he beats her…

"Daddy, please," I whisper. "Put the knife down. I'll come. I promise. I won't fight, but you have to let her go…" My fingers tighten around the Glock. "Let her go, please. You don't need to hurt her."

"That's where you're wrong," he snarls, but his reaction time is obviously lagged because Kitty elbows him in the gut.

That's when my life becomes more of a movie than reality as I jerk to my feet and take the stance the Disciples drummed into us.

I aim.

And I fire.

Then, I fire again.

And again.

Blood explodes around me. Like red maple syrup, it spatters the walls and stains the floors, coats Kitty and me as it bursts from him when he drops to his knees and tumbles forward.

"Get away from him, Kitty."

Did I just say that? How was that me—how did I sound so in control?

Kitty holds her neck where there's a bleeding wound and she scuttles over to her mom's side. Then, her eyes grow steadily wider as the Glock goes off again and again until it's done. Until he can't come back. Ever.

Dead.

At last.

As I stagger into the wall, letting it prop me up, I warble, "It's over, Mommy. He can't hurt us anymore."

And that's when my brain takes over.

Everything fades.

Black spots dominate my vision and I'm okay with that because I'm safe. I took out the danger. He can never hurt me again and I can finally let go.

23

CINDY/BELLE

"BELLE? ISABELLE?"

The next time I blink my eyes open, I'm looking straight into Patricia's and Kitty's worried faces.

"You fainted. Drink this," someone orders—a guy. When he appears next to them, my heart skips. *Cade.* Then I blink because that is *not* Cade.

What the hell is going on here?

I turn my head and recognize Patricia's couch—I'm lying on it. Then, after I blink a couple times, I realize it's Lucas who is staring at me. Much like the last time I saw him, he doesn't look happy.

"Lucas," Patricia tuts. "Get out of her face." When he doesn't move, she snaps, "Give her some room, son!"

Struggling to sit up, I stare straight into Patricia's eyes. "My dad?"

"He can't hurt you. You took care of him," Patricia assures me then helps me to sit up fully. "We're so proud of you, honey."

Kitty hands me a glass of what I guess is whiskey by the smell, and I shoot it back, not even feeling the burn and ignoring the numbness of my tongue.

"Where is… he?" I gulp. "A-Are the cops on their way?"

When his cell rings, Lucas steps out of the room. It makes it easier to breathe without him looming over me. Kitty sits beside me and grabs my hand.

"Thanks for saving our lives, sis." She winks. Her neck is bandaged. Otherwise, I'd think I'm dreaming. "You were fucking awesome. Bang, bang, bang. Like something from *Kill Bill*. Never seen anything as cool in my life."

Cool? God, I feel faint. "We need, I mean, the bodies. The cops…"

Kitty snorts. "My family's in the mob, babe. Don't you worry about that."

Squeezing my fingers, Patricia nods. "You just relax. We Frasiers have everything taken care of."

When Lucas comes back into the room, he informs us, "Cade is being released. I'm going to pick him up." He points at me with his bandaged hand as he slips into his coat. "Make sure she doesn't leave in the interim."

When he opens the door to leave, the smell of bleach hits me like a punch to the face.

Róisín shuffles past him into the room, ignoring her brother entirely. "That piece of shit was totally not FBI." Róisín's riffling through what I'm assuming is the dead bodyguard's wallet, pulling out the ID and scanning it with a sniff. She peers at me. "Hey, Belle. Great job, babe. Kitty said you were like something from a movie."

Kitty beams at me but I just feel— "Oh, my God, I'm going to be sick." I surge onto quivering legs, wailing, "I'm a murderer."

"Me too, babe." Kitty brandishes her bicep. "Took 'em out like Vinny taught me when I was a kid."

Patricia groans. "God, I remember that mess with the watermelon."

Neev cackles. "Vinny and his bats."

Feeling like I'm in a parallel universe, I shake my head.

Regular me pushes things away, locks them up in the back of my mind. Except, there's no hiding any of this. They all know. They saw. They're *proud* of me.

It's a surreal moment, but oddly empowering.

My stomach settles.

"Take it easy," Kitty urges. "You're safe, babe. Just you wait until I tell Cade what you did. Man, he's going to be so proud too. Here we were, thinking you're a Barbie doll, I mean, a cool Barbie doll, but ya know, a doll nonetheless, and here you are, fucking Catwoman instead." I just blink at her but she shoves another glass at me. "Drink.

"Hey, I hope you don't feel guilty. That fucking lunatic needed to be put down." She grabs my wrist and jerks me back down on the couch, forcing me to take the whiskey. "What are you so upset about? You fucking kicked ass. Lucas was impressed too."

"That was Lucas… impressed?"

She snorts. "Yeah. He's a miserable asswipe."

Patricia tsks. "Kitty."

"What? It's true!"

As they start bickering about inappropriate labels for siblings, I shoot the second shot of whiskey back, finally feeling the wonderful glow that only alcohol and Valium can give.

Still… "Where are they?"

"In our meat freezer," Patricia informs me, her voice as calm as if she's discussing the weather or a new recipe she's trying out.

"Oh." I lean back. "Of course." *Where else?*

Neev walks over with the bottle in her hand, grinning wryly at me. "Another?"

"I thought you were at work."

She pshaws. "Kitty texted us with the DL. I hauled ass back home to help out."

She says it so simply that…

This is what family does. At least, *this* family, that is.

I hold up my glass as she pours way too much whiskey into it and, all at once, even though I need the extra shot of whiskey, that whisper of a craving for Valium fades much as the nausea in my belly did.

The vague notion of acceptance, of being a part of something bigger than me, whispers into me. As does the fact that I'm safe. I can sit here with no fear.

He's gone.

Dead.

And I did it.

Me.

That man was a monster, a killer who kept me prisoner on the drugs he prescribed and his money. He stripped me of my self-esteem and terrorized me. Worse than any of that, he killed my mom.

And I took him out.

Me.

The loud chatter of Cade's family cocoons me like a warm security blanket as I bring the glass to my lips. This time, I don't sink it back, just sip.

I have nothing to worry about—they'll protect me.

I have nothing to run from—I dealt with him.

What do I do now?

I close my eyes and maybe it's the Jameson, but I see my mom, smiling at me.

"Live, Isabelle, just live…"

Despite the crazy day, I smile and gently tip my glass to her.

For the first time ever, that feels possible.

24

CADE

ACUIG

When our SUV got pulled over on the ride from Aidan Jr.'s building back to mine, it was only Lucas who stopped me from trying to beat the shit out of the cop who asked me for my ID when I wasn't even speeding and sure as hell didn't have a busted taillight.

At first, I'd thought it was about Davis, but the BS I was booked with were trumped-up charges that had that fucker Davis and his bloody stumps for fingers all over them.

Grateful that I'd stopped at Lucas's place to shower and clean up after the meeting with Davis or the situation would have been more difficult to resolve, my brother called in Aidan, who called in whoever, and within two hours, I was back out on the streets.

Yet, upon returning home, it's to find a cleanup crew in the hallway.

Gaping at Lucas as I practically trip over a member of the team scrubbing bloodstains out of the floorboards, I demand, "You didn't think to tell me there was a bloodbath in the front fucking hall at any point during the journey home?"

He shrugs. "Didn't want you freaking out in the cop station."

"Well, consider me freaked out. What about the ride home? You could have told me then, dickwad."

"You were too busy bitching about the situation." His eyes gleam, which tells me he did this on fucking purpose.

"You're an asshole," I growl. "What the hell happened?"

The gleam fades, and with a grimace that I can feel in my bones because today has been *long*, he rubs the back of his neck. "As far as I can tell, Davis hired a grunt to pose as a fed. When Ma didn't open the door fast enough, he opened it by force. The bastard knocked her out."

Eyes flaring wide, I bite off, "Goddammit, you should have told me sooner!"

"Nah, you can see for yourself that she's fine if you stop asking me stupid fucking questions and go into her apartment." He rolls his eyes. "I swear, half my job is crisis management and figuring out how to tell big kids shit in a way that prevents a gang war." He tugs his fingers through his hair and continues, "Anyhow, Kitty texted me and because I was near, I got here quickly but not quick enough to stop shit going down how it did.

"Davis forced his way in with the grunt. When I got here, Kitty proved her lessons with Vinny and watermelons hadn't been forgotten, but her throat was a mess because Davis held her at knifepoint before your woman took care of him. I have no idea why she was armed."

My woman.

Damn, I like the sound of that.

Then, the rest of what he said catches up with me.

"Is Kitty okay?"

"Her throat's sliced up some, but mostly, yeah. She's buzzing—you know what she's like. Fucking bloodthirsty. The doctor says she'll be fine, just has to keep it clean."

"And Ma?"

"Headache. The force left her bruised and stiff but she's good."

"You should have told me this before I got here instead of letting me walk into a hall that stinks of bleach."

When he rolls his eyes at me again, I flip him the bird and stride into Ma's.

On my way through the door, I freeze when a thought occurs to me and turn back to Lucas. "Is Belle in there? Or did she leave?"

Lucas, who's talking to one of our cleanup guys, arches a brow at me. "Kitty'd have messaged me if Belle tried to leave. I don't think she'll be in a good headspace," he warns.

Nodding in thanks, I barrel down the hall, knowing I'll find them in the kitchen—I'm right.

Neev and Kitty are making cookies of all things, Róisín is removing her makeup, and Belle is sitting so close to my mother that she's practically in her lap.

Over the past couple of days, I've noticed how she gravitates toward Ma and, considering her past, I'm thankful Ma is a source of comfort for Belle.

Ma's holding a bag of peas to the back of her head, and her color is bad—she's pasty as fuck. As for Belle, she looks dazed, as if the world is spinning around her and she can't make it stop. Still, she's not jumpy —if she were, Neev and Kitty's bickering would have her leaping out of her skin.

Aside from her expression, she's showing no signs of injury, which is a relief. Once I know she's safe and uninjured, pride replaces concern.

She took out the fucking trash, owned her shit, cleaned it up, and now, she's free. To live, to love. To be with me... or not.

My sisters don't notice me as I drift into the room, so I ignore them and place a gentle hand on Ma's shoulder and squeeze her there softly while ducking down to press a kiss to Belle's temple.

She jolts in surprise but settles when I whisper in her ear, "I am so fucking proud of you, baby."

Then, I switch sides, putting a hand on her shoulder so I can lean over Ma and kiss her cheek.

"And you wonder where we get our balls from, Ma."

She snorts at my cheek and swats me with a hand. "It certainly wasn't your da."

I grin at her, but it fades as I crouch at her side and settle my hand on Belle's knee so I can comfort them both.

When Belle immediately clings to it, I squeeze back, trying to be reassuring as I ask Ma, "How are you feeling?"

"Rough," she admits with a wince. "It all happened so fast. I didn't even get the chance to draw my gun."

"You didn't need to, Annie Oakley," Kitty drawls. "We had Belle on our team."

I cut my sister a look. "Shut up, Kitty."

Then I catch sight of the bandage around her throat and I wish to fuck I hadn't stopped with Davis's fingers tonight.

It would've saved my family a lot of trauma if I'd just superseded Aidan's orders.

Not realizing I'm thinking murderous thoughts, Kitty huffs. "I'm being nice."

I glance at Belle who's back to spacing out, but her hand is entwined with mine and she's clutching at me so hard that I know my palm will be studded with nail marks later.

Still, it's reassuring that she hasn't dissociated from what's happened today. Somehow, we need to keep that momentum going before—

Hell, I don't even want to think about it.

For someone with mental health issues, today has been disastrous. I can't imagine how tempting Valium might be right now to her, and I need to make sure she doesn't fall back into bad habits.

"I don't think your *nice* is compatible with how Belle's feeling," is all I say to Kitty.

"Cade's right," Ma grouses. "Shut your trap, Catriona."

Kitty huffs. "I think she was awesome. You should have heard the shit that fucker was spouting. Honestly, I've never met the man before and I wanted him to choke on his own vomit and die."

"Gruesome," Róisín drawls, shooting the eldest girl brat a dismissive glance as she does something weird to a cotton pad that has bubbles forming on it. "I know I didn't need to hear that, so I'm sure Belle would prefer you shut your trap too."

Belle bows her head and, in a whisper, says, "It's funny. I always felt like I ruined everything. That before I came along, his marriage to my mom was perfect, but I know that was a lie. Mom was scared of him for as long as I can remember. He was the snake who poisoned everything, not me…"

"Of course it wasn't you, baby. I think we need to get you upstairs so you can rest up." I shoot Ma a look. "Do you need anything?"

She shakes her head and grimaces. "Your sisters have been clucking around me like I'm a cockerel on the loose in their hen house—"

"Ew," Neev groans. "That's gross imagery, Ma."

I figure Ma knows that though. She looks pleased with herself.

If she's well enough to make lewd jokes, then I know she'll be fine.

"If you need me," I tell my sisters, "I'll be upstairs."

"Is your brother out in the hall?"

"He's dealing with the cleanup." I clear my throat. "Where are *they* right now?"

Belle's fingers tighten some more as she lets me know that she's not as out of it as I first thought. "Patricia said they were in the meat freezer."

"Just until the streets get quieter," Ma demurs.

I figured as much, but seeing Belle's reaction, I doubt she's as comfortable as I am with a corpse sharing space with the chicken for Sunday dinner.

With each passing moment, I can feel her fragility deepening. At first, I thought resting would help, but because I know about her dependency issues, I don't want to make this worse, so I decide to give her a Frasier special—*overwhelm her with family.*

Instead of taking her to my apartment, I pick her up, ignoring her yelp of surprise, then settle her on my knee. Immediately, she burrows her face into my throat while Ma leans against my side.

I raise my arm so I can curve it about her shoulders too, and Ma whispers, soft enough so only I can hear, "Good judgment call, son. I knew that time I dropped you on the head as a baby didn't cause too much lasting damage."

"Thanks, Ma," I drawl with a snort.

She smiles but it cracks some as she tilts her head to stare at Belle.

She doesn't think there's any risk of her overhearing because she whispers, "Belle needs family. If you can't give that to her, then you need to let her go."

Her words linger in my head as Belle starts crying. It has nothing to do with what Ma said and everything to do with the shock wearing off.

When her slim frame trembles in my hold, I know the only way I can help is to ground her and keep her from going off the rails.

From her current perfume—eau de whiskey—I already know she's three sheets to the wind, so when Kitty wanders over, a mug of hot cocoa in her hand and a cookie, I murmur, "Baby, Kitty's got something for you. It'll help sober you up."

When she doesn't move away from my throat, I grab the cookie and press it against her fingers. She sniffles, stays right where she is, but raises the cookie to her lips and starts chewing.

I don't even care that tiny crumbs fall down my collar—it must be fucking love.

Watching us, Kitty grins then pinches her thumb and pointer finger into an "O" shape. She prods the air at Belle then gives me a thumbs-up.

Róisín coughs, also gives me a thumbs-up, and Neev, who's watching me from afar, does too.

Why they think I need their approval is anyone's guess.

The bitch of it is, I don't have any say in whether Belle becomes a part of the family or not—that's down to her and whether she can forgive me my sins. Whether she's willing to move to New York. It's not like the Irish Mob comes with an option for a sabbatical...

With my mind wandering, I let my sisters do their thing. They start bickering with Ma and eventually with Lucas, who shows up stinking of bleach.

They talk about inappropriate shit and Neev's upcoming hair appointment.

Róisín complains about her boss at the bar where she works who keeps peering down her shirt. Lucas and I share a pointed look that communicates how the boss will be regretting his inability to keep his eyeballs under control.

Kitty whines about needing me to work with her at the gym again but doesn't say why—I figure it's because of what happened today.

It's easy and loving and just… life.

Okay, mob life. But life.

When Belle stops hiding in my throat, I don't acknowledge her reappearance other than to pass her another cookie.

Not putting any pressure on her to get involved, we talk around her until Kitty declares, "Neev, you need to get your hair dyed the same color as Belle's. If you go brown, it'll make you look ancient."

"Thanks," Neev snipes.

"I don't dye my hair," Belle murmurs. "I get streaks but I'm a natural blonde."

"God, you lucked out in the hair and the tits department, didn't you?" Róisín complains.

"Róisín!" Ma chides, but it lacks her usual heat.

"What? It's true. They're massive. If I were gay, I'd totally try to snag you from Cade, babe," Raisin jeers, making Belle snicker. But she blushes and I know she accepts the words for what they are—a compliment. Just Raisin-style.

"How's your head?" I ask Ma, concerned by her limp response.

She grimaces. "It's fine."

"Liar." Lucas grunts. "Come on, Ma, let's get you up and to bed. Raisin, you can do something useful for once and help me get her ready."

"Fucking raisin. Call me by my real name or I'll piss in your coffee the next time you're over."

"I don't want to go to bed," Ma grumbles, ignoring Raisin's warning. "The doctor says I need to be checked on every hour anyway. I might as well stay here."

"How about the sofa, Ma?" Kitty asks gently. "Neev, Róisín, and I will take it in turns to sit up with you."

"Yeah, that sounds good," she admits tiredly, and without uttering a word, she tells us how bad she's feeling by letting Lucas support her as he walks her down the hall to the living room. On her way out, she weakly calls, "I'll see you later, Belle. French toast tomorrow for breakfast."

Lucas argues, "No cooking for you for a few days."

"I'll direct the girls. You know they burn water."

"Hey, we didn't burn the cookies," Kitty gripes.

"Only because they're from a package," I retort.

"They were good cookies," Belle defends my sister, who shoots me a smug look. "They tasted great, Kitty. Thank you."

"Because they were Nestle's finest," I mock.

"Could you do any better?" Belle asks me.

Kitty scoffs, "He can't even turn on the toaster oven without setting fire to the building."

Glaring at her, I mumble, "That was one time."

"Dipshit put cheese in the toaster to speed up grilled cheese," Neev said with a chuckle.

"I was twelve!" I bicker. "Fuck, no one lets you forget anything in this house."

Then, Belle makes it worth being at the center of my sister's bullshit because she whispers, "That's the best part about being in a family. No one forgets you. Ever."

With my siblings, we're more likely to argue with one another until we're blue in the face, but I don't spoil the fantasy and press a kiss to her temple.

"You say that like it's a good thing," I tease. "Just you wait until you get your dress caught in the door and you end up flashing the neighbors—"

"Shut up, Cade!" Róisín growls.

I smirk at her, knowing I just declared war on my sisters who'll throw back twice as much shade as I can deliver, but it's worth it because Belle laughs and that's music to my fucking ears right now.

25

CADE
TWO DAYS LATER

"BELLE, baby, do you want to come to the gym with me?"

It's like I haven't spoken.

She just stares straight ahead. The TV's on, but I don't think she's processing what's happening.

Plunking my ass down on the couch, I reach for her hand. When she cringes, I immediately suck in a breath and try not to overreact.

"Belle?"

She swallows. "What?"

"Do you want to come to the gym? We can work out together," I croon.

Her head wobbles from side to side. "No, it's okay. You go."

Uneasily, I mutter, "Do you want to sit with Ma?"

"No."

Though I purse my lips, I get to my feet and retreat to the bedroom. Changing into sweats, a wifebeater, and some sneakers, I draw out the set of free weights I have in the closet and start a lighter workout.

Even though she has to hear me, she doesn't ask me what I'm doing, doesn't ask why I haven't gone to the gym.

I doubt she even notices I'm here.

Ma said she tried to get her to call her friends, but she was quiet all morning, just stared out the window…

Fuck, I want to help but have no idea how.

Stacking more weights on the dumbbells, I try to relieve some of my inner tension through heavy lifting, utterly unaware that I'm falling back into old habits, one that came about when Vinny died…

Right now, though, my mind is focused on her.

I hate that the only way to reach her is through sex, but I hate that vacant look in her eyes more. Hate it with a fucking passion. And she always reaches for me first, like she needs the connection too, and when we're together, it's as if she's back with me.

Like I didn't wreck her.

If I can ground her, if that's what she needs from me, then that's what I'll do.

Doesn't stop it from fucking sucking. Doesn't stop me from adding an extra ten pounds to the dumbbells, either, and from doing another round of a hundred on top of my five sets of fifty reps…

26

CADE

"BELLE?"

She flicks a look at me.

Progress.

"Kitty asked me if you wanted to head out with her for a drink? She said something about raining chaos on Manhattan. I thought you might enjoy being in on that," I tease.

But her expression is wooden. Blank.

My hope fades.

Her gaze flickers to the TV.

I guess I have my answer.

27

CADE

"BABY, YOU NEED TO EAT."

She peers out from the blanket cocoon around her. I woke up this morning and found her like this. "I'm fine."

"You're really not." I hesitate. "I'm here, you know?"

She blinks. "I know."

I don't think she does.

I don't think she gets it.

But I remember what it was like. I loved Vinny, and she hated her father, but when you kill someone for the first time, you—

I sigh.

I reach over and gently stroke a few strands of bright blonde hair from her forehead. "Just as long as you do. I'm going to get some work done, okay? Lucas wants me to see if this surveillance footage corre-lates with a—" I stop talking when I see her zone out.

She doesn't care that her father *was* behind my phony arrest. Doesn't care that the guy claiming to be a fed was a PI who'd been trailing her for months—he even had pictures of us fucking in his case files before his shitty home office in his trailer had burned to the ground thanks to me.

No, she doesn't need to worry about all that. I'll tell her over dinner —maybe she'll be more aware then?

Leaning down, I press a kiss to her forehead.

Maybe karma has fucked me over again—the one woman I want to let me in, I can't reach, and it's all my fault because I failed her.

Me. No one else. *Me.*

God, I'm so over fucking up with the people who matter the most to me.

28

CADE

WITH THE MUG of soup sitting on the coffee table waiting for me, I don't let her argue, just sit on the couch and drag her onto my knees. She's used to me hauling her around at nighttime when it's like another woman gets into bed with me—from this walking ghost to a nymph who wants to drive me mad with want and need for her.

"What are you doing?" she grumbles.

When I hear the slur in her voice, my brows arch. I trust that she hasn't been using, but...

"I'm feeding you," I retort. "Ma said when she came up at lunchtime you hadn't eaten any of the soup she made for you, so I'm not going anywhere until you eat."

Though I can tell she's not hungry, mostly, I get the feeling she's tired.

I'm not surprised—I'm fucking wrecked. I like sex as much as the next guy, but she's on me worse than poison oak through the night and then stares into space through the day. Ma says she comes up and finds her napping, but I think those bouts of sleep are few and far between.

I want her to reach out to me, want to help her talk about what happened, but I just fucking don't know how. In my family, we don't talk—we *do*. But Belle's not making that easy on me. I mean, that's her right, but it just leaves me out in the cold, unsure of how to help her, uncertain of how to improve this disastrous situation that's of my own making.

As I bring the mug to her lips, she turns her head to the side. Then, she nuzzles her face into my throat. When she kisses me there, I grumble, "Isabelle, eat the soup."

"You *drink* soup."

"Eat it, drink it, I don't care which verb so long as it ends up in your stomach and not down the garbage disposal again." I can't believe I'm about to say this, but when she starts pressing her lips to my throat, I state, "None of *that* until you've eaten."

She huffs.

But she *drinks* the fucking soup.

I'll take it as a win.

29

BELLE

"Cade, you awake?" I whisper into his neck and am rewarded with a mumble and his arms tightening around me, followed by the calming sounds of steady breathing.

I stare into the darkness.

My insomnia is back with a vengeance and, even with Cade fucking me exhausted, I can't seem to shake it. I toss the covers off and reach for one of his T-shirts then walk into the other room to get my phone, which is charging.

Jesus, I have to talk to Cade. All I'm doing is trying to pretend that I'm fine when in truth, I'm struggling.

I grab my phone and sink onto his couch. The screensaver lights up, revealing Cade and me from before the whole "I killed my dad" time when we ordered pizza and he fed it to me. He's laughing, showing off his dimples and golden brown hair. Absently, my fingers trace his face.

I lean my head into the soft cushions on his couch and turn to stare out the window. Morning light is arriving, accenting all the lights and sounds of New York beginning to stir for another day.

I don't think I can cope with watching this again. I'm exhausted and it's not getting better.

Maybe things *can't* get better here.

Maybe I need to go back to Los Angeles...?

The thought lifts a weight off my chest that I didn't know was there, and it's suddenly easier to breathe.

I've been so scared about calling them, sharing another mess I made with them, but I can't heal here. I need Charlie and my tribe and, for the first time in our friendship, I need to open up to them. Then, they'll understand. I know they will.

My hand tightens on my phone as I make my decision.

When I glance at his bedroom door, my heart aches, but this is the right thing to do for me. Even though I've let him have my body... I guess my mind hasn't forgiven him yet.

He lied.

And Cade doesn't talk about the future, which makes me feel insecure. The only time he told me he loves me was when he yelled that he *thought* he was "falling in love" with me to Lucas that one day, but other than that, nothing.

I rub my poor, tired eyes, wishing I could let go and sleep, but my mind can't seem to stop. It just races like a hamster on a wheel, over and over, replaying things that I need to let go of.

A week.

It's been seven whole days of sleeplessness since I killed my father, and everyone goes along like they're fine, as if I'm one of them, but I'm not. Would it be better if Cade claimed me? I don't know, but he hasn't, and I'm left feeling like I'm in limbo.

Sighing, I sit up and look down at my screen. 4:01 am. Too early to text Charlie, but I'm sure she'll have her phone on silent.

> Me: I'm coming home tomorrow.

It's 1:00 am in L.A. She's not going to be up, but that's okay. She'll respond in the morning. My fingers type American Airlines and I scroll through departure times. There's an 8:00 am nonstop flight to Los

Angeles. My fingers hover over the option, and before I can talk myself out of it, I make the reservation.

Standing, I move to the refrigerator for a bottle of water, wondering how I'll tell Cade that I'm going to leave today. I know I have to be honest, but have I ever been one-hundred-percent honest with anyone, even myself? Trusted someone so much that I let all my demons out?

No.

I haven't. The closest I've come is with Cade and Patricia, but I always held back, and now, I never will because he doesn't care enough to do anything more than fuck me.

Taking a drink of water, sighing when it cools me down, I set the bottle on the counter and make the walk back to the bedroom.

As I do, my eyes take in the sparseness of his dwelling. God, his dead brother Vinny's apartment has more furniture than Cade's. It makes sense that he can't offer me anything when, from his home alone, I can see he offers himself nothing too.

Cade stirs and kicks the white sheet off him. My eyes memorize every inch. I watch his hand reach over to my side as if even in sleep, he wants me near, and for a second, I almost falter.

But I can't.

I need to be able to think. If I stay here, I'll let him distract me with sex while I keep hiding years of pain and abuse. Which is why I need to leave. It's time I heal. I'm finally strong enough to do it. I guess I have him to thank for that too.

I sit down on the side of the bed. "Cade?"

His ridiculously long eyelashes flutter open and he grins, his dimples flashing. *For me.* Because he's happy to see me...

My heart skips a beat but I tame it. Sex won't fix things. It won't.

"You okay?" he mumbles, grin fading when he takes in my expression. His hands reach for me, though.

"I need to talk to you." I can't stop myself from caressing his hair. The waves seem to have a life of their own as they wrap around my fingers. "I'm going back to L.A." Even to my ears, my voice leaks exhaustion.

This time, he sits up, but he's still blinking back sleep. "Huh?"

"I need some space to think." I bite my lip at the confusion in his expression. "I can't do that here."

"What's wrong?" he rasps. "What can I do?"

He has no idea that he's a part of the problem.

I want nothing more than for him to fix everything, but if he can't see that he fucked up and it's made me insecure, that it's made me need certain reassurances from him, then there's no hope. All it'd have taken was "I love you." It wouldn't have made me sleep easier, but it would have made me feel as if it were a step forward.

Instead, I'm just staying in his bed rather than an AirBnb and replacing therapy with a ton of orgasms.

So, I just say, "A lot of things are wrong."

He grabs my hand. "You're not going to L.A. Not after everything. The last thing you need is to be alone. I can—"

My finger on his lips stops him and I lean forward to kiss him. "I won't be alone."

He scoffs. "Those people don't—"

That pricks my temper. "*Those people* are my family. Just like you and Kitty have your ups and downs, but she has your back, my family has mine too. I've fucked up and made it hard on them. Sometimes, you run out of free passes, and it's time I made things right. With them. With myself."

"What the fuck, Belle? You can't just wake me up and tell me you're leaving without discussing it—"

I scoff, "Sure I can. You're someone I'm hooking up with; you're not my man, Cade." Hurt leaches into his expression, but he defined the lines of our relationship, not me. Then, I feel bad because I could have brought this up sooner, mentioned that I needed more from him… On a deep sigh, I mutter, "I'm not Belle and I'm not Cindy. That's my point. I don't know who I am. But trying to pretend that I'm fine is not helping me."

"I've never needed you to pretend to be anything other than your-self. You're Isabelle. You need time? Fine, you can stay with Kitty—"

I shake my head. "Cade, listen to me. My whole life, I have been pretending to be someone, someone who isn't me. Do you get that?

I've pretended for so long that I don't know who the real me is. And I can't learn here, in a place that made me into what I am today. Not without a support system. I need to go home." This is it, time to lay it on the line. "What I do know is that I love you, but that's not enough if I'm on my own here."

He stares at me, his chest rising and falling as if he just ran up and down the stairs, but he stays silent.

He.

Stays.

Silent.

Heart breaking, I inhale then exhale. "All of this…" I motion back and forth between us. "…just happened so fast. I'm not gonna lie and say that what you did—lying to me about your intentions at the start—doesn't hurt. It does. It's made me second-guess everything—"

Shuffling to his feet, he crosses his arms. "You should have said. I tried—"

"No. I shouldn't have done anything. I've barely gotten through this week. If it doesn't make sense to you that a week ago, I put a bullet in my father's head and I might not be okay, then Jesus Christ, there's no helping you.

"Was he the worst man alive? Yes, but I still killed him. *I* did that."

His mouth works. "That was my fault. I should have been the one—"

"That's the thing, Cade. It's not your fault. None of this is your fault. Shit happens. You can't control everything. I don't blame you." *Not for that.* I grab his face with both hands, forcing him to look at me. My eyes swim with tears when he stares straight into them and hope leaps in my chest because it's there… *I can see it.*

"Say it, tell me your truths," I whisper, because maybe I don't have to leave. Maybe we can make this work—*together*.

He rubs my cheek with his thumb. "Belle…" He sounds as if he's in pain as he lowers his forehead to mine, and *I know* he's going to tell me that he loves me. My heart flutters, hope fills me, then… "How long do you plan on being gone?"

The need to scream is unreal. I can feel the hope inside me

deflating like he just pricked me with a needle.

My eyes flicker open and I shove away from him, not even trying to hide the fact that I'm devastated.

God, no wonder we suit each other—we're both fucked up. Broken. Just in different ways.

"As long as it takes. Forever." I shrug. "I'll find a way to pay you back for the hospital—"

For the first time, his temper flares and I start to hope *again*... but, no. "Don't insult me," he snaps.

"I owe you," I rasp.

"You owe me nothing."

Turning away from him so he doesn't see the tears in my eyes, I head to the bathroom. He doesn't stop me, and he didn't say it. So, I have my answer. I got my truths—we owe each other nothing.

Gulping, I turn on the shower and pull off his T-shirt, letting the hot water cleanse me as I wash, almost in a daze.

You need to do this.

Neither of us can think straight when we are close. We just fuck and that's never going to work.

I turn off the water and step out, not needing to call his name to know he's left the apartment.

I can feel he's gone.

But the emptiness in the bedroom is almost a relief as I brace my hand on the door and stare into a room we've shared for nearly two weeks.

Two weeks.

No time at all, but somehow, everything has changed.

I don't want to stay away forever, and I know that last argument was a cry for help—a plea for more—one he didn't answer.

I return to the sink, where I start to gather the products I need to pack. But when I next look into the mirror, I straighten my shoulders.

I'm done lying to myself.

It's time I take responsibility for my own life, for my future.

Whether he's in it or not is no longer down to me.

It's on him.

30

CINDY

"CINDY." I turn, trying hard not to burst into tears at Doug coming toward me.

Over the years, Doug and I have become super close. He's the best hair stylist in Los Angeles and an even better friend. I can't count how many times he's held me together when I thought Ryder had destroyed me.

I've just landed, and sheer exhaustion must have finally taken over since I don't remember the plane ride. All that matters is Doug and that I'm home and that I can start a new phase of my life.

"Hey, baby girl." Doug's warm arms go around me as I almost trip over my baggage to throw myself into his hug, burying my face in his neck at the same time.

"I got you," he whispers into my hair.

Clinging to him, I let the tears I've been fighting finally fall.

"Doug, I—" I swallow back all the things I need to say and let his calming presence infiltrate me.

"You're okay, just breathe."

I listen, taking a deep inhalation and slowly releasing it as I lift my head.

"Let me see you." He sweeps my hair off my shoulder and tucks a strand behind my ear. His eyes caress my face and for a second, I'm self-conscious. I'm wearing zero makeup since I pretty much grabbed my carry-on and left, but to be honest, Cade seems to like my face clean of it, and after this past week, I've gotten out of the habit of constantly wearing it. Doug's used to Cindy, though. Not... *Isabelle.*

I laugh but my voice cracks as I joke, "I know I look terrible."

Doug grabs my chin. "I don't think you've ever looked more beautiful." His eyes narrow, and he pulls me in for another tight hug. "Thank fuck. It's good to have my girl back."

When he kisses the top of my head, I sniffle. "I haven't been gone that long."

With a final kiss, he reaches for my baggage with one hand, and the other folds around mine.

"That's not what I'm talking about. It's been years since your eyes have been this clear. I've missed *this* Cindy." He stops at the crosswalk and then propels us forward toward the parking garage, stopping at his black Range Rover.

He holds the door open for me and I hop inside, asking, "Where's Robert?"

"At his parents' place," he replies before walking around to the driver's side and getting behind the wheel.

"What's going on?" I ask uneasily, certain I heard annoyance in his tone. Because Robert and Doug are perfect, literally. If they can't make it, nobody can. "Is everything okay?"

"Oh, his mom is throwing his sister-in-law a baby shower and she demanded he be there. It's boring as hell." He grins and starts up the vehicle. "Thankfully, you came through and saved me from needing to attend."

Studying him to make sure he's being serious, I take note of his dark hair, which he's wearing longer than usual, but he's still dressed in his signature head-to-toe black. There's something sexy about him: his attitude, probably. It's as if people can feel he doesn't give a shit, so that makes everyone, all sexes, flock to him like he's a magnet.

"So, you guys are fine?"

He puts his arm on my headrest and looks back to pull out. "Yeah, we're good."

Flipping the visor down, I study myself in the mirror and grimace. Reaching for my purse, I grab my makeup bag.

"Don't even think about it," he snaps, making me jump. "You don't need to dress up for me."

I sigh and zip the bag back up. I mean, he *is* just dropping me off at my condo. Why bother with the whole process of transformation? It's another habit I need to break.

Made-up Cindy is one of my many masks.

Not wanting to get into that, I ask, "How's the salon doing?" I cross my legs and lean my head back as he fills me in on all the gossip.

Apparently, Dolly and Doug are finalizing her hair product line. I knew they were working on it but had no idea it was so close to launch. It makes me realize how much I'd checked out on them. How much I'd let them down.

Resolving to be a better friend, to be worthy of them, I cheer, "Doug, that's amazing news! I'm so proud of you two."

He flashes me a grin. "It happened fast, but I'm happy. Your hair will love the leave-in conditioner."

"You going to give me a PR box?" I tease.

"For my best girl, of course." He grins again. "You hungry?"

He doesn't wait for my answer as he exits the 405 Freeway and pulls onto Ventura Boulevard. Then, he drives past my street.

What the hell?

"Where are you taking me?" I demand.

"Someplace that'll feed you," he drawls. "You look hungry. And sad."

When he leaves it there and doesn't fire off questions at me, I mutter, "Just lay into me, get it over with. I know you want to. I mean, I disappeared without warning and asked you to water my plants. I'm aware that I suck." Then, I sniff. "Though why Axel had to break into my apartment if you have a key, I don't know."

"It impressed the girls." He snorts. "Those are your issues, baby girl. If you want to tell me all your shit, I'm here to listen, but I'm not going to push when you look so..." He shakes his head. "I'm being serious. You don't need a lecture. Plus, it's easier if you tell us everything together. That way you don't have to repeat yourself." He drives into the parking lot of Casa Vega, our favorite Mexican food restaurant/happy hour hangout.

When I look around and recognize the tribe's cars, I groan. "No. No way, Doug. I'm tired." I did not mentally prepare for this.

Doug ignores me and pulls up to the valet.

"Me too. Fucking brutal week." Still ignoring me, he takes the ticket from the valet and snags my purse as he gets out of the Range Rover. "You'll feel better after a couple margaritas."

"It's barely noon!"

He snorts as he peers through the driver's window at me. "Since when did that stop us?"

"One drink," I snip, joining him on the sidewalk and snatching my purse from him.

Unapologetically, he holds the big wooden door open for me. "Of course."

"I knew I should have put on makeup," I grumble, running a hand through my long hair, which probably looks wild. "You're a jerk for stopping me."

"You've never looked more stunning." His earnestness calms me down before he propels us into the dark restaurant and my eyes adjust to the dimness.

Dolly waves at us from our usual booth to the right.

"About time, beyotch," Dolly screams and leaps up, throwing her arms around me until I'm almost choking. God, that feels good.

"Okay, give her room," Doug teases.

As he untangles Dolly's arms from my neck, I look over at the table. Eve, Charlie, and Antoinette are seated with margaritas and nachos in front of them...

No incoming hugs...

"Hey," I greet as I slide into the booth next to Charlie, who takes a sip of her drink as she studies me like I'm a lab rat that needs to be monitored.

"Okay, I'm getting all of us shots," Dolly declares. "Edge is taking care of the kids. I pumped my breast milk, and I'm going to enjoy myself. You are too. This is an alcohol intervention before this"—she waves her hand at us—"all turns into an argument." She sashays toward the bar area as I turn to my friends.

Perfect.

They're pissed, but I'm not sure that I care. With everything that has happened since I left, their disapproving vibes bounce right off me. I meant it when I told Cade that I need to repair things here, but I'm not going to take their crap either.

"Where's Julianna?" I ask.

Eve's blue eyes laser in on my face. "She thought you would be uncomfortable so she stayed home."

"Why would I be uncomfortable?" I reach for Charlie's margarita. "Her welcome home party couldn't be any worse than you guys," I declare, staring defiantly at Eve, who cocks her head, her long blonde hair spilling over her shoulder as her mouth twitches.

"Well, because you kissed her husband then disappeared, only to call and say you'd gone to New York without telling any of us and were staying with some stranger who's in the Five Points' Mob—"

"Look, I'm exhausted," I grumble. "If you guys don't want to listen to my side of the story, I'm going home for a much needed nap."

"Cindy, we thought you'd been kidnapped," Eve retorts.

"Phones work both ways. I didn't notice you texting me…"

There's a group inhalation as my words land the hit.

Antoinette reaches over to hold my hand. "What Eve is trying to say is we've been worried and are unsure about how to help you." Supportive, sweet, fierce Antoinette squeezes my fingers. "This was our way of trying… I suppose it was a kind of interv—"

"I'm a fuckup," I admit, not letting her finish her sentence. "Have been for a long time. I never told you guys about my past. Not because I didn't trust you, but because I was ashamed. Even knowing all your histories, I never could admit mine, because that'd mean I'd have to look at myself, and that was not something I could deal with. The funny thing is, my past, what happened, it wasn't my fault. I didn't do anything wrong…"

That's the moment I realize even Charlie is staring at me, and suddenly all these things that I've held in, pretended aren't a part of me, are a lie. They loved me before; they'll love me after. I'm strong and I deserve to be happy—they'll want that for me.

Reaching for a tortilla chip just so I can destroy it with my fingers, I realize this might be the first time I've ever acknowledged my right to be content.

"See, by focusing on you guys, I never had to face my own horrors. But I'm not scared anymore because I've faced the monster and I came out alive."

I must have stunned them silent because we all jump when Dolly sings, "Here we go." She sets down five shots on the table. "Wait. What'd I miss?"

"Cindy's having an epiphany." Doug grabs her wrist to pull her down into the booth. "So, shut up."

"Oh, thank God," she whispers, pushing the shot in front of me and doling the rest out to everyone else.

Eve frowns at her as Antoinette squeezes my hand supportively again.

"Well, I met Cade—"

"We know that part," Eve cuts me off. "What happened? Talk, Cindy. That last phone call you were hysterical, and I was getting ready to hop on a plane to rescue you."

My mind drifts back to that day that seems so far away yet was only a week ago.

There's no way to sugarcoat this… "I killed my father," I blurt out.

Besides the music playing in the background, it's like I blasted them with liquid nitrogen. Then, in a croak, Charlie grabs my arm and demands, "You… I don't know… Go on."

It's more of a plea than anything.

"He murdered my mom." I release a breath, ignoring their gasps of surprise. "God, that's good to get out. Good to share. My father came to Cade's building. See, he had gotten Cade arrested—"

"Wait. How did he know his address?"

"He was watching me, the sick fuck. He showed up at my place with this guy who Cade found out was a PI." I lean back and cross my arms. "This is why I've always been so paranoid and scared. I've spent half my life thinking he'd have me kidnapped and brought home. Little did I know, the guy I was fucking was hired to do exactly that."

"Oh, Cindy." Antoinette rubs my shoulder, urging me to go on. "Cade betrayed you?"

Whatever. Might as well tell them all of it. It's eating me up inside.

"He did, but it was a misunderstanding. My father was a successful surgeon, and he treated a lot of important men. The head of the Five Points' Mob was one of them, and he sent Cade to bring me back to New York.

"When Cade realized what was going on, that it wasn't just a case of some wild-child daughter being held against her will by a scary MC, he tried to make things right but it was too late. My father came to Cade's building and hurt his mom too.

"When he held Cade's sister, Kitty, hostage, I just snapped."

I look at the red tablecloth, but the red becomes the blood that puddled around the dead bodies, and the sounds of the gun, the smell of the cordite in the air… it overtakes everything.

"Cindy? Dammit, Cindy! Cade got rid of the body?" Eve's voice makes me jump. "Doug, nudge her before I lose my shit—"

"Y-Yes." I blink at her. "He did."

"No police were involved?"

"None."

She heaves a relieved sigh. "Thank fuck for that."

Doug clears his throat. "Why didn't you come back after everything went down?"

"Well, I was in shock at first. And then Cade's whole family rallied around me. They're so amazing. He has three sisters and a brother, and his mother is fantastic. They've been wonderful…"

"So, is Cade here?" Eve looks over her shoulder as if he's hiding behind the large plastic plant at the back of our booth. "He came with?"

"No, I… He's in New York." Grabbing the shot and downing it, I let the burn of the tequila distract me from their expressions.

"Why? He got rid of a body for you," Charlie wails, looking like she wants to shake me. "Why did you leave him?"

"Because… he lied. Not just about why he started up with me, but about his feelings. I know he has them for me, I saw it, but he couldn't say it and I'm not settling for a guy who won't tell me how he feels about me."

"Cindy," Doug says slowly, "all I'm hearing is that you ran away again." By the look on his pretty face, he's not even trying to hold back his disapproval.

"No. I did *not* run. I didn't even run the first time. I just needed some goddamn space." I point a finger at him. "I told him the truth, that I loved him, and he had ample opportunity to say it to me. I didn't need a fucking ring, Doug. Just confirmation that I wasn't wasting my goddamn time with him.

"I guess in the back of my mind, I was hoping he'd stop me." I shrug. "It's fine. I needed to come home. I missed you guys, and I wasn't happy with how I left things. I know I need to do better. I-I realized that in New York." I reach for another shot only to have Charlie grab my wrist.

"It's okay to feel all this. It's also okay to let him love you. You are worthy of that."

Her golden eyes hold mine as I set the shot down. "Well, that's just it. What if he doesn't love me? He's never said it to me. Sure, I saw it in his eyes, but that's not enough, is it?" Before she can reply, I retort, "And I agree. I *do* deserve to be loved."

She has no idea how hard that would have been for me to say just three weeks ago, but the words spill from my lips with ease today.

Today is what counts—not yesterday, hell, not even tomorrow.

One day at a time.

"You barely know each other," Doug points out.

"Doug!" Dolly hisses. "Shut up! That's not how love works."

"What? I'm just saying! He's a man. It's almost impossible to get a guy to admit he loves you after only a few months of dating, never mind *days…*"

"Look, I don't want to start crying, but I have over thirty years of self-doubt, pain, and destructive behavior to reconcile myself with. And Cade has his own shit he needs to fix in himself too.

"Sure, the chemistry is phenomenal, but that's not enough for me. I could see myself staying just because I love his family when he grows bored of me and gets tired of having sex with the same woman—"

"Cindy," Eve barks. "I completely get what you're saying, but Doug may be right. It took Blade forever to admit that he loved me. You need to fight for it."

"I don't have to do anything. I've been fighting to keep my head up my whole life and it never turns out how I want."

"Okay, that's fair, but look at the big picture. Cade didn't give you to your dad. He told his brother he loved you—"

"He said he *thought* he was in love with me—"

Eve cocks her head at me. "Really? Look, you might have started as a job but clearly, that didn't last long."

"Why are you trying to convince me he wants me when he literally let me return to L.A.?"

"Because you're sitting here, telling us the truth about your past, with no makeup on." Eve's bluntness has me sniffing at her. "He got rid of a body for you. You don't do shit like that when you're just all loved up with a woman's pussy."

"Eve's right, Cindy," Dolly remarks.

This is why I love them. No matter what I do or what happens, in the end, they always have my back. Even if I don't have my own.

"You love him." Charlie's words make my eyes dart to hers. "You're different, and it has nothing to do with the fact that this might be the first time I've seen you without makeup." She shoots me a soft grin. "You look… peaceful."

"Peaceful? Charlie, I'm hardly at peace. My whole life is exploding. I'm not sleeping and I'm miserable…"

I look around the table and find them smiling at me—God, it's borderline creepy.

"What is wrong with you?" I groan. A part of me wants to run and hide in the restroom then call an Uber.

"The thing about men," Eve points out, "is that just because you love them and they love you, they'll still drive you insane. This is that. It's a blip. You need to fix this so that this *you* becomes a permanent fixture."

I huff and because they're crazy, I mutter, "Guys, I need you to know I'm sorry for what happened before I left. I feel terrible that Julianna didn't come today because she thinks I'm in love with her man because I'm not. Not at all.

"I never wanted to hurt any of you, you're my family, but I did. I fucked up and for that, I'm sorry."

"Cindy..." Dolly covers her mouth for a moment, then she's riffling through her purse. "You... I can't... We need to call your Cade."

"Dolly, we're not calling Cade." I laugh, but it comes out as a sob because now that I've come clean and made my amends, it feels so *empty* without him here. I take a breath. "This is on him. It's not on me. I'm worthy of him bridging the gap that *he* put between us. I need someone to fight for a future with me, not someone so stuck in the past with his mistakes that he can't see that tomorrow is better than yesterday.

"I-I thought I needed him to fix things, to make everything better, but I realize that's on both of us." Saying it out loud fills me with resolve. "One more thing since I'm telling you guys everything. My name is not Cindy. It's Isabelle, but you can call me Belle."

"Oh, my God." Dolly digs her nails into Doug's arm again, causing him to grunt out in pain. "You *are* having an epiphany. I'm so happy for you," she cries as Doug detaches her hand and reaches for his shot.

"Okay, everyone just relax." Doug arches a brow then raises his tequila in a toast. "To Belle." And suddenly, I'm holding a shot glass in my hand as my tribe grabs their drinks too. "We love you."

The whole table yells, "To Belle! We love you!"

Then, Dolly hoots, "And to Cade pulling his head out of his ass so we can meet him!"

The others laugh and repeat, "And to Cade pulling his head out of his ass so we can meet him!"

I can barely shoot back the tequila because of the lump in my throat. When I close my eyes, a wave of pain, maybe even homesickness, flows over me. Not going to lie—I miss Kitty, Róisín, Neev, and Patricia, but that's nothing to Cade.

He may break my heart by not scooping me up, and that'll be on him, not me. Eve says I need to fight for him, however that goes both ways. I'm not the one who fucked everything up—he needs to fight for me too. And not just by cutting off people's fingers, either.

I'm done running—he knows where I am. It's time he showed up for me, and if that's the end, it'll hurt, but so be it.

31

TEXT CHAT

Kitty: BELLE!!!

Belle: What?!

Kitty: You left!

Belle: I said goodbye.

Kitty: Oh, I know. But I'm just reminding you that I need you to save me from my brother's stupidity so my letting you go is a favor I'll expect you to repay at some point in the future.

Belle: Lol, you're crazy. Which brother?

Kitty: The one you like.

Belle: I don't like either at the moment.

Kitty: To be fair, neither do I! STILL. You have to save me.

Belle: Honey, I have to save myself first.

Kitty: *pouts*

Kitty: How's it going with all that?

Belle: Not great. But I'm getting there. That's something, right?

Belle: Just concentrating on my friends, atm.

Kitty: Are you going to meetings?

Belle: Ugh, wish I hadn't told you about that.

Kitty: Caught you in a moment of weakness. I'm good at getting confessions out of people. I should have been a priest.

Belle: Jesus, the congregation would be overflowing if you were.

Kitty: I know. The Catholic Church doesn't know what it missed out on.

Belle: Lol.

Kitty: Anyway, I could lie and say it's the nurse in me, but it's not. I really care about you, Belle.

Belle: Thank you. <3 I care about you too. I'm going to meetings.

Kitty: Good. So proud of you. :*

Kitty: He's a moron, but he really likes you.

Belle: I don't want to talk about this, Kitty. Hey, I just got my nails done. Do you like them?

BELLE SENDS PHOTO

Kitty: Yowza. Those are some claws, and seeing as I'm the cat in this friendship, I should know. Hot date?

Belle: Hmm. "Scarlet Lady" red. Beautiful, isn't it?

Kitty: I repeat: he's a moron.

Kitty: Hey, I miss you.

Belle: I miss you too.

Kitty: I'm sorry he sucks.

Belle: Me too. <3

32

CADE

A WEEK LATER

"YOU'RE A FUCKING *MORON*."

I squint at the bright light as Kitty drags open the shades in my room and lets in the punishing sun that's hell-bent on melting my eyeballs. "Shut the fucking curtains, Kitty!" I growl.

"No. You deserve the pain." She kicks my foot. "You suck."

"Thank you," I mumble.

"That wasn't a compliment."

"Well, I'm taking it as one."

She huffs. "Go and get her."

"Go and get who?" I yawn as I cover my face with a pillow.

"Belle!"

There's a pain in my chest that's worse than the one in my eyes.

I shove it aside like I've been shoving it aside since Belle left. "Kitty, she didn't sleep in a week. Being here was bad for her health."

"She napped at Ma's."

"That's not enough for her to function. Something wasn't right for her here." I rub my temples where it feels like the seven dwarfs are attacking my optic nerves with their pickaxes. "New York was bad for her. She wanted to be around her family."

God, I was hoping she'd start to think of me as family.

"And you're just going to settle for that?"

"What else can I do?"

"You can stop being a dickwad and go and get her. God, maybe if this place didn't look like a room at the YMCA, she'd have felt more at home—"

"This *isn't* her home. L.A. is. And my lack of furniture doesn't make up for the shit I've done—"

"Home is where the heart is," she interrupts.

I toss the pillow at her. "Are you going to start quoting more proverbs at me?"

"If it'll get you to do something, sure. A stitch in time will save your ass because I'll beat it black and blue if you don't get on a plane tonight. How about that?"

"Original," I mock. "She bought a ticket without even talking to me first, which says it all. I lied to her, Kitty. I failed her. She even had to deal with her father; I didn't put that asshole down for her. I don't blame her for leaving. Especially after…"

"After?" Kitty prompts, though her scowl *has* lessened.

"Some days, I'd get back from work and she'd be pretty much catatonic. She didn't want to open up to me, and the moment I thought she was reaching out, she told me she was leaving." I don't tell her that she offered to pay me back for the hospital bill. As if I'd take her goddamn money. But that sealed it for me—a reminder of yet another way I'd fucking failed her. Disheartened but proud of her, I rasp, "She obviously decided to stop wasting her time with me and so she should. She deserves better."

Kitty's mouth gapes open. "Who are you and what did you do with my brother?"

I ignore her to state, "Do I miss her? Of course I do." I growl, slamming my hand into the comforter. "But I'm not about to put her in a bad place, not when she's got herself out of it. You didn't see her when she was like that. I did. The last thing I want is for her to start using again because of what I did."

"How can you read between the lines *so well* and *still* mess this up?" she snaps.

I glower at her. "I put her in danger, Kitty. I let her down. I told her I'd protect her, keep her safe, and I didn't. I failed her so it makes sense to me that she'd want to get away." I release a heavy sigh. "I'm surprised she stuck around as long as she did."

"She didn't want to get away, though. She was looking for a sign," she argues.

I rub my eyes. "What kind of sign?"

"That you cared!"

"I do care. Of course, I care."

"Did you tell her that?"

"I showed her."

"Dick-in-pussy action doesn't tell a woman she's loved," she scoffs. "Did you not pick up on that memo? And here I was thinking that having three sisters would give you some insight into womankind, but you're just as behind as every other dick out there."

I have no idea what it is about my expression that reveals it, but slowly, so slowly that I know to be wary, she rasps, "Did she tell you she had feelings for you, Cade?"

I grunt.

"She did, didn't she? And you, being a moron, didn't say anything back, did you?"

From out of nowhere, my head is slamming into the bed and my other pillow is being used as a missile.

Snatching it from her with a growl, I hug it to my chest so she can't steal it again. "What should I have said?"

"That you love her, asshole. Don't be such a guy. Christ on a cracker—"

"Be grateful Ma doesn't hear you blaspheming."

"I think on this occasion, she'd forgive me. You're an idiot, Cade."

"You said that already. *Repeatedly.*"

"You admitted that you were in love with her!"

"I didn't say it outright."

"She said *you* said you did."

"Well, not..." I clear my throat. "Not to her."

"Why not?"

"It didn't seem… There didn't seem to be a right time."

"When she was leaving you, it didn't seem like the right time?"

"The opposite, actually."

She throws her hands in the air. "You brought her here."

"I had to hide her—"

"Bullshit. You could have taken her to a hotel."

"I tried! There was a traffic jam."

"You suck."

"You said that already."

"She told me that you were in the city to visit your family."

I grunt. "I was manipulating her, Kitty. Yes, I know. I fucking suck. I get it. I fucking get it. And that's why I let her go, dammit. Because I *do* suck. By lying so early on, I broke something fundamental—"

"Shut up. That's defeatist and my brother is not easily defeated. Look, I'm not going to say you don't have some serious issues. You know, what with lying to her from the start and—"

"Covering up the murder of her father?" I drawl, rolling the pillow and tucking it under my neck.

Kitty hums. "Exactly. But you did cover up her tracks, and she kinda owes the Five Points some thanks for that."

"She owes us nothing."

"Her father got the Irish Mob involved in bringing her back to the city," she drawls. "You seriously think you didn't end up being a better option? Can you imagine if he'd worked on the leader of the Albanians' knee instead of Aidan's?" When I blanch at the notion, she nods. "Exactly."

"I shouldn't have seduced her."

"Look at my brother, thinking he's Casanova."

I glower at her smirk. "Shut up, Kitty. Leave me the hell alone." When she doesn't disappear and, instead, plunks herself down beside me, I mutter, "Maybe this is for the best."

"I don't think it is."

"She said she needed to find herself." I scrub a hand over my face. "I didn't even realize she was lost. I'm not an idiot, I knew she was bad, but I figured we'd work on that together."

"I hate to state the obvious, Cade, but she's a recovering addict who just shot her father. If that wasn't insane enough, that man murdered her mom and abused Belle as a kid. Can you blame her for feeling lost?"

I couldn't. "I don't, but she never talked about it."

"What did you do when you came up here after work?" She sighs. "And please don't tell me you were only fucking like rabbits."

"Of course we were."

"No wonder she left you. She thinks you're only interested in sex." When I don't contradict her, she frowns. "That's not all there is between you, right?"

I scrub a hand over my stubbled jaw. "No."

"Well, why did you make her feel like it was?"

"You want to know the truth?"

"No, I'd prefer you lie to me," she mocks.

"You're a pain in the ass."

"I know. Spill."

"I knew she'd leave eventually. It made sense from how we came together. She's the best sex I've ever had. I figured..."

When my words wane, she shakes her head. "You figured that you were the best sex she'd ever had, too, so you'd keep her busy until she forgot to leave?"

"Pretty much."

"That worked out well for you, didn't it?"

"What else was I supposed to do?"

"Talk to her? Tell her you didn't want her to go?" She sighs again, and somehow, those sighs make me feel like more of a moron than her whooping me with my pillow. "It's your life, Cade. I'd have left you alone if you hadn't spent the last week getting drunk. Lucas messaged Mom to ask what was going on with you because you called in sick for the second time in a row."

"So, what you're saying is that you're the lesser evil?"

"Yeah. You could have Ma up here instead."

I shudder. "Or worse, Lucas."

We both grimace at each other, but she murmurs, "I don't think you'd be this miserable if you were glad about Belle leaving."

"Why would you think I'd be glad?"

"Because, brother or not, you're a man and men are douches."

I roll my eyes. "Thanks for the vote of confidence."

"You're welcome. You lived up to my expectations and that's saying something."

Shifting onto my back, I stare at the ceiling and mutter, "My life is here, Kitty. Her life is there. It's not like you can resign from the Irish Mob."

"She can come back to New York."

"She hates the city. You should have seen what I had to do to get her here in the first place."

"Am I too young and innocent to know?"

I snort. "It involved fingers and a blanket on the plane."

"Ew, do they even launder those blankets?"

My lips twitch at her disgust. "They probably did after we used it."

"Jesus, Cade, I don't need to know anymore." She shoves my arm. "Do you want her?"

"Isn't that obvious?"

"Not really. Not from where I'm standing and, to be honest, not from where she's sitting either. Ya know, on the other coast of our massive country.

"I mean, you didn't tell her you have feelings for her when she told you she did, despite your rusty beginnings. You didn't run after her when she left…"

"Has she texted you?"

"Yeah."

Hope filters through me. "What did she say?"

"Nothing. She showed me her new manicure and they're not the kind of nails you wear to a job interview."

I frown. "What does that mean?"

"Well, she needs to get a new job, doesn't she? She got fired from the diner. She never said if her friend hired her back."

Blinking at her, I rumble, "Damn, you guys talked more than I realized. And no. Her father was richer than Midas. She's his only heir."

She sniffs. "It takes more than two weeks for an inheritance to come through. To job interviews, you'd go with classic French tips."

"What are those?"

"The white ones."

"Okay. What did she go with?"

"Coffin-shaped, 'Scarlet Lady' red."

"Scarlet Lady?"

"That's the name of the nail polish. She specifically told me." She prods me in the arm. "You know what that means, don't you?"

"No."

"For fuck's sake, Cade!" Róisín yells from the living room. "Isn't it obvious? She's going out and trying to get laid!"

"Raisin, what are you doing eavesdropping on my conversation?" I holler back.

"She and Neev are both out there waiting for you to come to your senses. We like Belle," she admits. "And I like you around her too."

"What do you mean?"

"You're a bit of an asshole with women, Cade. It's because you're so pretty. You don't have to treat them mean to keep them keen. They just float around you like flies around a turd."

"Gee, thanks—"

"You know it's true. But with her, you were kinder, gentler. It was a good side of you to see. You were attentive and reactive instead of just, I don't know, passive?"

"Passive? What the hell does that mean?"

"You know what it means. I don't think there's much about your life that you care about, Cade. You've been that way since Vinny—"

"Don't bring him up."

"No? I think you and Belle have a lot more in common than you realize. Something broke both of you when you were young. Something made you realize that life isn't perfect and the people you can rely on aren't always there for you." She shoots me a look from under her lashes. "I-I know you got a lot of the blame for what happened with Vin."

Rolling my forearm over my eyes, I mutter, "Lucas wouldn't speak to me for months."

"I remember. You were a kid, Cade. He shouldn't have done that. Maybe your broken pieces and Belle's rub up nicely together and that's why you were so insistent about fucking her into oblivion."

Though I've got a frog in my throat, I have to chuckle. "You're such a jerk."

"I learned from the best. I'm just the one who pulls your head out of your ass. Are you going to go and get her?" she asks, tone hopeful.

"No—"

"Is he going to go see her?" Róisín calls from the other room.

"Tell him we'll make his life hell if she's already banging a biker by the time he gets his ass over there!"

"Neev!" I snap. Before Kitty gives me any more shit, I get out of bed, dragging the sheet with me.

Kitty scowls at my bare ass. "You're naked?"

"Of course. I was in bed," I argue.

"I sat on the bed."

"I can guarantee that my dick has touched most of the bedding—"

She gags and rushes out of the bedroom. "I saw Cade's dick. I'm going to puke."

Neev snorts. "I saw it when he was banging Mary Elizabeth that time against the locker in my junior year. I still can't believe you got away with that."

"She said she was pregnant?" Róisín inquires.

"No. But the principal walked past and I think even *he* didn't believe Cade had the audacity to fuck a girl in—"

"Do we need to be having this conversation?" I growl, tucking the top sheet around my waist as I wade into the living room.

"Yeah, we need to stay focused. You know he has the attention span of a gnat. Cade says he won't go visit her."

"I won't." When the three witches start hissing and spitting at me, I snap, "She said she needed to find herself. I'm not going to fuck with that."

"Finding herself is a euphemism for finding another guy to get under so she can get over you."

"Raisin," I snarl.

"What? It's true!"

"It is," Kitty agrees. "Especially with nails like that."

"I'm going to call her."

"Call her?" Neev repeats, shaking her head. "That's not the big show that every woman wants."

"We need to make him watch *An Officer and a Gentleman*," Róisín whispers.

"He's not going to war," Neev says.

"Every day's a war. He could get shot whenever he goes out. Or arrested."

"Cheerful, Raisin," I mutter.

"It's true," she defends.

"I've seen that movie."

Kitty arches a brow. "*You* have watched *An Officer and a Gentleman*?"

"Yeah. Richard Gere, right?"

"Yeah."

"He goes into that factory and sweeps her off her feet. That Deborah chick."

"Deborah Winger." Róisín chuckles. "You *have* watched it."

"Probably to ensure he got laid afterward."

Scratching my chin, I admit, "It probably did involve a date, Neev." My brow furrows. "She meant it."

"Meant what?"

"That she doesn't know who she is. Isn't that something you have to figure out on your own?"

"Never seen you be more 'Cade' than when you're around her."

My frown deepens as I stare at Neev. Kitty said something similar, but Kitty is Kitty. If Neev thinks it too, maybe I should be listening. "What are you talking about?"

"You used to be so sweet, Cade. After…" She clears her throat. "You know, everything, it made you a jerk with women. Heck, with most people who aren't family. You were sweet with her, though. Maybe you shouldn't be trusted to find yourselves when you're on your own. Maybe you're better people together, you know?"

"That's flawed logic," I grumble.

"It's logic nonetheless," Kitty crows. "Now, we told Lucas you caught the plague, and we've booked you a flight that takes off in four hours—"

"What?!"

"You heard us. You're going to go there, sweep her off her feet, and bring her back HOME."

"I should drag her here kicking and screaming?" I drawl.

"If you need to. You should never have let her go in the first place." Kitty prods my shoulder and gets in my face. "You tell her how you truly feel, Cade Frasier. Whether you've got feelings or whether it's love, it doesn't matter. She just wants to know that she wasn't a piece of ass."

"And if she doesn't come back with you," Róisín says helpfully, "you did a nice thing and shored up her confidence, so you didn't ruin her for the next guy who taps that patootie and realizes what the keeper she is."

I flick her on the end of her nose. "Thanks, Raisin. You always keep my ego in check."

"What are little sisters for?"

"Apparently, they're good for raiding your wallet and buying air tickets for their no-good brothers," I retort, but my words drift into a sigh. "I fucked up at the beginning—"

"You fucked up at the end too," Neev points out. "This doesn't have to be the end though, does it? Maybe you haven't gotten deep into the beginning, but if you don't act now, that's it. It's really over…"

Her words resonate.

I didn't want Belle to go, but I didn't know how to get her to stay. Didn't think I was worth her trouble, to be honest.

Scraping a hand over my stubble, I can't deny that I want more.

Jesus, that I want everything. But I'm used to people distancing themselves from me when I screw up, and I thought she was no different.

But my sisters are right.

If she doesn't want me, I should shore up her confidence, seeing as I'm the one who messed with it in the first place. She doesn't deserve to have any baggage after what I put her through.

And secondly, this could just be a little mishap in our beginning. It's only the end once we both say it is…

That's why I mutter, "I'd best get ready for my flight."

As they whoop and cheer behind me, crowing about bringing me in line, I head into the bathroom where I stare blankly at my reflection for a couple of minutes.

The truth is, I'm pretty damn sure that what I feel for her *is* love, but I also know that she has every right not to believe me after we met under false pretenses. I guess I have to prove my feelings to her, but I don't really know how to go about doing that.

My sisters have ovaries, and they think that a grand gesture will be enough… I guess I'll find out soon—

"I don't hear that shower working!" Neev shouts outside the door, making me jump in surprise.

"Fuck's sake," I grouse under my breath as I drop the sheet and head into the shower to switch on the spray.

As it blasts me in the face, I feel a little more awake, a little more aware.

Neev's right about one thing—I don't want this to be the end, and Belle has made it clear that the ball is in my court.

A smile curves my lips. "Good girl," I mutter, "knowing your worth. It's about damn time."

33

CADE

THE L.A. SUN on my face feels good after freezing my balls off in New York, and a part of me admits that I could get used to this—sun in the winter—if I had the choice.

Not that I do.

The Five Points is my future. I tied my fate up with them a long time ago, and the Irish Mob isn't something you simply waltz out of.

If Belle does want to be with me, sun in the winter is not going to be something we get to appreciate for a while.

As I rent a car and make my way to Burbank, the thought of being with Belle long enough to become snowbirds has me hiding a sheepish grin.

Kitty was right about me being a moron—I should never have let her get her ass on that flight without knowing when she was coming back. Without pinning down a date. But she'd taken me by surprise and mostly, I'd just been reeling about how fucking easy I was to walk away from.

Riding through the city, I make my way to the diner where she used to work. Kitty only mentioned job interviews, nothing concrete, so I'll start at Charlie's diner.

If not, I can always go to her place, but I don't feel like showing up there out of the blue. She might feel cornered, and after what she's been through, after what I've put her through, she doesn't deserve that.

When I stroll into the diner a couple hours later—traffic in L.A. is worse than in NYC—the place has quieted down after the lunch rush.

I take my usual spot and that's when someone rolls up beside my table and slips into the seat opposite me without asking if it's taken.

At first, I think it could be Belle, but this broad's got a scowl meaner than a pissed-off pit bull and her nails roll along the Formica table as she drums her fingers, demanding, "What took you so long?"

I frown. "Do I know you?"

"I'm Eve."

"So?"

"So, I'm one of Cin—I mean, Belle's best friends."

My lips twitch with pride. "She wants you to call her Belle?"

"She does." Her eyes narrow. "It's been a week since she got back."

"I know."

"Took a week for you to figure out you were a complete ass?"

I don't like being interrogated, but I admit, "Yeah."

"Would've taken my stubborn-ass man a lot longer, so I can commend you for that." She smirks. "So, do you have good intentions?"

"What is this? An interview?"

"Yep. I never met you before and Belle's still in a fragile head-space. She told us what happened between you."

"She did?"

"After a half-dozen shots of tequila, sure." She purses her lips. "You fucked her instead of kidnapping her."

I scrape a hand over my face. "When you put it like that, I have to wonder what the hell I'm even doing here."

"The truth hurts."

"It does."

She arches a brow at me. "Do you have feelings for her?"

"I do."

"She said you didn't tell her you loved her."

I tip up my chin. "That's between me and her."

"You made it my business by breaking my girl's heart," she retorts.

"She's the one who left. She could have stayed—"

"In a place that's not her home?"

"*I* could have been her home," I snap, the words rawer than I meant for them to be.

But, goddammit, it's true.

"You couldn't even tell her you loved her."

"It's too soon for that." I heave a sigh. "I want to make things right."

"How do you intend on doing that?"

"I'm gonna woo her."

A laugh escapes Eve. "You are, huh?"

"I am. Dates at the movies, carriage rides around the park, the whole nine yards."

She looks at me suspiciously then says, "Belle'd probably like that."

"I know. That's why I'm going to do it. She's a girly girl."

Eve snorts. "You've read her well."

I shrug. "Circumstances dictated that I look deeper into her life than she's aware of."

"Wait, you snooped?"

I grunt.

She hums her disapproval but looks more thoughtful. "You're a mobster. You can't just roll up into Burbank and stick around."

"No, I know. She has to come back to the city with me if she wants us to be together."

"She wants to be here," Eve counters. "With us. We're her family."

"And she can be. I'll make sure she can fly back whenever she needs to be in Los Angeles, with her tribe, but my place is in New York, just like your man's is here in California."

"What do you know about my man?"

"More than the feds do."

She surprises me by smiling. "I think I like you."

"You going to tell Belle you approve?"

She cocks her head and then stands. "Where'd be the fun in that?" Leaving me gawking at her, she strolls off toward the counter. "Belle!" she calls out, uncaring that there are a few stragglers still trying to enjoy their cheeseburgers. "Get your butt out here."

"I'm coming, Eve! Jesus, what's up?"

"I've got a surprise for you," she singsongs.

Belle steps out, huffing and swiping those scarlet nails through her hair as she fluffs up her bob—a new haircut too? Christ, my sisters were right about her getting back into the dating game. "What kind of surprise?" she demands.

Eve smiles and points at me. "The kind that's shaped like a groveling dick."

Though my heart feels like it's sunk to the bottom of my stomach, I get to my feet and amble over to the counter.

Belle's eyes are big and round in surprise—she didn't expect me to come for her. Or at least, she gave up hoping I would.

"Belle," I rumble.

"Ooh, that's hot."

"Shh, Dolly," Eve hisses, drawing my attention to where a cluster of women is watching us from the other side of the counter.

I have no idea where they came from and wish they'd go back to wherever they were before I showed up.

"What? I love it when guys growl."

"Dolly." The woman I recognize as Belle's bestie slaps the tiny brunette's arm.

I look at Belle. "Can we take this somewhere private, please?"

"I'm at work."

Her blunt answer has me pursing my lips. "It'll take five minutes."

Eve snorts, calling out, "You think it'll take five minutes to get back in her good graces?"

I grit my teeth because this sucks, but if this is what it takes to win Belle... Clearing my throat, I start, "I should never have let you come back here—"

Much like my sisters did, they boo and hiss at me.

"Let me finish—" I snap, skewering the cluster with a scowl. "I shouldn't have let you come back here without talking about an end date."

Belle frowns. "I don't know what you mean."

"I mean, I asked you when you were coming back and you didn't give me an answer."

"Because there wasn't an answer that you'd have accepted—"

"And that's my point." I aim a finger at myself and then at her. "This isn't over, Belle. You know it. I know it."

"I know no such thing, Cade. You can't even tell me you have feelings for me after..." Belle glances around but the diners are gathered near the exit, not the counter, and no one apart from her friends can hear us. "...the murders and getting rid of bodies for me."

"That is end-game material," Eve concurs. "It's not like that's something you do for just anyone."

Dolly grins. "It's just so romantic, in a morbid way."

Charlie pipes in, "It'd be even more romantic if he had nothing to do with why the dead guys were there in the first place."

"She's right," I admit, wincing. "I manipulated things, manipulated you into being with me, and that's why I let you come back here. Because I could see the sense in that, could understand why you'd need to find a new balance, but..." I suck in a breath. "My sisters told me that I'm a better guy around you."

"See. He listens to his sisters. I love that!" Dolly whispers as she grabs ahold of Charlie's arm. "I knew I was right to root for you, Cade."

Belle ignores them. "How are you a better guy?"

"They said I was a jerk before, but with you, I'm different. I know why too—from the minute I set eyes on you, Belle, I won't lie, I knew you were a walking disaster." I dismiss the boos and hisses from the audience with a snarled, "I'm going somewhere with this. Give me a chance to explain."

"Explain fast," Eve says coolly. "No one talks to our girl like that."

I raise my hand. "Look, you guys are not perfect. There are a lot of reasons she went with me to New York. She had her stomach pumped because she OD'ed. If that's not a cry for help, I don't know what is. Then her so-called BFF's man fires her in the goddamn hospital."

Charlie blanches. "I apologized for that."

"Too little, too late," I sneer. "She came back to L.A. because she thinks you're her family, but all I can see is that you let her down as much as I did. Belle had a reason for being fragile, and maybe you guys didn't know that reason—"

Slamming her hands on her hips, Belle argues, "Cade, you can't say stuff like that. It's called an intervention for a reason. You don't know everything I put them through."

"I can say whatever I need to in my defense of *you*." I tip up my chin. "I know I let you down and I'm here to admit it. To say sorry for lying, for manipulating you. To prove that I'm sorry for fucking up and allowing you to come to L.A. without an expiration date on this trip."

"He's right."

It doesn't escape my attention that Eve is like the Solomon of this bunch—her word is law.

I cut her a look. "Bet your ass I'm right."

Her lips tighten. "We should have been there for you more, Belle. We knew you were struggling but didn't know what to do to help you other than..." She shrugs awkwardly. "...how we did."

Heartfelt "sorries" whisper from Antoinette, Dolly, and... huh. It's the first time I realize there's another woman there as well—I recognize her as Ryder's woman. Julianna.

Belle's cheeks are fire-hydrant-red as she mutters, "It's hard to care for addicts. You guys did the best you could."

With a grunt, I reach over and snag her hand. She tries to pull away, but my grip is too firm as I tug her nearer to the counter. "I never asked you about the drugs, didn't think I had a right to, considering everything, but have you stayed clean?"

She swallows. "Yes."

I look at her, really look, and can see that she's at least been sleeping because she doesn't seem exhausted, just harried. "Good girl."

"Damn, that's sexy," Dolly mutters. "I love it when Edge calls me that."

"Shut up," Charlie hisses.

"I don't want this to be the end, Belle."

"You can't even tell me you have feelings for me, dammit!"

"How can I tell you that I care about you when everything we have was founded on a lie? I'm not going to do that to you." Her eyes turn big. "I want a second chance. I might not have earned one, but I'll make sure that I do because I want to be able to tell you those words without you questioning them."

"A-A second chance? Y-You..." She blinks at me then whispers, "He loves me," under her breath.

I swallow because she read between the lines. "You heard me. I know L.A. is your home, but I can't... My work... I can't leave. It's not the kind of job you can quit. My place is in New York, but I'll never stop you from visiting L.A. so long as I know that you'll be coming back to me." Hands balling into fists, I lay it on the line. "I want to date you, Isabelle Davis."

She looks completely confused. "You want to date me?"

"I do."

"Tell her about the carriage rides," Eve cheers me on.

"Carriage rides?" Belle questions, her eyes big. Her inner romantic is already coming out to party. "In Central Park?"

My lips twitch. "One and the same. I want to grab a coffee with you and I want us to go to the movies. I want to take you to dinner and I want us to eat pizza before a basketball game. I want to take you"— fuck me—"dancing." Her eyes light up. "I'm going to prove to you that I'm the best man for you and then, when you say those words, I'll know I've earned them. And when I say them back to you, you'll know I mean them."

"*When* you say them... not if? Because you will? *Soon?*"

"When," I confirm, watching her throat bob in response. "And no sex until then."

"Wow, he means business," Dolly states.

Belle pouts. "No sex?"

"No sex."

She bites her lip and then peers at her friends. Charlie's smile is sheepish and laced with guilt, Eve mostly looks regally amused, Antoinette's grin is dazzling, Dolly is nodding and doing a happy dance, and Julianna seems hopeful—I don't think that has anything to do with her not wanting Belle to kiss her man in public anymore either.

"What do you guys think?" she questions, but I don't think it's to string me along. More like she wants their approval.

We'll work on that together—her believing in herself and having faith in her own ability to make a decision.

Just like I need to work on sharing more, on believing I'm no better than the teenage punk who got his brother—

I stop that thought process in its tracks.

There's plenty we need to work on.

Together.

Breaking into my thoughts, Eve declares, "I think he means it."

Belle wrings her hands. "It's not too soon?"

"Nah." Dolly shakes her head. "He said 'no sex.' That's like the bro code for 'I'm going to marry this chick once she forgets I screwed up.'"

Charlie shakes her head at Dolly. "I swear you don't speak the same English as me."

"Charlie?" Belle asks warily.

Sighing, Charlie flicks a look at me, then, catching Belle's eye, she nods.

"Julianna?" she whispers.

"I think he means every word he says and I think you deserve every last bit of it."

Belle's eyes glisten with emotion. "Really?"

"Really."

I'm not a fool. I know I've got her friends' approval, so while Belle confirms that, I make my move.

Within seconds, I'm around the other side of the counter, and as Julianna says that final, "*Really*," I'm there, in front of her.

The next moment, Belle's shrieking as I grab her by the ass and haul her into me. Her girls cheer and laugh, maneuvering her to the other side of the counter. As she clutches her arms around my neck, knees pinning my hips, ankles crossing over my ass, I tell her, "I think it's time to give your notice."

Belle stares at me, a silent plea for me not to hurt her in her eyes. That look breaks me, especially when she whispers, "You are sure about this, aren't you? I don't think I can take it if you don't mean this."

Her confidence is so fragile at that moment that I could kick myself for making her feel that way. But we're going to work on writing a better beginning for ourselves together. So, while I know there's plenty to make right between us, while I know it'll be hard for her to leave L.A. behind and move permanently to a city that's full of bad memories, I have no compunction in telling her the truth: "Sweetheart, I haven't been surer of anything in my whole life."

Her smile lights me up from the inside out. "Charlie?"

"Yeah, yeah, I know. I need to find another waitress."

Belle beams at her from over my shoulder then presses her lips to my ear, whispering, "We need to discuss the 'no sex' part of this dating deal you've offered me."

As I let my mouth find hers, I mumble, "I'm open to negotiations."

34

BELLE

EIGHTEEN MONTHS LATER

NEW YORK, NY

"OKAY, there. I think she's perfect." Dolly steps back to observe me as Doug and Antoinette walk around the chair I'm sitting in.

"Definitely perfect," Doug agrees.

"Oh, my God, Belle, you're so beautiful." Antoinette screams, "Eve, Charlie… come here."

"You guys are killing me. I need to see." I go to stand, only to be pushed back down by Doug as his eyes take in my entire face, hair, body…

His smile is mischievous. "Our work here is done." He dramatically steps back as Eve, Charlie, and Kitty come walking into the bedroom of the suite carrying Cristal champagne and some strawberries. Nicole, Eve's daughter, follows them, her blonde hair swept off her face as she stops and runs over to me.

"You're a princess, Auntie Belle!" Her hands reach out to touch my satin gown. "So pretty!"

Dolly nods as she grabs her shoulders and pulls Nicole in for a hug. "She's like the real Belle, except this one hates reading and Cade is definitely no beast."

Snorting at her, I retort, "No, my man is 100% beef hunk."

As the others catcall me, I grin unrepentantly. But I can't wait any longer. I walk slower than I'd like, so I don't wreck my hair, toward the large full-length mirror Patricia had Lucas bring over this morning when Doug demanded one.

I just stare at myself, vaguely hearing the pop and screams as the champagne spills out and drips to the floor. Because here I am, wearing a beautiful dress on the day I have dreamed about my whole life.

I might have given up at some point, but Cade made me a believer again.

"Well?" someone demands, but all I can do is stare at my reflection as I lose myself in the past year.

In memories of the dates we've enjoyed in overpriced carriage rides and quick hookups in the back of our SUV after we tease each other in a fancy restaurant. The coffees we shared and the time he had the barista write "I love you" on my coffee cup instead of my name then, as I cried, whispered it as he spoon-fed me cake.

Cake—for the longest time, I didn't share the negative connotations I have with it because of my dad, then I opened up to him later that evening and he held me as I cried. *Again.*

Just one instance of many where he consistently shows up for me.

I think about how he proposed in one of our favorite restaurants, Glas, and how we devoured the leftovers from takeout cartons later that night after we left no surface untainted in our apartment.

Sure, we've been through good and bad days, but somehow, with each moment, each second, we learned how to heal and trust.

With each day, we grow stronger, until here I am, on the brink of walking down the aisle to pledge my eternal love to Cade.

My partner.

My anchor.

There's an irony in the fact that I'm a runner and when he fucks up, he's used to losing people… It's made us both aware of how easily we could ruin *this*, and we work double hard to fix things before they can break.

So, when life's trials hit us, I don't run away from him—I run to him. If he fucks up because he *is* a man, he apologizes straight off the bat. No bullshit, no lies. He owns it. And we move on.

Together.

It's a learning curve, but it's working.

"Are you okay?" I blink at my reflection then down at Nicole who stares at me worriedly. "Auntie Belle?"

When I nod, she beams at me, which makes me feel weepier than before.

"Don't you dare start crying." Dolly sniffs as she takes a glass of champagne from Charlie. Both are a vision in their pale pink brides-maid's dresses. "If you do, then I will, and we don't have time to fix my makeup."

"Why do you want to cry?" Nicole frowns at me then Charlie and Dolly as they both burst out laughing. "Isn't it a good day?"

"You're right, Nicole. It's a great day. It's just that Cin—*Belle* looks so beautiful because she's happy." Charlie wipes under her eyes then gives her glass to Dolly as she throws her arms around me. "I miss you so much," she chokes out. "But, God, it's worth the distance just to see you like this."

I nod, not trusting myself to speak, and squeeze her back, tighter than ever because I miss her too. So freakin' much.

When Cade proposed, he said I could have the wedding wherever I wanted and that he would marry me anywhere, but New York felt like the right place to be. It's where everything went wrong, but where it all came together too.

I'm lucky they could all make it up here.

"I miss you too," I manage to get out. "Thank you for coming. I know it's been a pain—"

"Hush. As if we'd miss it," she chides with a sniffle.

"Break it up. We can all cry after she says I do." Doug intrudes upon our lovefest as we give each other a supportive squeeze before letting go.

Despite the distance, our friendship has blossomed. I think it's because you can't bottle things inside when you're so far away from one another. You have to talk, otherwise you don't connect. Ever. I probably talk to her more now than I did when I lived in Burbank and worked for her.

"What's the holdup?" Patricia demands, bursting into the room followed by Róisín and Neev. "The wedding planner is—" When they see me, all three grab one another's hands and Patricia stands there, speechless.

Having come to know her better than ever, I know how rare that is.

Patricia has her opinions and the family listens. Or else. God, I love her.

"Isabelle," Patricia whispers brokenly as she takes a step closer. Her hand wisps over my hair, not touching, stopping a scant inch before she does. "You're stunning. I couldn't be prouder to call you my daughter."

I reach for her hand while I gaze at my reflection again. "Thank you, Patricia."

The woman who stares back at me is barely recognizable as the same one who hid in bathrooms and panicked about visiting New York at boarding gates.

I'm wearing a white satin gown, tight in the bodice, allowing my breasts to spill forward in a way I'd never have done before, which has the added benefit of accenting my small waist. I turn slightly to admire the long train in the back.

My hair is up, and I decided to go without a veil so I could wear my mother's diamond tiara, which I found in my father's safe.

After the NYPD declared the case closed, saying Father died of natural causes—I don't care how the Five Points made that happen when he'd been stored in a freezer overnight—I inherited all his worldly goods. The first thing I did was put the townhouse up for sale. That townhouse was the basis of my worst memories and I couldn't wait to get rid of it.

But, after watching the realtor screw up two offers, I decided to get my license and sell it myself because I needed it off my hands.

Not only did I get more than the asking price, I also realized I had a gift for sales. That was almost a year ago and I'm going strong. I just got my real estate license to sell in L.A. too, and I'm getting ready to start flipping houses with the "3 Designing Blondes," Eve, Antoinette, and Julianna's interior decorating company.

"Um, I don't want to be a buzzkill…," Neev announces, looking up from her phone and wiggling it at me. "…but Cade is freaking out. Not sure, but I think my brother might come and get you if we don't go now."

"You ready?" Charlie asks.

I take a breath and surprise myself with how calm I feel. But then, this is the right move for me. This is *it*. What I've been waiting for since I met him. We've been racing toward this from the start—I figure we'll always do everything hella fast.

I smile. "I'm ready."

"Okay, traffic is a bitch, and it hasn't been easy—what, with all the Five Points being inside and a lot of Disciples—but I think it's gonna be fine." Kitty plasters on a smile as she reaches down to help Dolly carry my huge train out the door.

Doug grabs the makeup case, which is so big it has wheels, and Eve carries the champagne.

"It's two blocks away. How bad can traffic be?" Charlie screams over all the horns blaring as soon as we exit the hotel.

A long black limo waits for us, and we climb in. Dolly touches me up as Eve and Antoinette talk on their phones and for a second, I let myself have this moment. Because every single person in this vehicle is someone I love. It's been a crazy week, with parties and Disciples flying in. Blade and Axel had to spend hours talking to Aidan Jr. Not sure about what, but I didn't ask. They came, though, and for that I'm grateful.

"So, who is the hottie with the blond hair and the laidback surfer vibe? Please tell me he's single?" Róisín leans forward so she can look at me as Dolly fixes my lipstick.

"Rip?" I mumble, trying not to move my lips.

"Sweetheart, trust me, you do not want to hook up with a Disciple. They are nothing but heartache," Doug schools her.

Róisín smiles like a satisfied cat and leans back in her seat. "Maybe he just hasn't met his match." She arches a brow when we gape at her. "What? All right, geez, I'll stay away."

The limo pulls up and a guy who's part of the Five Points opens the door—I swear they all buy their designer suits from the same tailor.

My stomach flips with excitement when Patricia pats my hand and exits, Róisín, Neev, and Kitty behind her.

"Holy shit. I'm getting married," I whisper with a grin, bouncing in my seat.

"Eve, finish the champagne," Dolly orders over her shoulder.

"No! I'm happy. I don't need it."

Doug alights from the limo and holds his hand out for Antoinette. Her long pink skirt dances around those ballerina legs of hers, and it's such a feminine color against the Armani black tuxedos the men are wearing that I take a moment to just appreciate my good taste.

"Wait until you see your flower girls." Eve smiles, knowing where my mind is at before she climbs out with Nicole, leaving me with Charlie and Dolly.

"This is happening," I say around a chuckle.

"Belle, this is your moment. You deserve all of this." Charlie presses a kiss to my cheek that has Dolly screeching and patting my makeup with a beauty blender.

"Enough, Dolly!" Doug chides, shoving his hand in my face so that I can take it.

As he helps me out of our ride, it's like time speeds up.

Suddenly, we're all making our way to the door of the church. Lots of passersby stop and stare and a few cheer, but the massive amount of security makes most keep walking.

I look around and find Antoinette holding Michelle's and Juliet's hands as they get in place, both looking beyond adorable in their pink tutus, their flower baskets filled with pink roses.

As everyone gets into place, I'm on my own for the first time in days.

I'm walking myself down the aisle, but now I'm wondering if I'm fool because these are five-inch heels, for fuck's sake. I could at least have leaned on Doug so I didn't fall in front of two hundred guests—

"Here we go," Doug drawls, kissing my cheek as the large wooden doors open to the old church. "You got this, baby girl!"

I hear everyone stand. The organ chimes its first note.

This is it.

Our day—the first step toward a future I never thought I'd have.

"I'd say good luck, but you don't need it," Doug tells me before he starts to walk down the aisle with Eve on one side and Patricia on his other arm. I thought it would be best, and Cade was fine making Doug one of his best men. He knows it's best not to piss off the Disciples.

I was a little worried all the guys would say no to letting their women walk down the aisle with a Five Points' mobster, but so far, no one has killed anyone, so I'm rolling with it and taking it as my dues as the bride.

I watch as Dolly, Kitty, Neev, Róisín, and Charlie line up, getting ready for their moment in the spotlight, and I smile as I hear Antoinette instruct the twins, "One foot in front of the other so Auntie Belle can walk on the petals."

It's that simple.

One foot in front of the other until I stand before him. A light bit of warmth makes me glance up and a tiny ray of sunlight spills down through the gray sky, hitting a piece of stained glass just so. A sign? It's as if my mother is here with me... shining her light on my face.

I hope so.

Then, it's my turn. I'm all alone at the church's entrance aside from the guards, and I'm ready to never be alone again.

One foot in front of the other... I take a deep breath and step forward, nodding at all the smiling faces. The music sounds louder as I enter the large church, which is filled with more beautiful stained-glass windows and flowers. I hear murmurs of, *"Stunning,"* and, *"So elegant,"* as I move toward Cade until my eyes connect with his blue ones.

Time stops, "Canon in D" evaporates, as does the smell of roses, and it's just Cade and me.

Those damn dimples flash as he grins, then he mouths, "I love you," at me. The words arrow straight into my heart, making my chest hurt.

God, I love him so much.

I need nothing more.

Just him. Just us. Forever.

35

CADE

SEVERAL YEARS LATER...

BURBANK, CA

"ARE you going to come for me, beautiful?" I rumble in her ear, sliding my hand around her throat to tilt her head back. "Look at me, Belle, look at me."

Her dazed eyes find mine.

Fuck, she's a beautiful, sleepy mess.

There's something delicious in wrecking her.

In seeing my pretty wife, always so pristine and perfect from years of ingrained grooming by her fucker of a father, even before goddamn bed, be messy for me.

I nip on her earlobe, sucking it into my mouth as I whisper, "Maybe I shouldn't let you come, hmm? Not if you won't tell me what I want to hear."

She whimpers at the purred warning. "I want to come, please, Cade, please."

Smirking, I tut. "I don't think that's enough. I think you need to beg."

She groans. "You bastard."

My smirk morphs into a grin as I start to retreat, pulling my dick free until the tip is almost out in the cold. Her cunt clasps around me, holding me in, and she shrieks, "Give me your cock, Cade. Don't you take it away. Don't you fucking dare!"

"That's more like it," I croon, giving her what she wants. "What's the rule?"

"I take what I want," she says thickly.

"So?"

"I want you to fuck me, Cade. Fuck me. Hard. Fast. Rough."

Immediately, I comply, snapping my hips back so that I can ram into her deeper, slamming her forward so that the headboard rocks into the wall.

"I want you to kiss my throat. Bite me there."

I burrow my face into her neck and start to suck on that sensitive spot where it meets her shoulder.

"No, no sucking," she cries. "Bite me. I want your mark. Later, I want everyone to see."

That immediately makes my blood pressure shoot sky-high.

We're in L.A. for Suzanna's birthday party, so that means we're in Disciples' territory in the house we own here.

I have no self-esteem issues with how badly my wife wants me, but that doesn't mean I don't enjoy rubbing it in their faces that they were the ones who let her get away.

Hey, what can I say?

I'm proud of my wife.

I'm proud of the woman she's become without the shadow of her father haunting her.

I'm proud of the steps she's taken in her recovery where every-fucking-day she puts in the work and stays strong for us.

I'm proud of how she can let herself be imperfect around me (even though her imperfect is still fucking pristine), and I'm prouder still of what she's achieved in her real estate business.

More than that?

I'm fucking *thankful* for her.

She gave me Suzanna—my pride and goddamn joy.

I've already proven that I'll shed blood and break bones for my woman, but there is nothing I won't do for Suzanna. And despite Belle's growth, I know she'd want it no other way.

Her father was a piece of shit.

I am *not*.

My baby girl is safe, secure, and loved. So goddamn loved. She's like her mom—spoiled—but fuck if I care.

Her guttural moan brings me back to how I spoil my wife the most.

"What's this, Belle? The second? Or the third?"

"S-Second." She bows her head as I bite her throat harder, nipping until I know the ring of my teeth will be visible. "I-I don't know if I can," she keens. "Oh, God, Cade. How do you feel so fucking good? Why can—? How—? You—?"

Her muffled screams are swallowed by the pillow she shoves her face into as she shatters around me.

While her orgasm nearly brings me to the edge, I reach down, circle where I'm claiming her, get my fingers sticky with her juices, then gently rub her clit.

The immediacy of her tension has her jerking like she's been electrocuted.

"No, no, no, no," she whines, gasping as I rumble, "One more, baby. You know you can give it to me. Don't you want to please me?"

Mouth gaping, her fingers dig into the sheet, tearing at it in her wildness, dragging it off on one of the corners and revealing the mattress beneath.

"I can't!" she cries.

"You can. If you want to please me, I want your cunt to drag my cum from me, Belle. I want you flooded with me." Her raw growl has me smirking as I rake my teeth down her throat again. "Don't you want that, babe?" I don't let her answer. "I know you do. I know you want my cum."

She shudders. "I do, I do, I do. I want… Fuck. Cade. I-I want—"

I press a tender kiss on her shoulder. "What do you want, beautiful?"

"A baby. A b-boy. With your eyes."

I still.

Freeze.

Everything inside me is breaking and making and coming back together again.

Suzanna was a happy accident.

This…

"Are you being serious?"

"I could stop taking the pill today," she whispers, her head rolling so that she can look up at me.

There's a gleam in her eyes, one that tells me she planned this.

She planned to wreck me with the greatest gift of fucking all—*her goddamn trust.*

I suck in a breath. "Are you sure?"

Her cunt clamps down around my dick. "I'm sure. I want your cum, Cade. Please. Can I have it?"

Shuddering, I rasp, "It's yours. I'm yours. Fuck, you own me, Belle. You know that, right?"

It's her turn to groan. "O-Oh, God, I love it when you say that."

For someone who's never belonged to anyone since she was a child, I know what those words mean to her.

My fingers start up again.

Faster, hungrier than before, if that's even goddamn possible.

Hips snapping, I rock into her, thrusting harder, deeper, wanting to come inside her, wanting to fill her, wanting our family of three to grow.

As she clutches at the sheet, I growl, "I won't give it to you unless you come again, beautiful."

That's when she finally gives me what *I* want—she fucks me back.

Hard enough that our skin claps and that sweat binds us together in places she'll grimace about later but doesn't care about now.

My woman, *my wife*, loves it when I make her filthy.

This time, when the rhythmic pulsing of her cunt sets off, I know I'm going to lose it. I do not need to hold back. Not now that she's glutted on pleasure.

When she screams my name into the pillow for the third time, I let go.

For a moment, it's like heaven and hell collide and the firestorm that sets off through my veins is something for the ages.

Then, reality sets in and I let my head fall back on my shoulders as the momentousness of what just happened floods me.

I roll us so that we're on our sides and, in her ear, I mutter, "Minx."

Her soft laughter is exhausted and the day hasn't even begun yet. "Not a minx."

"Such a minx." I kiss her cheek. "Don't change. I fucking love you as you are."

She shivers. "I just feel like it's the perfect time to start trying again."

"Is this because you hit your fifth year of sobriety?"

Belle yawns and shrugs. "Maybe? Maybe it's because I love seeing you with Suzanna and I just... I want to see that again. Or, I guess, *more* of it."

"You like me being a daddy?" I tease.

Chuckles cascade from her as she slaps the thigh I curved over her hip. "Don't be gross!"

"I'm not being gross! I'm stating a fact. You like it."

She snorts. "You keep telling yourself that, bud." Turning her head to the side, she peers at me. "You're not averse to the idea?"

"Fuck if I am. And if I need to roar louder the next time I get to come in you unprotected, I'm ready to be the star of the show." As she chuckles, I settle my hand on her belly. "You know I'd have you barefoot and knocked up in the kitchen if I could."

"Yeah, that's not happening. But the family part? I don't know. Especially with Patricia and Kitty around..."

"Kitty's popping out Irish-Sicilians like there's a shortage," I grouse, thinking of my twin nephews and the third kid that's on the way.

"I want Suzanna to have what you had, not what I—"

"You want Suzanna to be plagued by siblings, is what you're saying? You want her teased and pranked and to be the butt of jokes, huh?"

Belle snickers. "You did most of that to them. Don't pretend like you were an angel."

Though I huff, I hide my grin in her throat. "You ready for today?"

"A yard full of Disciples and their spawn running around like they're on real Coke and not just Coke Zero? Nope."

"Tonight's your treat, no?" I offer, because as much as she's a sociable creature, even I'm overwhelmed with the small army of kids the Disciples have popped out over the last couple years.

I swear there's something in the water in Burbank...

Hey, that might work in our favor while we're in the area.

She hums. "Definitely my treat. I can't wait to see The Stuffed Muffins play—"

Before she can finish that sentence, the thudding of little feet sounds down the hall.

Accustomed to this by now, we separate like the well-oiled machine we are. She dips down and grabs her sleep shirt that's on the floor for these occasions only, I quickly shuck on last night's boxer briefs, and she sorts out the sheet she dragged from the mattress while I rearrange the comforter so we're covered.

Just in the nick of time, too.

Ten seconds later, the door slams open.

"DADDY! MOMMY! It's my birthday! It's my birthday! It's my birthday!"

My lips twitch. "I didn't know that. Mommy, did you?"

Flopping a hand to her chest, Suzanna gasps—she's already trying to outpace the drama queen in her mom. "Mommy, Daddy's lying! Tell him that's bad. Put him in timeout!"

"He's already been in timeout, Suzanna. Unfortunately, Daddy is a lost cause."

"Hey!" I argue, but Suzanna's caught the giggles from Daddy being told off rather than her, and that means she hops, skips, then jumps onto the bed and bounces up and down like it's the bouncy castle she's requested for her birthday party.

"Daddy's naughty, Daddy's naughty, Daddy's naughty," she shrieks with each jolt of the mattress.

"Mommy can confirm that Daddy is very, very naughty," Belle teases, quickly snagging Suzanna and hauling her onto her knee. "Are you ready for your special day, birthday girl?"

"I am," she cries. "Can I have two slices of cake, Mommy? No, three! Three!"

Grinning, I rest a hand on the mattress and lean into it. "I think three's fine, don't you, babe? You're only five once, Suzie."

I have no idea why Belle gasps at that, but she does. Then she curls her arm around my shoulder and drags me into her. I'm not averse to being manhandled by my wife, especially when it means my face ends up in her tits with Suzie cackling as she smacks kisses onto my cheek, but I've no idea why.

Still, I know it's best not to ask.

She'll tell me when she's ready, but share she will.

"I love you," she growls fiercely in my ear. "And I can't wait to have another baby with you."

To lighten things up, seeing as Suzanna's looking at us with confusion because of her mom's ferocious tone, my lips quirk into a cocky grin. "I *do* make pretty babies, don't I?"

Belle laughs and strokes a hand over our birthday girl's chubby cheeks. "*We* do, Cade. We do."

SERENA AKEROYD BACKLIST

When **FILTHY DISCIPLE** reaches 500 reviews, head to my Diva
reader group for a bonus chat with the Frasier siblings!
www.facebook.com/groups/SerenaAkeroydsDivas

**THE CROSSOVER READING ORDER WITH THE FIVE
POINTS' MOB, A DARK & DIRTY SINNERS' MC, &
VALENTINIS…**

FILTHY
FILTHY SINNER
NYX
LINK
FILTHY RICH
SIN
STEEL
FILTHY DARK
CRUZ
MAVERICK
FILTHY SEX
HAWK

FILTHY HOT
STORM
THE DON
THE LADY
FILTHY SECRET
REX
RACHEL
FILTHY KING
HERE —> FILTHY DISCIPLE <— HERE
THE CONSIGLIERE
THE ORACLE
FILTHY LIES
FILTHY TRUTH

CASSANDRA ROBBINS BACKLIST

CHECK OUT THE REST OF MY BOOKS...

THE DISCIPLES
LETHAL
ATONE
REPENT
IGNITE
FORCE

FORBIDDEN STANDALONES
POWER
RULE (COMING APRIL 28, 2023)

THE ENTITLED DUET
THE ENTITLED
THE ENLIGHTENED

ROCK GOD SERIES
RISE

CONNECT WITH SERENA

For the latest updates, be sure to check out my website!
But if you'd like to hang out with me and get to know me better, then
I'd love to see you in my Diva reader's group where you can find out
all the gossip on new releases as and when they happen. You can join
here: www.facebook.com/groups/SerenaAkeroydsDivas. Or you can
always PM or email me. I love to hear from you guys: serenaakeroyd@
gmail.com.

ACKNOWLEDGMENTS: SERENA

I've said goodbye to so many characters this year and there was such joy in returning to the fold with *Filthy Disciple*. I hope you fell hard for Cade and Belle, and that you loved their crazy!

Thank you so much to Cass for bringing the Disciples into my life. Belle completed Cade in a way that made my heart (and his) happy. They truly were perfect for each other.

I have to thank Anne for her bloody patience. Life has knocked us both for six (more like twelve) over the past three years since our friendship began, but we're still surviving and thriving. For your support, love, friendship, research skills, and memory, lol, ability to function on ice tea, and Milady's snoring as a soundtrack to our editing calls, THANK YOU. Never mind, of course, your sharp eye and your *pink* pen without which this story wouldn't have flowed so beautifully. <3

To Norma, thank you for always fitting me in when I need you the most. You and Norma's Nook are a Godsend and, as always, you polish my books up to perfection.

To my posse, MWAH from QB. You girls have my back, and for that, I'm beyond grateful. Love you, ladies!

Thank you so much to Gel for the teasers, and Letitia for bringing Cade to life and making him hot AF. Ah, Cayman, thank you for having Cade's pretty face, too. ;)

So much gratitude to Valentine's PR, Wildfire Marketing, and Candi Kane for their PR support for this release. And to the bookstagrammers, bloggers, and Tiktokers who have spread the word, THANK YOU. From the bottom of my heart. <3

And finally, to my Divas and readers. Couldn't do this without you, and wouldn't want to either!!

I hope you're excited for more… Especially after those Easter eggs. :P

ABOUT SERENA

I'm a romance novelaholic and I won't touch a book unless I know there's a happy ending. This addiction is what made me craft stories that suit my voracious need for raunchy romance. I love twists and unexpected turns, and my novels all contain sexy guys, dark humor, and hot AF love scenes.

I write MF, menage, and reverse harem (also known as why choose romance,) in both contemporary and paranormal. Some of my stories are darker than others, but I can promise you one thing, you will always get the happy ending your heart needs!

CONNECT WITH CASSANDRA

I HOPE you enjoyed Cindy and Cade's love story!

If you're curious and would like to know more about Cindy's past, you can find her along with my hot bikers in my Disciples MC series.

https://www.cassandrafayerobbins.com/the-disciples-series

Ways to stay connected with Cassandra:

www.cassandrafayerobbins.com

cassandrafayerobbins@gmail.com

Join my reader group, Robbins Entitled, on Facebook!

ACKNOWLEDGMENTS: CASSANDRA

First and always, to my husband and my two beautiful children. Their patience when I'm trying to figure out how to do this self-publishing journey is amazing. I love you guys more than you can imagine.

My brother Chris, my baby brother Duke, and my cousin Jake: I'm so lucky to have you. My dad, and my Minnesota family: thank you for all your support.

To my co-author, Serena Akeroyd: Thank you for asking me to collaborate on this story and allowing Cindy to find her happily ever after with Cade.

To my editor Nikki Busch: You are the best at what you do. You truly make all my stories incredible. Not only are you a wonderful friend, I would be lost without you. Anne-Geneviève Ducharme-Audran – I thoroughly enjoyed our chats and working with you during this project. Your hard work and dedication will never be forgotten. Thank you.

Michelle Clay and Annette Brignac: What can I say besides you two complete me! I'm beyond honored to be part of our Tribe but also to call you both my best friends. When I ask for one-hundred-percent, you give me one-hundred-and-fifty percent, and I love you both so much.

To Candi Kane PR, my master at calm: You're simply fantastic! To our incredibly talented cover designer Letitia Hasser: Thank you for bringing our smoking hot Cade to life. Gel Mariano, your teasers are perfection! Thank you for creating them. Thank you to our photographer, Wander Aguiar for your wonderful photography skills and making sure Cade was immaculate. Thank you to Cayman Cardiff for being the incomparable Cade!

To my incredible Team: Without you I could not do this. You're all so special to me. Megan, Kelly, Teresa, Melinda, Cameel, Heather, Cat, Cindy, Erin, Gladys, Rebecca, Stephanie, Tammy, Jennifer, Robyn, Myen, Chayo, Stracey, Violet, Nichole, Mandy, Melissa, Tiffany, Laura, Lucia, Danielle, Clayr, and Sophie: Any magic that happens to me, just know that all of you are part of it. Your friendships and support mean the world to me. Love you all so much.

To my reader group, Robbins Entitled: I adore all of you and am honored to be able to get to know you all. It makes my day to get up and talk to you.

Huge thank you to all the amazing bloggers, IG bookstagrammers, and TikTokers, who supported this release. I'm beyond grateful for you.

Lastly, and most importantly, I thank you, our readers.

ABOUT CASSANDRA

Cassandra Robbins is a *USA Today,* Amazon Top 20, KDP All-Star, and international bestselling author. She threatened to write a romance novel for years, and finally let the voices take over with her debut novel, *The Entitled.*

She's a self-proclaimed hopeless romantic, driven to create obsessive, angst-filled characters who have to fight for their happily ever after.

Cassandra resides in Los Angeles with her hot husband, two beautiful children, and a fluffy Samoyed, Stanley, and Goldendoodle, Fozzie. Her family and friends are her lifeline, but writing is her passion.

Made in the USA
Columbia, SC
25 September 2024